PRAISE FOR THE *NEW YORK TIMES* BESTSELLING
CAT IN THE STACKS MYSTERIES

"Courtly librarian Charlie Harris and his Maine Coon cat, Diesel, are an endearing detective duo. Warm, charming, and Southern as the tastiest grits."

—Carolyn Hart, *New York Times* bestselling author of the Death on Demand Mysteries

"Combines a kindhearted librarian hero, family secrets in a sleepy Southern town, and a gentle giant of a cat that will steal your heart."

—Lorna Barrett, *New York Times* bestselling author of the Booktown Mysteries

"James should be on everyone's list of favorite authors."

—*New York Times* bestselling author Leann Sweeney

"Ideal for Christie fans who enjoy a good puzzle."

—*Library Journal*

"[A] pleasing blend of crime and charm."

—*Richmond Times-Dispatch*

"Humor and plenty of Southern charm. . . . Cozy fans will hope James will keep Charlie and Diesel in action for years to come."

—*Publishers Weekly*

"James just keeps getting better and better. . . . It's an intelligent read, so well-written that I couldn't stop reading it. Every single time I turned out my light for the night, I found myself thinking about the story, flipping the light switch again, and reading just 'one more chapter.'"

—MyShelf

A Cat in the Stacks Mystery

THE PAWFUL TRUTH

Miranda James

BERKLEY PRIME CRIME
New York

BERKLEY PRIME CRIME
Published by Berkley
An imprint of Penguin Random House LLC
penguinrandomhouse.com

ISBN: 9780451491145

Berkley Prime Crime hardcover edition / July 2019
Berkley Prime Crime mass-market edition / May 2020

Printed in the United States of America
5   7   9   10   8   6   4

Cover art by Dan Craig Inc.
Cover design by Katie Anderson
Book design by Tiffany Estreicher

This book is dedicated to the memory of my beloved aunt, Faye Williams Cook, 1940–2018.

ACKNOWLEDGMENTS

First, thanks to my editor, Michelle Vega, and the terrific team at Berkley—Jennifer Monroe, Tara O'Connor, and Elisha Katz—for taking such great care of Charlie, Diesel, and me. Special thanks also to my agent, Nancy Yost, and her amazing associates, Natanya Wheeler and Sarah E. Younger. Nobody does it better.

The support of friends makes everything better, and I have some pretty amazing friends: Patricia Orr, Terry Farmer, Julie Herman, Carolyn Haines, John McDougall, and Don Herrington. Thanks for all you do for, and give to, me. I am truly blessed. The readers who are so devoted to Charlie and Diesel (not necessarily in that order) make the hard days so much easier. Thank you for your continuing love and support for the series.

ONE

What did you get yourself into?

That thought had run through my mind several times for the past few days, but never so often as it had during the ten minutes I waited for class to start.

Staring at the eager young faces and listening to the chatter of voices rise and fall around me, I felt increasingly out of place. I had not failed to notice the covert glances, the occasional grimaces, and the *what is* he *doing here* tilts of the head in my direction. Not much subtlety.

Stop being so self-conscious, I chided myself. *You have every right to be here, even if you are three decades older than the rest of the class. Focus on why you're here and remember the excitement you felt when you finally decided to do this.*

Good advice, I realized, and I felt the tension begin to ebb away. I had long been fascinated by medieval history and sometimes wished I had majored in history, rather than in English, during my undergraduate days here at Athena. I had heard great things about the young professor who taught this course on the history of England from the end of the Roman occupation until the Norman Conquest. He offered a second course that picked up with the aftermath of the Conquest through the accession of the first Tudor monarch, Henry VII. When I saw the course listed for the spring semester, I decided to give myself a belated Christmas gift and sign up to audit it. If all went well with the first course, I would sign up for the second one the next time it was offered.

Dr. Warriner's courses always filled quickly, I had learned. I managed to squeak in before the class closed admissions. I hoped he lived up to his reputation because I was so interested in the subject and anticipated filling in the gaps in my knowledge.

A late arrival caught my eye when she slipped into an empty seat to the left a row ahead of me. A voluptuous blonde with a head of curly hair, she appeared to be in her thirties. Still younger than I, but at least there would be one other older student in the class. As if she felt my speculative glance on her, she turned to look my way.

A cool, assessing gaze met mine. She smiled briefly, then turned back to face the front of the classroom. That one glance revealed a stunning face, makeup so expertly applied that she appeared cosmetics-free. Perhaps Dr. Warriner's reputation had drawn her in as well, I mused. Or she might be a graduate student.

Conversation ceased suddenly as a tall, muscular man strode into the room to the front of the classroom. Had I not already seen Carey Warriner around campus a few times, I would have been more struck by his appearance. I heard the slow exhalation of sighs around me, and I glanced around. The female students raked him with their eyes, and I understood why. Warriner was easily the most handsome man I had ever seen in the flesh.

Broad shouldered, he stood at least six foot four and had the dark hair and eyes often referred to as *black Irish*. His chiseled features brought to mind the stars of Hollywood's Golden Age. With his sleeves rolled up to expose bronzed forearms, he favored the class with an engaging smile as he surveyed the room. Perhaps it was my sometimes overactive imagination, but I thought the smile slipped briefly when his gaze rested on the attractive blonde to my left.

The smile quickly returned, however, and he perched on the corner of the long table at the front of the classroom. "Good afternoon, everyone. I am Professor Warriner. Welcome to my course on the history of early medieval England."

His beautifully modulated baritone elicited a few more audible sighs from around the room, and his smile broadened. He appeared appreciative of this reaction. He reached for a folder he had laid on the table beside him.

"First things first, of course," he said. "Let's get the dull stuff out of the way. When I call your name, please raise your hand."

He extracted a piece of paper from the folder and began to read the names. The blonde lifted her hand to the name *Dixie Belle Compton. Talk about a Southern name*, I thought. *Dixie Belle.* I noticed that Warriner did not look at the students when he called this name. Perhaps he already knew her? That would explain the brief change of expression.

So engrossed in contemplating this, I nearly missed my own name. I jerked my hand up, and Warriner nodded. He soon finished his roll call and laid the paper aside. He rose from his perch and went to the board. Here he wrote his e-mail address. Turning back to face the class, he said,

"You will use this to submit your written assignments. You will find the syllabus for this course, if you haven't already, on my page in the history department website. This course requires a substantial amount of reading, some of it translations of primary sources; others are monographs by historians covering particular subjects." He paused to the sound of a few subdued groans.

"This course is no sinecure," he continued. "If you don't know the meaning of the word, I suggest you look it up. You will have to work, and work diligently, if you expect to do well in this class. If you aren't willing to work, I suggest you go ahead and drop the class today." He paused for a moment as he assessed the class with a measuring glance. "I am passionate about my subject, and while I don't expect my students to share my passion to the same degree, I do expect dedication to your work in this course. There will be no online instruction in this course. I prefer the old-fashioned methods, and that means I expect to see you in class at every scheduled meeting, on time, and ready to participate. Do not be late."

Warriner's uncompromising expression did not daunt me. In fact, I admired his standards, well familiar with them from my own college years here, thanks to several of my toughest professors. I had to admit to a certain amount of surprise, however, because of the prevalence of online education these days and the use of chat rooms and so on for group assignments.

I heard the rustle of movement around me. No doubt a few students were squirming a bit, and I wondered how many of them would return for the second class. Might as well weed out the less serious students right away.

"Now," the professor said, "on to the scope of this course. We begin with the departure of the Romans in the

fifth century of the Common Era. We will not discuss in
detail why the Roman Empire abandoned its province of
Britannia. That is the subject of a course taught by my
colleague Professor Fischer."

A hand shot up from the front row.

"Yes, what is it?" Warriner asked.

"Um, I was wondering, you know," a lanky young man
said, his words hesitant, "if you're going to talk about King
Arthur? I mean, you know, this is the period when he
lived, right? Once the Romans left, you know." He stam-
mered to a halt, and he appeared to shrink under the now-
harsh gaze of the professor.

Warriner stood and folded his arms over his chest. He
surveyed the room before he again focused on the student
with the question. "This is not a course on fantasy and
myth. A professor in the English department teaches a
course on English folklore. I suggest you take that if you
want to read about Arthur and his knights." He paused
briefly. "Now, back to reality. There well could have been
a warlord in the aftermath of Roman withdrawal who attempted to take control of parts of Britain, but if he ex-
isted at all, he was nothing like the legends that have
grown up around the fantasy of Arthur."

I felt the tension in the room. Perhaps the young man
had hit a sore spot with Warriner by asking his question.
Based on my own reading, admittedly limited, I agreed
with the professor, as much as I enjoyed tales of Arthur
and the Round Table. I loved the movie *Excalibur*, for
example, but I viewed it as fantasy, as I did Mary Stewart's enthralling Arthurian tetralogy about Arthur that I
had read years ago.

Warriner suddenly smiled, and the tension I had felt
dissipated. "I get a similar question every time I teach this

course," he said to the student, "and thank you for getting it out of the way so quickly. Now we can begin to focus on the real meat of the course."

The professor spent several minutes discussing the assignments for the course, from assigned readings and the reports to be written about them, to the number of tests, including the final exam, and the research paper due by the end of the course. Students could choose their topics, but he must approve them, and for those who needed help, he had a list of suggestions they could consult.

He paused for questions, and after he had answered three, he began his lecture. I had my pen and notebook ready. Many of the students, I had already observed, had brought laptops or tablets with keyboards with them. At first I found the clicking and tapping of keys and screens distracting, but I quickly became absorbed in Warriner's lecture. My hand began to cramp after about twenty minutes. As accustomed to the keyboard as I was, I had not written this much by hand in years. I decided I would bring my laptop from now on.

I did my best to keep up with my note-taking, but occasionally I found myself so intent on the lecture I forgot to write anything. Warriner spoke with passionate interest in his subject and shared fascinating details about life in fifth-century Britain. His lecturing style made the past come alive, and I enjoyed every moment that he spoke. The bell rang far too soon.

"We'll continue the topic on Friday," Warriner said as students began to gather their belongings and stow away their devices.

I flexed my cramped writing hand and then massaged it. While other students filed out of the room, Warriner did not move from his position at the front of the room. I glanced up to find him regarding me. "Mr. Harris," he said, "I would like to talk to you, if you have a moment."

"Certainly." I stuffed my notebook and pen in my brief-case and rose from the desk to join him at the front of the room.

Warriner perched again on the table and regarded me with a frown. For a moment I wondered if I had somehow offended him, or if he didn't care for older students in his classes.

"Is there a problem?" I asked.

The professor shook his head. "Not at all. I am wondering, however, why you are auditing my class rather than taking it for credit. Though we have not met before today, like everyone at Athena I am aware of your reputation for assisting in local murder investigations. Surely you're not intimidated by the intellectual demands of the course."

"No, it's not that," I said, somewhat defensively. His tone had not been dismissive or in any way negative, and I suddenly realized that my initial reaction was due to my own insecurities, not to his remarks. "I haven't been in the classroom for over twenty-five years, and though I am thoroughly interested in the subject, I'm not sure I want to work that hard."

"Doing well in this course takes effort and ability," Warriner said. "Don't underestimate yourself. I think you should consider taking the course for credit."

I shrugged. "I'll think about it, but I don't believe I'll change my mind. If you'd rather I dropped the class because of that, I will, though I'd be deeply disappointed."

Warriner flashed a smile. "No need for that. How about this? You turn in the first two assignments; let me see what you can do with them. If neither of us is satisfied with the results, I won't push you into taking the class for credit, and you can audit."

I considered that for a moment. I wondered why this mattered to him, but I had to admit he intrigued me with his offer. "All right, I'll do that."

"Good." Warriner nodded and rose from the desk. "Then I'll see you here on Friday."

I nodded and turned away. At the door I almost ran into Dixie Belle Compton, who had apparently been lingering there. She brushed past me and strode into the room. She jostled my arm, and I dropped my briefcase. She didn't pause in her progress, and I suppressed a rude comment.

As I bent to pick up my briefcase, I heard Warriner say, in a savage but carrying undertone, "What the hell are you doing in my class?"

TWO

||||||||||||||||||||

I didn't wait to hear Ms. Compton's response to Carey Warriner's question. I grabbed my briefcase and headed rapidly down the hall. I couldn't help but speculate, however, about Warriner's behavior. That he and Ms. Compton knew each other was obvious. I wondered *how* they knew each other, and how *well*. The tone the professor used had sounded both nasty and angry. What prompted it?

Not your business, I reminded myself. I walked quickly from the social sciences building back to my office in the antebellum mansion that housed the library director's office, along with the archive and rare book collection. I would do better to focus on my work than to speculate idly on the private lives of people I barely knew.

Diesel ran out of the administrative suite as I approached the outer office where my friend Melba Gilley, the director's administrative assistant, worked. My Maine Coon child, as I sometimes thought of him, warbled and trilled to let me know he was glad I hadn't abandoned him after all. He walked beside me back into Melba's office, chattering all the way. No doubt he was regaling me with his activities with his buddy Melba.

"Hello," I said. "I'm back to take this rascal off your hands."

Melba looked up from her computer to grin at me and the cat. "He's been a perfect gentleman, as always. Haven't you, sweet boy?"

Diesel trotted forward to rub his head against Melba's outstretched hand. He looked at me, his expression smug—or so I interpreted it.

"I'm sure he has," I said. "I appreciate your looking after him while I'm in class."

"Glad to do it," Melba replied. "How was the class?"

"Fine. He's an excellent lecturer." I debated whether to tell her what I had overheard between the professor and Ms. Compton. If anyone in town knew of any connection between professor and student, Melba would.

"He has a great reputation," Melba said, rubbing along Diesel's spine. "He's about the most gorgeous man I've ever seen, but he doesn't act like he's the Lord's gift to women, I'll say that for him." She giggled. "Not like some men I know who aren't anywhere near as good-looking as that man is."

I laughed. "There were plenty of young women in class today, and I heard them sighing when he walked into the room." I hesitated again, about to mention the other *mature student*, as we were called to my chagrin, but Melba forestalled me.

"His wife is every bit as beautiful as he is," Melba said. "From everything I've heard, she's nice, too. Teaches medieval English lit, I think."

"Irene Warriner." I nodded. "I believe she's a specialist in Anglo-Saxon literature."

"Everyone says they're devoted to each other." Melba looked hesitant.

"You're obviously dying to tell me something," I said. "What have you heard to the contrary?"

"Do you know Viccy Kemp?" Melba asked, but continued before I could respond. "She's the administrative assistant in the history department, and she and I go back a long way together. I had lunch with Viccy last week, and she brought along Jeanette Larson, who's the admin in the English department." She paused to look at me expectantly.

"I've spoken to Ms. Kemp," I said, "when I went by to ask a question about auditing the class. I don't know Ms. Larson."

"They're just about two of the biggest gossips on campus." Melba wrinkled her nose. "They're like this." She twined two fingers together. "Anyway, what one of them doesn't know, the other one does, and they don't hesitate to talk about it to anyone who'll listen."

"And you were listening."

Melba shrugged. "I couldn't very well tell them to stop talking."

Not when you were dying to hear what they had to say. I prudently kept that to myself, however. "Go on," I said. "What did they have to say about the Warriners?"

"Jeanette said that Carey Warriner has taken one of the English professors to lunch several times lately," Melba said. "She wasn't talking about his wife. It was Barbara Lamont."

I shook my head. I didn't recognize the name. "Maybe they're just friends."

"Could be," Melba said. "But then Viccy chimed in to say that Irene Warriner has been going out to lunch with one of her husband's colleagues in the history department, Daniel Bellamy."

"I don't know him," I said. "I haven't met him, but I read one of his books on Regency England." I laughed. "You know, that's probably the reason Irene Warriner is having lunch with him. The Regency connection."

Melba shook her head, obviously puzzled. "What are you talking about? What Regency connection?"

"The Regency period in the early nineteenth century when George the Third was mad and his son served as his regent," I said.

"Okay," Melba said, "but I still don't see the connection."

"Remember that book by Lucy Dunne I gave you a few weeks ago?" I asked.

Melba nodded. "I haven't gotten to it yet. What about it?"

I grinned. "I can't believe I know something you don't about someone on campus. Lucy Dunne writes historical romances set in the Regency period. Lucy Dunne is Irene Warriner."

"Well, I'll be," Melba muttered. "I had no idea she was a writer. Guess I'll have to read that book next. So I guess you think Dr. Bellamy is helping her with her books?"

I nodded. "Stands to reason, doesn't it? The period she teaches is many centuries earlier than the Regency, and he is an accomplished historian. The Lucy Dunne books are excellent, and I think you'll enjoy the one I lent you."

"Why doesn't she write about what she already knows?" Melba asked.

"The market is better for Regency- and Victorian-set romances," I said. "At least, according to Jordan Thompson, and she ought to know. Jordan told me not long ago that she—Irene Warriner, I mean—had recently signed a big contract for more books. She didn't know how much, but apparently it was at least a healthy six figures. So she must be doing really well with her books." Jordan Thompson owned the local independent bookstore, the Athenaeum, and I had always found her extremely helpful and knowledgeable about books of any genre.

"Okay, so maybe that explains Mrs. Warriner having lunch with another man besides her husband," Melba said, "but what about her husband having lunch with another woman?"

"Could be something similar, I suppose, but I don't know what Barbara Lamont's specialty is." I had a feeling this one might be more difficult to explain than the Warriner-Bellamy connection.

"Hang on a minute, and I'll look her up." Melba turned to her computer and started tapping at the keys. After a few clicks of the mouse, she evidently found what she wanted to know. "Barbara Lamont teaches twentieth-century American literature," she announced. "Her specialty is Edith Wharton. Also Henry James, it says here."

"Maybe Carey Warriner is a big Edith Wharton or Henry James fan. The two of them knew each other, I believe," I said. "There are probably a dozen reasons—perfectly innocent reasons—that the two of them might have lunch together. Men and women can be friends without there being anything more than friendship between them. Like you and me, for example."

"I know that," Melba said. "And I pointed out that exact same thing to Viccy and Jeanette, but they don't believe it. According to Viccy, Carey Warriner has a roving eye."

I debated again whether to tell Melba about the incident between Carey Warriner and my fellow student Dixie Belle Compton. I decided I wouldn't. No need to fan the flames of gossip any further, although I knew Melba wouldn't share it with her friends if I asked her not to.

"That may well be," I said, "but as long as it doesn't

interfere with his duties as a teacher in the class I'm taking, I'm not going to spend any time thinking about it."

My tone must have been sharper than I realized, because Melba shot me an injured look.

"You don't need to get all pious on me," she said.

"I'm sorry. I didn't mean for it to sound that way." I offered a rueful grin, and her expression lightened.

"I can't stay mad at you, Charlie." She laughed. "If you weren't interested in what I know about people, you wouldn't hang around here listening to me, now, would you?"

"'A hit, a very palpable hit,'" I quoted—my daughter Laura's influence, for she liked to quote Shakespeare, and I had picked up the habit from her.

Melba ignored my little sally and glanced around her feet and mine. "Where's Diesel?"

I squatted to look under her desk. My cat was snoozing on the carpet. "He's napping." I stood. "Come on, boy, let's get upstairs to the office. Time to get some work done. It's already two thirty, and you'll be leaving in an hour."

Diesel emerged from beneath the desk and yawned. He paused to stretch before he trotted to the door. "See you later," I said as I followed him out of the office and up the stairs.

I unlocked the door and turned on the lights. Diesel headed for his litter box and water bowl, both placed discreetly out of sight in a corner behind a low range of shelves. After a quick check of my e-mail, having found nothing that needed an immediate reply, I set to work cataloging more Southern fiction given to the rare book collection the previous year.

As a librarian, I loved nothing better than cataloging old books. I never knew what surprises lurked between their pages. I had found old tissues, bookmarks of various kinds, more than a few pressed flowers, and many inscriptions and annotations. The latter made each book a special object to me and not simply a generic copy of a title like its many fellows printed at the same time. Occasionally a book contained a review by a previous reader, either written in the book itself or on a card stuck between the pages. My favorite of these reviews, found several weeks ago inscribed in the front flyleaf of a novel, was *Utter hogwash, but good hogwash nevertheless*, followed by initials and a date.

I focused on the task at hand and spent a pleasurable hour cataloging while Diesel napped in the wide window embrasure behind my desk. He loved this particular perch because there were trees outside the window. I heard the occasional muttering when he spotted a bird or a squirrel, but he was smart enough to know that he couldn't reach the creatures. Muttering at them seemed to satisfy him, for which I was grateful. He had on occasion gone hunting in the backyard at home and brought me trophies, like small lizards, mice, and unlucky birds. Although I thanked him for the gifts, I quickly disposed of them, much to his consternation.

My cell phone rang a few minutes after three thirty, moments after I had put away the book I had finished cataloging. I recognized the number as that of the bookstore, the Athenaeum—Jordan Thompson or one of her staff no doubt calling to tell me they had books for me.

Jordan Thompson greeted me, and after an exchange of pleasantries she informed me that she had several items for me. "Plus, when you get here, I'll tell you about a special event we just added today. I know you'll want to attend."

"What is it?" I asked, intrigued.

Jordan laughed. "I'll tell you when you come in. Bye."

I would have gone by the bookstore anyway this

afternoon—I never could resist the lure of new books—but Jordan's comments added piquancy to my decision.

Melba was not at her desk when Diesel and I reached the ground floor, so we headed out the back to the small parking lot next to the building. I had driven to work today instead of walking as I usually did because I had an errand to run. Conveniently for me, that errand would take me to the town square, where the bookstore was situated. I decided I'd go to the bookstore first.

For once I found a parking space directly in front of the bookstore. I held the car door open for Diesel, and he jumped to the pavement and onto the sidewalk with alacrity. I had already told him we were going to visit his friend Jordan, and he was looking forward to the treats she never failed to provide.

I swung open the door to the bookstore, and Diesel loped inside. I paused, however, my attention caught by an announcement taped to the inside of the door, facing outward. Lucy Dunne would be appearing at the store this Saturday evening to sign her newest release, *A Night of Dark Deceptions*. Appearing with the author would be noted Regency expert Dr. Daniel Bellamy of Athena College, for a discussion of the historical background to Ms. Dunne's books.

So much for romantic intrigue between the two professors, I thought. They had been lunching to discuss their presentation at the bookstore. What a perfectly ordinary—and innocent—explanation. I'd have to text Melba about it later.

THREE

When Diesel and I walked into the kitchen after our book-store visit, we found Azalea Berry, my housekeeper, sing-ing to the latest addition to my family. Ramses, an orange tabby kitten about five months old, watched Azalea while she worked and sang at the stove. His tail twitched almost in time to the rhythm of the old hymn.

Azalea broke off when she realized Diesel and I had entered. I tried not to chuckle. This wasn't the first time we had caught the housekeeper singing to the kitten. Un-like Diesel, Ramses didn't go to work with me. The kitten was far too mischievous, and even with Diesel's willing help, I'd never accomplish much in the office while trying to keep track of Ramses.

After greeting Azalea and Ramses, I set my bag of books on the kitchen table. Somehow, I always managed to bring home two or three times as many books as I in-tended to purchase when I entered the bookstore. Jordan always had *just one more* I really should consider. Given that she had rarely steered me wrong over the years, I didn't often demur when she told me I needed to read a particular title. She knew my likes and dislikes well.

"Has Ramses been behaving himself?" I watched Diesel and the kitten greet each other. My large Maine Coon considerably dwarfed his adopted sibling. Ramses rubbed his head against Diesel's chin, and my big boy allowed this. He tolerated the kitten's antics better than I had expected.

"Oh, he's always trying to get into something," Azalea said. "I had to put him in time out at least three times today. He is a scamp, but he is mighty entertaining to have around."

Azalea's *time out* for Ramses consisted of shutting him in the utility room with his food, water, and litter box for about ten minutes at a time. She swore it was effective—at least for a few hours.

"You can't get bored with Ramses around," I said. "Is he still trying to climb into your bag?"

In addition to her leather handbag, Azalea always brought a large woven straw bag, the contents of which remained a mystery to me. Ramses had been fascinated by this bag from the get-go and tried to get into it at every opportunity. He had even sneaked into it and gone home with Azalea several times without her realizing it until she reached her house. After the first time, Azalea told me not to worry about retrieving him. She would keep him overnight and bring him back the next morning.

"Every chance he gets." Azalea chuckled. "Reckon I ought to put it up in a high cabinet somewhere, but that little imp would probably still find a way to get into it. The good Lord only knows why he likes that bag so much."

"With cats, you never know." I chuckled. "They get these fixations sometimes, but most of the time, they do wear off." Privately, I thought Ramses liked Azalea better than he liked me, though he was affectionate enough with me. Azalea was the one who slipped him treats, however. That little belly showed no signs of diminishing anytime soon.

A couple of times I had almost suggested the idea of Ramses's going to live with Azalea, but while she tolerated the kitten on the occasional sleepover, I wasn't convinced that she wanted him as her own. Before I could give the kitten away, however, I felt I needed to consult the young person who had first given Ramses to me. I wouldn't want him to think I hadn't appreciated his gift. The next time he dropped by to visit Ramses and Diesel I would broach the idea with him, I decided.

Diesel headed for the utility room, and Ramses, shadowlike, accompanied him. "I'm going to put these books away in the den," I said to Azalea. "Have you heard from Laura or Alex today?"

"They both dropped by a little while ago with the babies," Azalea replied. "Thank the Lord Miss Alex is doing so much better. She's looking almost back to her old self again."

Alex, married to my son, Sean, struggled with postpartum depression after the birth of their daughter three months ago. Thanks to the help of a therapist and the support of family and a live-in nanny, Azalea's niece, Alex had improved significantly. Charlotte Rose Harris, whom we all called Rosie, was thriving. Her cousin Charlie, aka Charles Franklin Salisbury, the son of my daughter, Laura, and her husband, Frank, was several months older. Laura thankfully hadn't suffered the way Alex did. Both mother and child were healthy and happy.

"Too bad Diesel and I missed them," I said. "It's been a few days since I've seen either of the babies." Every time

I gazed down into those small faces, I felt a sense of wonder. *My grandchildren*, I thought, still a bit bemused by the fact that I was a grandfather.

"Little Charlie and Ramses played some," Azalea said. "Made Miss Alex laugh, and that was good."

I smiled at that. "Yes, that's great." I picked up the sack of books and carried them with me to the den. My cell phone rang while I pulled out my purchases and stacked them on the desk. I answered the call, happy to see by the caller ID that Helen Louise Brady was on the line.

"Hello, love," I said. "How are you? Worn out from the lunch crowd?" Helen Louise owned one of the most popular lunch spots in Athena, a French bistro on the town square.

"*Mais oui*," she said. "I'm getting too old to be on my feet this much."

"Now, now," I said teasingly, "you're several months younger than I am, and *I'm* not old."

Helen Louise laughed. "True, but you sit at your job. I don't."

"These days I do." During my years in the public library system in Houston, Texas, I spent much of my time on my feet. I was happy now to have a more sedentary job, working with archives and rare books.

"Maybe it's time to think about adding another part-time worker for the lunch shift," I said. "Business is holding steady, isn't it?"

"Thank the Lord, yes," Helen Louise said. "With college classes back in session, it's better than ever. I've been thinking about putting an ad on the website and in the local paper. I should bite the bullet and get it done."

She had been saying she was cutting back on the hours she worked ever since she hired a full-time manager and another full-time staff person. Some weeks she did manage to take time off, but she had a hard time letting go of control of her business. I understood that. She had worked hard to establish it and took great pride in her accomplishment, as well she should. She needed time for a personal life, though, and as that personal life involved me, I was definitely in favor of her cutting back. I didn't want to pressure her, however, because I knew it had to be her decision.

"I think it's a good idea to place those ads," I said. "You're run off your feet during busy times, and you don't want customers to feel like they're kept waiting too long for service."

"You're right." Helen Louise sighed. "Thanks for always helping me put things in perspective, sweetheart. Having you there for me makes all the difference."

"That works both ways," I said. "Are you going to be free for dinner tonight? I'm not sure what Azalea has on the menu, but it's bound to be good."

Helen Louise chuckled. "Lure me away from work with good old-fashioned Southern cooking, is that your game? This time, it's going to work. Yes, I'll be there around six."

"That's fine," I said. "I'll let Azalea know, but I'm sure she's cooking enough for the two of us and several more besides."

We said good-bye, and I headed back to the kitchen to tell Azalea that Helen Louise was coming for dinner.

My boarder Stewart Delacorte, a professor of chemistry at Athena, arrived home around five thirty.

"How was the second day of classes?" I asked after he greeted the four of us in the kitchen.

"No more exciting than the first day," Stewart muttered darkly. "I'm getting too old to put up with freshmen anymore. They seem to be getting younger and younger, and more ill-mannered every year."

"You said the same thing last year," I said in a mild tone.

"And I'm another year older," Stewart replied, obviously intent on being grumpy.

"Retire then," I said without much sympathy.

"I'd like to retire from teaching freshmen," he said. "The juniors and seniors are fine, and I'm happy with my crop of graduate students this year."

"Then talk to the department chair and ask not to teach the freshmen again." We went through a similar routine at the beginning of each new semester. Even Diesel, normally sensitive to any kind of intense emotion, ignored Stewart in this mood. Instead he focused on slapping at Ramses.

I knew Stewart needed to blow off a little steam, so I played along. In another week he would be in a better mood, after terrifying the freshmen in his classes into what he considered proper classroom behavior. He was a tough professor, I had heard from more than one source, but I knew that his students had a high rate of acceptance into top graduate programs and medical schools.

Suddenly Stewart grinned at me and Azalea. "Thanks for listening. I'd better run up and get Dante out for his walkies. Haskell won't be here for dinner. All deputies got called in for some kind of meeting. He couldn't tell me what the meeting is about." He headed out of the kitchen, and moments later I heard him run up the stairs. He, Haskell, and Stewart's poodle, Dante, occupied a suite on the third floor of the house.

I sniffed appreciatively while I set the table for three. To judge by the aroma wafting from the oven, Azalea had made one of her staple chicken casseroles with the addition of rice, cheese, spinach, and mushrooms. A good old rib-sticker, as my father would have called it.

Helen Louise arrived a few minutes after Stewart returned from walking Dante. Azalea set the casserole on the table, along with salad and hot, freshly baked rolls. After ensuring that we were all happy with the meal, Azalea retrieved her purse and the straw bag—sans Ramses—and headed out the door. I had tried in the past to get her to have dinner with us. I knew she and my late aunt Dottie had often shared meals, but for whatever reason, she always declined.

After a few minutes of the usual polite dinner-table chitchat—along with the surreptitious offerings of chicken to Diesel, Ramses, and Dante—Helen Louise asked me how my first day as a student had gone.

"Fine," I said. "The professor is a great lecturer. I can see why his classes are so popular."

Stewart shot me a look of feigned disbelief. "You mean he actually has something interesting to say? Students aren't there just to ogle the movie star of the history department?"

I rolled my eyes at Stewart.

Helen Louise laughed. "I'm sure Charlie isn't there to ogle, so the professor must be good."

"I have no doubt some students are there to sigh and gaze at Warriner," I said. "He is handsome, I grant you, but he has a brain."

"Like me." Stewart sighed in dramatic fashion.

"I'll come to one of your classes and ogle you." Helen Louise batted her eyelashes at Stewart.

He grinned. "I have a better idea. Let's go to Charlie's class with him and ogle Warriner. He is almost too beautiful to be real."

"I've seen him," Helen Louise said. "He and his wife come into the bistro on a regular basis."

"That's interesting," Stewart said. "Whenever I've seen Mrs. Warriner out and about, she's always with another

23

man. Their body language makes me think they're really into each other. Touching each other's arms and gazing at each other without talking." He shrugged. "Makes me wonder about the state of her marriage."

Helen Louise glanced down at her plate. When she looked up again, her expression was troubled. "I wasn't going to say anything, but she's come into the bistro a few times recently with another man. I've noticed the same kind of behavior."

I put down my fork. "Irene Warriner is a novelist and writes as Lucy Dunne, you know. She's doing a talk with Daniel Bellamy, a history professor whose specialty is Regency England, for the bookstore soon. I'm sure they were just meeting to discuss their program."

Stewart shook his head. "I know Dan Bellamy. The man I saw her with is someone else entirely."

FOUR

I prepared for bed half an hour after Helen Louise went home. Diesel already lay stretched out on his side of the bed, his head on the pillow, with Ramses curled up beside him. I couldn't help smiling at the picture the two cats made, one so large, the other still quite small in comparison. That smile aside, however, I felt troubled by the gossip Helen Louise, Stewart, and I had discussed over the dinner table.

Though I barely knew Carey Warriner and knew his wife only by her novels, I disliked the thought that their relationship might be complicated by an extramarital affair. I hated to see unhappy couples, since my marriage to my late wife had been a truly happy one. I also, rather selfishly, didn't want to have to deal with a distracted professor this semester after I had finally decided to audit a history course.

After reflection I determined that, should Carey Warriner start behaving erratically in class, I would simply withdraw from the course. This was taking a pessimistic view of what might be nothing more than a mare's nest, as the old saying went. The fact that Helen Louise and Stewart had each seen Irene Warriner in the company of different men who were not her husband could have a perfectly innocent explanation. Men and women could be good friends, with nothing romantic or sexual attached to the relationship. Melba and I served as an example.

Suspicious minds—those who preferred always to look for a seamy side to any innocuous situation—might think Melba and I were more than friends. Anyone who knew either Melba or me at all well would find that laughable. At least, I hoped they would. I couldn't be responsible for the way others might interpret my actions.

And you should stop trying to interpret the actions of people you don't even know.

I could hear Aunt Dottie's voice almost as clearly as if she had been in the room with me. I knew what else she would say. *Other people's messes—if they* are *messes— aren't your business.*

No, they weren't, I told myself firmly. I turned off the bedside lamp and made myself comfortable. Sometime later I dropped off to sleep with Diesel and Ramses lying quiet beside me.

The next morning I woke resolved to put all thoughts of the Warriners and their private lives out of my mind. During breakfast Diesel begged for bacon, and Ramses generally followed his big brother's example. I saw Azalea slip tidbits to Ramses when she thought no one could observe and smiled. As long as she didn't overdo it, I didn't have a problem with her giving treats to either of the cats.

Diesel and I left for work at the archive office at the usual time. We walked this morning because the day bid fair to turn out sunny, although a little cool. Diesel loved the walk because we invariably ran into someone who wanted to talk to him and give him attention. For that reason I allowed for several extra minutes for the brief walk up the street the few blocks to campus.

We stopped to wish Melba a good morning before we continued upstairs to my office. The moment I unleashed Diesel he loped toward the window and jumped into his spot. I racked my coat and got ready for the day's work.

Perhaps half an hour later, while I was engrossed in deciphering the cramped handwriting in the margins of the book I was cataloging, the office phone rang. After identifying myself, I said, "How may I assist you?"

Melba said, "You've got a visitor this morning. Is it okay to send her on up?"

"Who is it?" I didn't have any appointments that I could recall. The few visitors I had were usually students or the occasional potential donor of books or papers for the archives.

"A Ms. Dixie Compton," Melba said.

I could tell by my friend's guarded tone that there was something about this Ms. Compton that bothered her. "Yes, send her up," I said. "Thanks, Melba." Frowning, I puzzled over the visitor's name, then recognition came. The blonde woman from Carey Warriner's class. Why did she want to talk to me, of all people?

I cradled the receiver and turned to Diesel. "We've got a visitor this morning, boy."

Diesel yawned and stretched, all the while regarding me with an expression of mild interest.

I remembered that Ms. Compton had stayed after class yesterday to talk to the professor and that his reaction to her presence in the class had sounded angry. The incident puzzled me at the time, but I had let it go. Now that it came back to me, I was even more curious to find out why Ms. Compton had sought me out like this.

I rose as she entered the office. "Good morning, Ms. Compton." I moved around the desk to take her outstretched hand. "Please, won't you sit?" I indicated the chair in front of my desk.

"Thank you, Mr. Harris." She set her purse on the edge of my desk. "I know you're wondering why I just popped up out of the blue, so to speak, but I wanted to talk to you about something."

"You're welcome, ma'am," I replied. Diesel had jumped down from his perch in the window and walked around the desk to examine the visitor. She glanced down at him and smiled.

"This is my Maine Coon cat, Diesel," I explained. "He comes to the office with me."

Ms. Compton nodded. "Yes, I've heard about him. If you'd had him with you in class yesterday, I wouldn't have had to ask anyone who you were. Even I've heard of you and your cat." She held out her hand and let Diesel sniff her fingers. After a moment, Diesel rubbed his head against her hand, and Ms. Compton scratched behind his left ear. He chirped for her before going back to his window. "He's a gorgeous cat."

"Thank you," I said. "He goes almost everywhere with me, but I didn't think the classroom would be suitable." Diesel had obviously approved of my visitor, otherwise he would have stayed in the window. Usually he stayed beside people he approved of, but evidently he wasn't interested enough in Ms. Compton to forgo the pleasures of napping in the window and watching any birds or squirrels nearby.

"What is it you'd like to talk about?" Now that we sat face-to-face, I had a clear look at her and could watch her expressions. At the moment she appeared nervous, though I couldn't imagine why. The fingers of her right hand played with the necklace of irregular-shaped blue and green stones she wore, alternately rubbing and fingering them.

"It's about the class we're taking," she said after a moment's hesitation. "It's been a long time since I was in school." She broke off.

When she didn't continue right away, I said, "I understand. It's been even longer for me. It can be intimidating coming back after an absence." I chuckled, hoping to set her at ease. "I'm only auditing the class at the moment. Are you taking it for credit?"

Ms. Compton nodded. "Yes, along with another one in the English department, the one that goes with it, I guess. You know, the one about Old English and medieval literature."

"I saw that course in the catalog. *Beowulf* and Anglo-Saxon poetry," I said. "It looked interesting, but I was more curious about the history, I guess." When would she get to the point of this conversation?

"They're both interesting," Ms. Compton said, "but I'm wondering if I maybe got in over my head by taking two classes. Maybe I should have stuck with just one."

Given what I had overheard yesterday after class, I had begun to wonder if she had chosen courses by husband and wife deliberately. She obviously had some connection to Carey Warriner, one that had angered Warriner. The inevitable interpretation had already occurred to me. Had Warriner and Ms. Compton had an affair?

"You can always drop one if you decide that it's too overwhelming for you."

She nodded. "Yeah, I can, but I don't want to. Now that I've got up my nerve to go back to school, I want to stick with it. I really want to finish my degree."

"Very admirable," I said.

"The thing is," she said, then seemed to falter. After a brief pause she resumed while she continued to fiddle with her necklace. "The thing is, I might need someone to study with. And you being the only other mature student." She broke off with a sudden laugh. "I hate that term, don't you?"

I nodded and smiled, and she continued. "Anyway, I can't see myself buddying up with one of the kids in the class, and I wondered whether you might be interested in having a study partner."

After she mentioned mature students, I had guessed where she might be headed, so I wasn't surprised by her request. Unless I did as the professor urged and enrolled in the course for credit, there didn't seem to be any point in my having a study partner. I had never done that in the past, and I hadn't given it any thought for the present situation.

I understood her reason for wanting to work with another older student, but I had little desire to do it. I wasn't sure how to respond. I had trouble saying *no* when asked for help, and even now I hesitated to say it outright. Then another thought struck me. How would Helen Louise react if I told her I had a study partner? A young, attractive woman study partner?

I decided I had better say *no* this time. "Since I'm only auditing," I said, "I probably won't be taking any tests or writing any papers. It's really kind of you to think of me, but I don't really need a study partner for auditing."

Ms. Compton sighed. "I guess not."

I decided, on impulse, to probe a little, though I could almost hear Aunt Dottie whispering in my ear that I should mind my own business. "I'm sure if you talk to the professor about your concerns, he can probably suggest someone who could work with you."

That earned me a startled glance from my visitor, and her expression hardened, but only briefly. She emitted a short, guttural sound that could be interpreted as a laugh.

"Yes, I *could* do that," she said. "Tell me, do you know much about him?"

"Warriner?" I shook my head. "I met him for the first time yesterday. I've heard great things about his courses, though."

"Yeah, I guess he's supposed to be good in the classroom," she said. "But outside it?" She shrugged.

"Then you must know him personally." I took those three words to mean that she did—and they weren't on the best of terms, if the beginning of the confrontation I had overheard was anything to go by.

"Yes, I know him," Ms. Compton said. "Let's just say I have personal reasons for not wanting to talk to Dr. Warriner about it."

What lay behind all this reluctance? Had Warriner and this woman had a really *personal* relationship? I couldn't help but wonder.

I kept my tone bland as I responded. "In that case, you should talk to your advisor," I said. "Surely you have one."

Ms. Compton nodded. "Yes, I have one." She rose abruptly. "I've taken up enough of your time, Mr. Harris. Thank you for talking with me." She grabbed her purse and left my office in a hurried manner, barely giving me time to respond.

"You're welcome," I called after her.

Behind me Diesel meowed as if he were asking me a question. I swiveled in my chair to regard him thoughtfully.

"I wish I knew, boy. That was a strange conversation."

The cat meowed again, perhaps in agreement.

"What did she want?"

I turned back to see Melba approaching my desk. She took the seat so recently vacated by Dixie Compton.

"Did you let her get out the front door before you made a beeline up here?" I asked.

Melba rolled her eyes at me and then waited for an answer to her question.

"She says she's concerned about the class we're both taking," I said. "She was wondering if I would be interested in having a study partner."

Melba frowned. "You turned her down, I hope."

"I did, actually," I replied. "What would have been your objection if I hadn't?"

"Because that woman is nothing but trouble, and you'd better not have anything to do with her."

FIVE

"That's pretty strong," I said in response to Melba's assessment of Dixie Compton. "What do you know about her?"

"She's been married twice, and she's been mixed up in at least two divorces that I know of." Melba shook her head. "She stirs up trouble, and you don't want to get too friendly with her."

"I'm hardly likely to." I was tempted to ask Melba whether she knew anything about Dixie Compton and Carey Warriner, but decided against it.

"I reckon you wouldn't be the first man to say that," Melba retorted, "and then find yourself hip-deep in all kinds of mess. Helen Louise will know what I'm talking about."

"You think I should talk to Helen Louise about her?" I asked, trying not to grin. "Maybe warn her that Dixie Compton is on the prowl, and that she's got me in her sights?"

Melba shot me a withering glance. "You think you're

so funny sometimes. Don't try to act all superior with me, Charlie Harris. I know what I'm talking about. If that woman ever turns up dead in a ditch somewhere, I'm not going to be surprised. She's pissed off way too many women, and probably a few men, in this town." With that, she got up and hurried out of the room.

Carey Warriner could be one of those men. That thought came unbidden, and I dismissed it. I had a tendency to occasionally let my imagination run away with me. No doubt the result of my experiences with murder the past few years.

I felt guilty over being facetious with Melba. I knew better than to respond this way when she was in one of these moods. I'd give her a little time to cool down, and then I'd apologize. She meant well, I knew, but frankly I had a hard time seeing myself as the target of a femme fatale's designs.

I had to wonder, though, whether Dixie Compton's invitation to be her study partner was her only purpose in coming to see me. I couldn't put a finger on it, but the whole episode felt slightly off to me. Her relationship with Carey Warriner—whatever it was, or might still be—made me leery. There was no point in my spending any more time analyzing it. I could sit here for way too long wasting my time.

"I need to get back to work," I said to Diesel. "We'll go downstairs in a bit, and you can work your magic on Melba and get her to forgive me." He gave me a lazy chirp in response and resumed snoozing.

I worked steadily until lunchtime with no further interruptions, other than the occasional muttering from Diesel whenever he spotted activity in the trees outside his window. He jumped down when he saw me making preparations to leave and beat me to the door. While I locked it, he scampered down the stairs. He knew we were headed home, where treats awaited him. Fried chicken, if I remembered Azalea's plans correctly.

Melba's office stood empty, and I supposed she had already left for her own lunch. Diesel waited patiently for me to put on his harness and attach the leash, and then we set off down the sidewalk toward home. Before we reached the first street crossing, a tall, attractive blond man who looked vaguely familiar nodded to me as he passed by, with only a cursory glance at Diesel. Usually strangers stopped, struck by the sight of a cat on a leash, but this man was either not interested or in too much of a hurry to comment or question.

That sense of vague familiarity nagged at me as Diesel and I continued toward home. I tried to recall the context in which I had seen the stranger but none came easily to mind. I paused to glance back, but he had disappeared from view. At some point I would recall where I had seen the man before, I knew. I thought instead about Azalea's delicious fried chicken and mashed potatoes with gravy and biscuits. Several minutes later we reached home and headed inside for our meal.

We found Stewart seated at the kitchen table, a pleasant surprise because it wasn't often that he came home from campus for lunch. I expressed these thoughts while Diesel, with Ramses meowing enthusiastically by his side, went to the utility room. Dante was not present, so I presumed that Stewart had left him upstairs.

Stewart grinned. "I had a hankering for fried chicken, and nobody's is better than Azalea's."

Azalea made a sound vaguely like a snort as she set a platter of chicken on the table, along with bowls of green beans and potatoes and a gravy boat. Next came glasses of sweet tea and a plate piled high with biscuits. I could feel my waistline expanding from merely inhaling the delicious aromas.

While I washed and dried my hands at the sink, Stewart continued talking. "It's a shame you weren't here a few minutes ago, Charlie. I had a visitor who is interested in renting a room for a couple of months. I thought you might be willing to rent Justin's old room."

Justin Wardlaw, a student at Athena who had boarded with me for several years, had recently moved in with family who lived near campus. I missed having him around the house, and Diesel certainly missed him, but I was happy for Justin.

"Who is it?" I asked as I returned to the table and took my usual seat. "If it's someone you know, I'm certainly willing to consider it."

"Dan Bellamy," Stewart said. "I don't know him really well, but we've been friendly for several years now. He goes to the same gym where Haskell and I are members. He works out sometimes when we do."

I stared at Stewart, a forkful of green beans halfway to my mouth. "The Dan Bellamy that we were talking about before?"

Stewart grinned again. "He's the only one I know. He apparently needs a place to stay temporarily while he has some work done on his house. Extensive renovations, he said, and there's too much noise and confusion. He needs a quieter space until it's done."

I chewed on my beans and didn't respond until I had swallowed and had a sip of sweet tea. "If you think he's okay, then it's fine with me. I'd like to talk to him first, though."

Stewart pulled out his cell phone. "I'll text him. He hasn't been gone long. He might have time now to come back and talk."

"Or just have him come by my office sometime this afternoon," I said.

Stewart nodded, his thumbs quickly tapping away on the screen of his phone. I envied him his ability. I remained firmly stuck in the one-finger style of texting.

Azalea had been doling out bits of chicken to the two cats while Stewart and I talked. The housekeeper noticed that I was watching, and she wiped her hands and held them up to let the cats see that they were empty of treats.

"That's all, you two. I can't stand around here all day just giving you chicken."

Diesel meowed, and Ramses started rubbing himself against her legs. Azalea glanced at me, and I shook my head. "Go on, you two, now scat. Blame Mr. Charlie, not me."

Diesel left Azalea and came to me, quickly followed by Ramses. I looked down at the two expectant faces. "No, you've both had enough. Despite what you are thinking, you do *not* need any more chicken."

That stern comment earned me an indignant trill from Diesel, while Ramses decided to scale my leg and scramble into my lap. Stewart watched, laughing the whole time. Then his cell phone buzzed, and he picked it up to glance at the screen.

"Dan," he said as he looked up at me. "Says he'll drop by your office around one thirty, if that's okay."

I nodded. "Fine."

Stewart tapped on his phone again, then set it aside.

Ramses kept trying to climb from my lap into my plate, and I put him down on the floor, looked at him, and said in my firmest tone, "No, Ramses, no."

Ever the optimist, Ramses attempted to climb my leg again, but this time Diesel batted him down. Diesel understood what I meant when I told him *no*. Ramses wailed indignantly, but Diesel kept pushing him away. Finally, the smaller cat gave up and went back to Azalea.

I didn't see the housekeeper give Ramses any more chicken, but he stayed near her until she left the kitchen for another part of the house. Ramses went with her. I wouldn't have been surprised to find out she had chicken in her apron pocket. She spoiled the kitten unrepentantly.

Now that Ramses was out of the room and Diesel had stopped pestering me, I could focus my thoughts on my prospective boarder. Suddenly my brain connected my encounter with the vaguely familiar stranger to Stewart's relaying of Bellamy's request.

"On the way home for lunch," I said, "a tall blond man who I thought looked familiar passed us on the sidewalk near campus. I wonder if that might have been your friend Bellamy."

Stewart shrugged. "Very possible. The timing would fit. He is tall and blond. Muscular and handsome, too."

I nodded. "Fits the man I saw. I can't figure out why he looked familiar, though. I've never met Dan Bellamy that I can recall."

"Didn't you read one of his books?" Stewart asked.

"Yes," I said. "Excellent book." Then light dawned. "There was a picture of him on the book jacket. Now I remember. I looked at it briefly, but I don't usually pay much attention to pictures of authors."

"Mystery solved then." Stewart grinned as he picked apart a drumstick and placed the meat on a saucer. "I'm taking this up to Dante. He was a good boy this morning and didn't eat any of my shoes."

I laughed. "One thing I don't have to worry about with Diesel. Ramses, however, is another matter. I caught him sharpening his claws on an old pair of dress shoes in my closet yesterday."

We finished our meal, continuing to chat about our pets and their quirks, some adorable and others downright annoying. My philosophy had always been, however, if you had something valuable you didn't want a dog or cat to play with, then it was up to you to put it safely away. You couldn't blame the pet for taking what was available for a plaything.

Stewart said he would clear the table while Azalea was busy elsewhere, and Diesel and I left him to it. I wanted to track down my Lucy Dunne books and put them together in anticipation of the coming event. The last two had been published in hardcover, while the first few had been paperback originals. I knew where the hardbacks were, but the paperbacks could be in several places.

I quickly found the hardbacks and pulled them from the shelf. Diesel watched from the sofa, stretched out and yawning, when I placed the books on the desk. I rooted among the shelves that covered one whole wall of the den and found two of the paperbacks. Another one was upstairs in a shelf in my bedroom, and after thinking about it for a bit, I remembered that I had taken one to Melba a couple of weeks ago. I would have to remind her to bring it to me before the event.

I had borrowed Daniel Bellamy's book from the college library. I imagined Jordan Thompson would have copies for sale at the event, and I might consider purchasing one and having the author sign it.

A check of my watch alerted me to the need to head back to the archive. "Come on, Diesel," I said. "Time to go back to work."

Diesel perked up and hopped off the couch. Two minutes later, the cat back in his harness and leash, we headed up the street to campus. Time to apologize to Melba.

SIX

Melba had returned from lunch. She glanced up as we approached the office suite's open door. She frowned at me, but she had a smile for Diesel when he ran to her after I let him off the leash. I followed the cat slowly and stopped a couple of paces from her desk while she scratched Diesel's head and crooned to him.

"I'm sorry," I said, my expression penitent. "Friends again?"

Melba rolled her eyes at me. "Of course we are. You need to be reminded every once in a while you can be a little too much of a smarty-pants, that's all. When I tell you something I know about a person, am I usually wrong?"

"No, not usually," I said. "In fact, I have a hard time recalling a time when you *were* wrong."

Melba shot me a glance full of triumph and a lot of *I told you so*. I held up my hands in a gesture of surrender, leash dangling.

"Diesel, would you like to visit Melba awhile if it's

okay with her?" I looked directly at the cat. He knew what I was asking him, and he responded with a loud meow. I glanced at Melba, who nodded.

"All right then," I said, turning to head upstairs. Almost to the door, I paused and looked back. "I have a visitor coming around one thirty. Potential new boarder."

"Anyone I know?" Melba asked.

"History professor Daniel Bellamy, the one you were talking about yesterday," I said. "That reminds me. Do you mind bringing me that Lucy Dunne book you borrowed?"

"How did that remind you of the book?" Melba looked puzzled.

"Lucy Dunne and Daniel Bellamy are doing an event this weekend for the bookstore," I said. "I'd like to take my books and get them signed."

"I don't know Dr. Bellamy myself, only what I've heard mostly from Viccy and Jeanette. I'm curious to see him." Melba pulled out a drawer and delved into it. Her hand emerged with the book I'd lent her. "I read it last night, stayed up until midnight. Really good. I need to read more of her books."

I walked back to retrieve the book. "You can borrow mine, if you like, after the event."

"I think I might go to this event myself," Melba said. "I might even buy my own copies."

"And check out what goes on between Lucy Dunne, aka Irene Warriner, and Daniel Bellamy." I grinned.

"Ha-ha," Melba said, her tone sour.

Ignoring that, I gave her the details of the event.

"I'll put it in my calendar," she said. "Now go away."

"As you wish, Your Highness." I headed upstairs to my office.

After checking e-mail, I returned to cataloging more of the collection. Absorbed in my work, I paid little heed to the time until Diesel caught my attention by meowing loudly from beside my chair. Startled, I glanced down at him, and he meowed again.

"Did you have a good visit?" I asked. He chirped and jumped into the window. I took that sound to mean *yes*.

A cough from the doorway alerted me to the presence of another person. I looked toward the door and saw the man Diesel and I had encountered on our way home for lunch. I rose from my desk and went around to greet him.

"You must be Daniel Bellamy." I extended a hand, and he accepted it with a firm grasp. "Please, have a seat." I indicated a chair.

"Thank you," Bellamy said, his voice a resonant bass. He made himself comfortable in the chair while I resumed my own seat. "That's quite a cat you have. I'd heard he was big, but I hadn't imagined quite how large he actually is."

"Diesel is above average size for a Maine Coon," I replied. "He's about ten pounds heavier and several inches longer from nose to tip of the tail than other males usually are."

"He's definitely handsome," Bellamy said. "He greeted me downstairs, then showed me the way to your office." He smiled at this. "He let me rub his head."

I regarded him across my desk. A handsome young man, perhaps thirty-five or forty, I calculated, he had darkish blond hair and deep-blue eyes. His hair, short on the sides but thick and slightly long on top, flopped toward his eyes. He brushed it back with his left hand. He looked back at me, his gaze direct, his smile friendly.

"Stewart Delacorte told me you might be able to help me out for a couple of months," he said.

"He mentioned that you're having renovations done to your home," I said.

Bellamy nodded, his left hand raking his unruly hair

back off his forehead again. "It's an older house, a Crafts-
man, built around 1925. It's been pretty well maintained
over the years, but some of the flooring needs to be replaced, and some of the plumbing, too, I'm afraid." He
grimaced. "The kitchen's going to be a mess, and so are
the bathrooms. I'd just as soon not try to live there while
all this is going on. It ought to go faster if I can stay somewhere else for two to three months."

"I can certainly understand that," I said. "I'm not sure
how much Stewart told you about the arrangements for
boarding."

"The bare bones, probably," Bellamy replied. "As long
as I have a comfortable room with a good bed and a bathroom, I'll be fine." He smiled. "I backpacked around Eu-
rope as a student, staying in hostels, so I can adapt to
pretty much anything."

I laughed. "The room I have in mind will certainly be
more comfortable than a youth hostel. It's on the third
floor, down the hall from Stewart's suite. Other than Stewart and his partner, there's no one else up there, so you'd
have your privacy. And, of course, a bathroom to yourself."

"Sounds fine to me." He hesitated. "Are there any meals
included? They're not necessary, but it would be convenient."

"Breakfast and the evening meal," I said. "I have a
wonderful housekeeper, Azalea Berry, who is a first-class
Southern cook. If you're depending on health food, I'm
afraid you're out of luck."

Bellamy laughed, his hand once more going to his head.
"Good Southern home cooking is fine with me. I work out
almost every day at the gym. That's actually how I got to
know Stewart and Haskell. Plus climbing two flights of
stairs every day can only help offset the calories."

"Climbing one several times a day hasn't helped me that much." I grinned. "But I don't go to the gym, either." Enough chitchat. Time to settle the details. "When would you like to move in?"

"Would this evening work?" Bellamy asked. "I've already packed most of what I need in hopes that you would agree to let me board with you."

"Five o'clock?"

He nodded. "That's fine."

"Good. I'll have a key for you and also a form you'll need to fill out and sign." I named the amount for a month's board, and he seemed surprised.

"That's not very much," he said.

I shrugged. "It's not really a moneymaking venture. I'm continuing what my late aunt started. She rented rooms to students and the occasional young starving professor, and I've kept it up. Though I haven't had that many boarders, come to think of it, other than Stewart, Haskell, and a student named Justin Wardlaw."

"Justin is a first-class student," Bellamy said with obvious pleasure. "He took two of my classes and did outstanding work. I had no idea he had boarded with you."

We chatted for a moment about Justin, and then Bellamy took his leave. I got back to work after calling Azalea to let her know there would be an additional person for the next couple of months for breakfast and dinner most days.

Occasional thoughts about my new boarder intruded while I tried to keep my focus on work. Bellamy had charm, I had to admit, an affable, outgoing man, based on this initial interaction with him. I could certainly understand his attraction for women, and I briefly speculated about his friendship—or more—with Irene Warriner. I had continued to feel a sense of familiarity with Bellamy while we talked. Based most likely on my having seen his photograph on the jacket of the book I had read, I told myself. There was more to it, though, I was sure, but I couldn't imagine what it was. Perhaps it would come to me later.

Diesel drowsed in the window behind me while I worked steadily. When I felt a paw on my shoulder, I checked my watch. Nearly four. Past time to pack up and go home.

Downstairs we paused to bid Melba good-bye. As she rubbed Diesel's head, she said, "Did your appointment show up?"

"Yes," I said, thinking it an odd question. "You didn't see him?" That wasn't like Melba.

She looked uncomfortable, then blurted out, "My stomach's a little upset this afternoon. The deviled eggs I had at lunch aren't agreeing with me, so I've been in and out of the office all afternoon."

"I'm sorry, that's not pleasant," I said. "He's a personable young man. You'll get a chance to meet him at the event, if not sooner."

"Did you accept him as a boarder?" she asked.

"I did," I replied.

"Don't be surprised if Irene Warriner shows up at your house, then." Melba arched an eyebrow.

"Ha-ha," I replied airily.

"We'll see," Melba responded.

"Come on, Diesel, time to get home," I said to the cat, and he followed me out of Melba's office.

On the walk home in the now-chilly afternoon air, I considered Melba's comments about Irene Warriner and Daniel Bellamy. I continued to believe that their relationship was most likely professional, perhaps a friendship and nothing more. Should it prove to be more than that, however, I would put my foot down about Bellamy's entertaining a married woman in his room. I wouldn't have a problem with her visiting him downstairs. On the other hand, if she were single, I wouldn't have a problem with her visiting him in his room. Then I chastised myself for wasting time on something that was only a slim possibility. I doubted whether the issue would arise while Bellamy resided in my house.

When Diesel and I arrived home, we found Azalea at the stove. Her faithful shadow, Ramses, lay curled up on the floor under a chair where he could keep a close watch in case anything dropped to the floor. He yawned and stretched, then ran over to Diesel. The two cats sniffed at each other while Azalea informed me that dinner was under way. Tonight's entrée consisted of baked chicken spaghetti, to be served with broccoli salad and fresh cornbread.

"Sounds fine to me," I said. "Do you know whether both Stewart and Haskell will be here?"

Azalea nodded. "Yes, they'll be here."

"Good, and of course the new boarder, Dr. Bellamy. This will be his first meal with us, and he told me he was looking forward to whatever you would serve."

"Any special requests for breakfast?" she asked.

"No, he didn't mention anything. I think whatever you decide will be fine." Only occasionally did I make requests for a particular food. Not that Azalea wouldn't be amenable, but the menu presented one less decision I had to make, and that worked fine as far as I was concerned. I was grateful that she continued to take care of the house, although I knew she did it mostly out of her love and friendship for my late aunt Dottie. She had promised Aunt Dottie she would look after the house and me as long as she could.

Diesel and Ramses tussled on the floor under the table. I left them to play while I went to the den and fired up my laptop. I could have rummaged in the desk for a copy of the lease I had all boarders sign, but I had the file on the laptop. Once everything was set, I printed the lease, then found a folder and labeled it with Bellamy's name. I took it back to the kitchen with me and laid it on the table.

I encouraged Diesel and Ramses to come back to the den with me. Diesel came readily at my call, but Ramses appeared reluctant. The standoff ended when I scooped him up and carried him off to the den, Diesel by my side. I closed the door firmly behind us and set him down. He meowed at me and stared at the door, but when Diesel and I made ourselves comfortable on the sofa, he decided to join us. I picked up a book from the table and began to read, while the cats snoozed beside me.

We stayed there, with me checking my watch occasionally to keep track of the time. A few minutes before five, I laid aside my book and headed toward the kitchen. Diesel and Ramses followed, my dogged minions.

The front doorbell rang, and Diesel ran to the door. Ramses continued to the kitchen, ever hopeful of treats, no doubt. I opened the door to find Dan Bellamy, his hand raised to ring the bell again. Beside him stood a woman I did not recognize.

"Good evening, Mr. Harris," Bellamy said as he and his companion stepped into the hall. Each carried a suitcase, and they set them down. "My friend Mrs. Warriner kindly offered to help me bring a few things over. Let me introduce you."

SEVEN

||||||||||||||||||||||||||||||||||||

Later, looking back, I recalled standing and staring at them beyond the point of politeness, but nothing in the demeanor of either Dan Bellamy or Irene Warriner suggested they found me rude. The latter's presence took me aback considerably, given the tales Melba shared with me and my own worries on the subject. I had to remind myself sharply of my own conclusion that their relationship was mostly professional because of their shared interest in the Regency period.

I recovered myself while Bellamy completed the formalities. When he concluded, I said, "Dr. Warriner, it's a pleasure to meet you. Lucy Dunne has entertained me for many hours, and I'm delighted to have the chance to tell you how much I've enjoyed your books."

Irene Warriner, a trim brunette with a creamy, pale complexion and a soft cloud of dark hair framing her face, smiled graciously. She extended a hand, and we shook. "Mr. Harris, it's always a pleasure to meet my readers, and I continue to be surprised by the number of men who have enjoyed my books. Many men turn up their noses at romance novels."

"A well-written book that tells a good story is what matters to me," I said warmly. "I don't pay much attention to the genre as long as I enjoy what I'm reading."

During these amenities, in the back of my mind I couldn't keep down the little voice that wanted to know the exact nature of the relationship between these two people. Nosiness was most definitely my besetting sin, and I readily confessed it.

Dan Bellamy smiled at Irene Warriner. "Thanks for the ride, Irene. I'll walk back to the car with you and retrieve the suit bag. I know you're anxious to get home." He shot me a sideways glance, and I wondered uneasily if I had somehow betrayed my thoughts.

That little voice in the back of my mind went silent. *I told you so*, I thought, relieved.

Irene Warriner smiled. "Carey made lasagna for dinner tonight, and if I don't get home in time, he'll have given half of it to the dog." She glanced down at Diesel, appearing to notice him for the first time, though he had waited patiently by her to be acknowledged.

"Goodness," she said. "So this is the famous Maine Coon. Diesel, isn't it?"

Thus acknowledged, Diesel chirped at her and allowed his head to be stroked. He seemed taken with her, butting his head against her hand when she attempted to remove it. "You are quite a handsome fellow."

"He won't argue with you over that," I said wryly.

Irene Warriner laughed. "When I get home smelling of feline, Jonesy—that's our dog, a terrier mix—will have a fit. He'll think I've been unfaithful."

Dan Bellamy shook his head. "You and Carey and that

dog, the way you both carry on over him. I've never seen anything like it." He nodded toward the door. "Come on, you'd better get going."

"Good-bye, Mr. Harris," she said. "And a special good-bye to you, handsome." She gave Diesel one last pat before she turned and walked out the door.

Diesel and I waited until Dan Bellamy returned with his suit bag, and then we escorted him up the two flights of stairs to his new temporary living quarters. I brought one of the suitcases, and Bellamy brought the other. I paused at the top of the second flight in order to regain my breath while Diesel and my new boarder waited. After about fifteen seconds I felt sufficiently recovered to continue. My knees, I decided ruefully, were not happy about all those stairs.

A wave of nostalgia washed over me when I surveyed the room. This had been Justin's room for three years, and I fancied I could still feel his presence. Diesel walked in and sniffed around, no doubt detecting traces of the young man he had quickly come to adore. After a moment I set down the suitcase and turned to Bellamy.

"You have an en suite bathroom, and there is a walk-in closet, so I hope you'll have enough space for your needs while you're here." I explained a few of the routine rules, and he nodded to acknowledge his acceptance of them. "If you'll come down by a quarter to six, we can go over the lease form before dinner."

"Thanks, Mr. Harris," he said. "I'll put away a few things and be down soon."

"Call me Charlie, if you like," I said.

He grinned. "If you'll call me Dan."

I nodded. "Come along, Diesel. I don't think Dan needs any help unpacking."

Diesel meowed loudly and preceded me from the room.

He hurried down the stairs well ahead of me. I followed in a more leisurely fashion. When I reached the kitchen, I had to step quickly aside to avoid Diesel as he charged out of the doorway and across the hall to the living room, Ramses trying in vain to match the big cat's longer stride. They loved chasing each other, and I was amused to see it. The more Diesel wore the kitten out with exercise the quieter Ramses would be later on. A quiet Ramses was a good thing.

Dan came downstairs a few minutes before the appointed time, and we went over the agreement. He signed and gave me a check for two months' boarding. Stewart and Haskell came down promptly at six, with Dante on their heels. Haskell and Stewart dished up our food, and the four of us—attended by three hopeful four-legged beggars—sat down to dinner. Dan proved an entertaining dinner companion, talking easily on various subjects, and I thoroughly enjoyed the meal. He volunteered to clear the table when we finished, and Stewart assisted.

I went to bed that night reasonably content with my new boarder. His easygoing nature seemed to blend well with the comfortable rapport among Stewart, Haskell, and me. Dan had evinced no problems with the cats or the dog, even rubbing heads when presented to him. He did not, I was pleased to notice, slip the supplicants any food. They already had enough hands willing to do that.

Before bed, however, I had homework—the first two chapters of the text assigned as required reading for the history course. Propped up in bed with my two bedmates beside me, I read the chapters, even going on to the third one, so engrossed was I in the book. I put the book aside when my cell phone rang—my nightly chat with Helen Louise.

We shared tidbits of the day, including my new boarder.

The news surprised Helen Louise, but I explained Dan Bellamy's need for a quiet place to work during renovations. Helen Louise, who'd had to do extensive renovations before she opened her bistro, said, "I pity the poor man. If they told him it will take two months, you can count on his being your boarder for five or six months."

"Unless he causes problems," I replied, "that's fine. He doesn't seem like the kind to do such things, though." Even as I said those words, I felt an uneasy stirring in the back of my mind.

"I can only hope you're right." Helen Louise chuckled. "Wouldn't it be lovely to have a few months trouble-free? No murders, everyone well and happy, no drama?"

"Yes, it certainly would." I spoke firmly and sent up a silent prayer that Helen Louise's words foretold reality.

We chatted desultorily for a few minutes more, then Helen Louise began yawning and bade me good night. I laid my book on the bedside stand, placed my phone atop it, and turned out the light. Ramses decided to snuggle against me, with Diesel on his other side, and I soon drifted into sleep.

I awoke the next morning with a tickling sensation on my nose. I opened my eyes to find Ramses sniffing my face, his whiskers brushing against my nose. After removing him gently from my shoulder—and getting his tail out of my ear—I rubbed my eyes and pushed myself up in bed. Who needed an alarm clock when you had a kitten in the house?

While I showered and dressed for the day, Diesel and Ramses headed downstairs. I knew Azalea would be in the kitchen preparing breakfast, and Ramses no doubt was eager to see her and find out what treats might be in the offing.

I heard footsteps on the staircase above me when I headed downward, and Dan Bellamy overtook me.

"Good morning," he said. "That's a mighty comfortable bed. I slept well, and I don't usually do so in a strange
bed. At least, not on the first night."

"Glad it was comfortable for you." I glanced sideways to
see that he too had dressed for the day, wearing a suit but
no tie, his collar open. "I wasn't sure if you were an early
riser," I continued. "If you usually don't get up until later,
Azalea will be happy to make breakfast for you then. You
don't have to eat this early if you're not accustomed to it."

"No, this is fine. I've already had a good run this
morning. I'm used to being up early."

When we reached the kitchen, I introduced Dan to
Azalea, and he greeted her pleasantly and thanked her for
the delicious dinner the night before. "After that, I'm really looking forward to breakfast."

Azalea nodded to acknowledge the compliment. "If
there's anything particular you like for breakfast, you let
me know."

"Thank you," Dan replied. "I will, but I'm always happy
with coffee, eggs, and bacon or sausage."

Stewart joined us about ten minutes later, explaining
that Haskell had been called out early to assist with a fatal
accident on the highway. Stewart grimaced. "I don't know
how he does it; they're always so tragic." He eyed his plate
of scrambled eggs and bacon slightly askance. Despite his
comment, however, he did not seem to lack his usual appetite.

The three of us chatted over breakfast, accosted frequently by Ramses and Diesel, though Ramses directed
most of his attention to his least resistant target, Azalea.
With breakfast finished, I put Diesel in his harness and
leash, grabbed the lunch bag Azalea had prepared for me,
and we drove to the public library, where I volunteered on
Fridays.

For the spring college semester, I would be working only from nine until noon instead of my usual nine to three. Although I didn't like depriving the staff of half the usual hours, the head of the library, Teresa Farmer, waved away my concerns.

"You have been such a huge help to us, Charlie," she said. "None of us is going to begrudge you the opportunity to take a class for a semester." She grinned. "If you start taking classes every semester, then we'll talk."

"Not anything I'm anticipating doing," I had assured her.

Diesel, as always, enjoyed his time at the library, thanks to all the attention he received from the library staff as well as the patrons. He was the most popular attraction at the library for many people, and he adored the adulation he received. When he needed a break, he retreated behind the service desk with me or another staff member and rested until he was ready to greet his public again.

A few minutes past noon found us in the car on the way to campus. I parked in my usual spot behind the administration building. We met Melba on her way out to fetch something for her lunch.

"I'll be back in time for you to get to your class," she said after greeting us.

"I really appreciate your help with this," I said, "otherwise Diesel would have to stay home on my class days."

"We can't have that, now, can we, Diesel?" Melba said.

Diesel warbled an indignant response, and we both laughed. The cat chirped as if he understood.

I took Diesel upstairs to the office so that I could eat my lunch and he could snack on the dry food I kept there, as well as perform other necessary functions as he needed. At a quarter to one we went downstairs and found Melba at her desk, eating a salad and turning the pages of a magazine.

"See you a little after two," I told her and Diesel before I made my way to the building where history classes were held.

I took the same seat I'd had on Wednesday and prepared my notebook and pen. The classroom held only about half the students that had been present at the first class, but more appeared a minute or two before the bell rang and Carey Warriner entered the room.

I glanced around but didn't see Dixie Compton anywhere. I wondered whether she had decided to withdraw from the class. If she had done so because of insecurity over her fitness for the course, I hoped my declining her invitation to be her study partner hadn't contributed to that decision.

The bell rang, and the professor began to take roll. As each student responded, I half expected Dixie Compton to slide in at the last moment, but she failed to appear, even several minutes after Warriner began his lecture.

I couldn't explain it afterward, but I had the uneasy feeling that something had befallen Dixie Compton that prevented her from coming to class this afternoon. But what could have happened?

EIGHT

I had little time to consider reasons why Dixie Compton had ducked class today. Once Professor Warriner launched into his lecture, I was too busy concentrating on his words and trying to transcribe them to think about much else.

When the bell rang at ten minutes before two and the lecture ended, I let go of the pen and massaged my right hand with my left. I had meant to bring my laptop today and type the notes, but I had forgotten to grab the computer before I left home this morning. Either my hand would soon get conditioned to the amount of writing I was doing, or I would have to figure out the best mnemonic to ensure that I remembered my laptop on class days.

I had halfway anticipated that Carey Warriner might approach me again today after the class to inquire whether I had made a decision about taking the course for credit. To my great relief, he did not. I hadn't given it much further thought since Wednesday, and at the moment I had no desire to respond in the affirmative. I didn't feel that I needed to put to the test my ability to make the kind of grades I had many years ago at Athena. I certainly didn't need another advanced degree. I was perfectly happy with my master's degree in library science.

But never say never, as my aunt Dottie always told me.

As the students left the classroom, Warriner called out a reminder to check the syllabus for our reading assignments for Monday's class. I remembered vaguely that the syllabus included occasional discussions throughout the semester, and I wondered briefly whether Monday would bring our first one.

I gathered my things and left the classroom. During the walk back to my office, I thought again about Dixie Compton's failure to show up for class. I had to wonder, given what I had overheard after class on Wednesday, whether Warriner had managed to discourage her after all. She had exhibited bravado with me, asserting that she was not going to let him intimidate her. Perhaps he had managed to do so anyway.

But why didn't he want her in the class? The only reason I could imagine involved them in an extramarital affair. Whatever the reason, I felt bad for Dixie Compton. I had little sympathy for Warriner if he had indeed been unfaithful to his wife. Though, I realized, the affair could have happened before he married Irene Warriner. I had no idea how long they had been married.

My nosiness often tended to get the better of me, and I pulled myself up sharply over the direction of my thoughts. These people's private lives were none of my business. Their actions did not affect me in the least, as far as I could determine. I should therefore banish further such thoughts from my mind and stick to my own concerns.

That resolution made, I forced my thoughts onto more personal matters. My plans for tomorrow included visits with my grandchildren. Sean and Alex had promised to bring Rosie over for me to babysit while they ran errands together. Laura had said she would come over with Charlie at the same time, while Cherelle, the nanny, enjoyed a much-deserved weekend off. Tomorrow night I intended to attend the Lucy Dunne event. On Sunday I had planned for the usual dinner with the entire family, and unless there were last-minute changes, everyone should be there.

Diesel hurried to meet me when I entered the building, trilling and meowing to fill me in on the details of his time with Melba. I paused to rub his head a few times before I proceeded to Melba's office.

When I reached her door, she glanced my way. She shot me an arch look and said, "How are things with you and your new girlfriend?"

I suppressed a flash of annoyance at this tired joke and replied with a frown, "Candice Bergen? Haven't seen her for weeks."

Melba rolled her eyes. "So funny. You know who I'm talking about."

"Yes, I do," I said, trying to keep from sounding testy, "and I wish you'd drop this thing. It's not that funny. As a matter of fact, Ms. Compton wasn't in class today."

A slight flush crept over Melba's face. "Sorry, Charlie, it's in poor taste. You're right. I won't joke about her again."

I smiled. "Thanks. Apology accepted. I don't mind if you tease me. We've always picked at each other, but some subjects aren't that amusing."

"Like infidelity," Melba said.

"Exactly." I didn't tell her that subject had occupied my thoughts far too much recently. Perhaps that was why I was overly sensitive to Melba's attempts at humor. Normally I didn't let her rattle me. "Thanks for looking after Diesel for me."

Melba waved that away. "No need to thank me every time. You know I love spending time with this handsome boy. He's always good as gold for Aunt Melba." As if in agreement with her, Diesel meowed loudly, and Melba chuckled.

"All right, then," I said. "Come on upstairs with me, boy, and let Melba have a break."

Diesel chirped at me and headed out the door. I smiled a farewell to Melba and followed him.

While the cat napped in his window, I settled down to work for the next ninety minutes. By the time I thought to check my watch, I found it was nearly three forty-five. I could easily have worked for another hour or more, but this was Friday afternoon, after all.

"Come on, boy, time to go," I said to Diesel.

A few minutes later, we were in the car, headed to the town square. Our destination this time was Helen Louise's bistro. I thought I would pick up one of her cakes to take home for dessert tonight. I wasn't sure whether Dan Bellamy planned to eat his dinner with us, but if he did, it would be nice to have a special offering as a kind of welcome, since we hadn't had one last night.

Trying to find a parking spot on the square on a Friday afternoon could be considered a health hazard, I sometimes thought. I had on more than one occasion witnessed shouting matches between drivers who disagreed on the ownership of an empty place. Today my luck held, however, and I didn't have to come to fisticuffs with anyone for a place in front of the bistro.

Diesel jumped to the pavement, and, leash in hand, I led

him into the bistro. Technically it was against health regulations for an animal, even one as well behaved as my cat, to enter a food service establishment. Helen Louise had in the past informed persons who complained about Diesel that they were welcome to go elsewhere. Diesel never went anywhere near a food preparation area. We generally sat at a table in one corner where there was practically no chance we might contaminate anyone's food. By now the bistro regulars had become accustomed to his presence, and many of them stopped by to say hello.

Helen Louise, busy at the cash register, nodded as she spotted us. I saw that our usual spot was available. The bistro was only about half-full, the lunch crowd long since departed. Once she finished with the customer at the register, Helen Louise came over and greeted me with a kiss. For Diesel, she had a few scratches for his head and chin that made him purr with happiness.

"Have you had a busy day?" I asked as Helen Louise took the chair to my left.

She nodded. "Typical Friday crowd. People were waiting as much as twenty minutes for tables. Thank goodness it wasn't raining today."

"Everything you serve is worth waiting for," I said, "like the chocolate cake I'd like to take home with me for dessert tonight."

An expression of dismay crossed Helen Louise's lovely face. "Oh, Charlie, if only I had known. Henry sold the last one about half an hour ago."

"Darn," I said. "I really wanted one for tonight, but I'm sure you have something else nearly as good."

Helen Louise looked thoughtful for a moment. "I tell you what, I have time to make one for you. There's only one thing."

"What's that?" I asked, puzzled.

"I'll make it for you if you invite me to dinner." She grinned impishly.

"Silly woman," I said in mock exasperation. "You know I can't be bribed by chocolate cake alone."

"I guess I'll have to up the ante," she replied. "Hmm, now, what else can I offer?" She chuckled. "How about three kisses?"

I pretended to consider the offer. "Make it seven, and it's a deal."

"Seven it is," she said. "Here's the first one." She bussed my cheek.

No doubt anyone else privy to this exchange would think Helen Louise and I thought we were giddy teenagers. I didn't care. We had fun with these little exchanges, and that's all that mattered.

"Dinner at six as usual?" she asked.

"Yes," I replied. "I don't know if there will be anyone besides the two of us, but in case Dan Bellamy is in, I thought it would be pleasant to have a special dessert for dinner since we didn't have one his first night."

"Then you shall have it," Helen Louise said. "I'll bring it with me." She rose from the table. "I'd better get back to work."

"Yes, you should. You don't want Henry to catch you slacking off." I winked. Henry was her full-time manager, the extremely dependable employee who had made it possible for her to cut back her hours at the bistro.

Diesel and I headed for the car after another kiss for me and a head scratch or two for him from Helen Louise. I had to wait for a pause in the traffic around the square to back out of my space, and I kept watch in the mirror with occasional glances over my shoulder. Finally a lull occurred, long enough for me to reverse the car and then start moving forward.

A sudden movement in front of the car caused me to hit my brakes hard. Diesel grumbled from the backseat, and I glanced quickly back to make sure he was okay. He didn't seem hurt in any way, only startled. I looked at the street ahead, and the two people who had dashed across it in front of me had now reached the sidewalk, apparently oblivious to the car that had nearly struck them.

I felt like getting out of the car right then and reading them the riot act. The man and woman stood on the sidewalk in front of the bistro, talking to each other. With a shock, I realized I knew the man—Carey Warriner. I didn't know the woman with him, but I thought I had seen her on campus before. What was the name of the English professor Melba's friends had mentioned?

Barbara Lamont, I recalled after a moment. Then the loud honking behind me caught my attention, and with a jerk I started forward again. I would have a few words to say to Carey Warriner the next time I saw him. What a foolish thing he and his woman friend had done. Had I not been paying attention I could have struck them both, and I felt sick to my stomach at the thought.

I checked in my rearview mirror as I paused at the light. I could no longer see them on the sidewalk, and I wondered where they had gone. I decided I would ask Helen Louise at dinner tonight whether they had gone into the bistro. Not in the presence of Dan Bellamy, however.

As my anger with Warriner faded during the drive home, I decided that I should let well enough alone. No harm was done, after all. No one had been hurt, and I would assure myself that Diesel was fine when we got home.

I turned down my street two blocks from the house. I spotted what looked like two sheriff's department cars parked near my place, and my heartbeat quickened. The closer I came to home, the faster my heart beat. The patrol cars did indeed occupy space on the street right in front of my house.

What on earth had happened here?

NINE

After a quick check to reassure myself that Diesel hadn't been hurt during the abrupt stop, I hurried him into the kitchen. I tried to settle my chaotic thoughts by focusing on a quick prayer that everyone was okay, but even that didn't work. I thrust open the door and stumbled into the kitchen, almost stepping on Diesel. Thankfully, before I could, he hissed and darted aside.

Haskell and his boss, Chief Deputy Kanesha Berry, sat at the table. Azalea stood by the stove, her arms crossed over her bosom, glaring at her daughter. I began to relax. Perhaps Kanesha had simply stopped by to check on her mother.

But why would she bring Haskell with her? And why two cars? I wondered.

"Afternoon, Charlie," Kanesha said, her tone as usual betraying nothing.

"Good afternoon, Kanesha, Haskell," I said. "How are y'all?" I nodded to Azalea and wished her good afternoon as well.

Ramses darted out from under the table and headed for Diesel, and Diesel ran out of the room. Ramses chased after him. Kanesha grimaced, whether in response to the feline antics or for another reason, I had no idea.

"I was about to call you, Charlie," Kanesha said. "I need to ask you a few questions."

"Do you mind if I sit down?" I asked. "This sounds serious."

"It is," Haskell said, and that earned him a frown from Kanesha.

I pulled out a chair and sat. "What's going on? Has there been an accident?" My heart began pounding again. *Please let my children and grandchildren be okay*, I prayed.

"There has been a death," Kanesha replied. "No family member, if that's what's worrying you. A death that we are considering a suspicious one."

"Thank the Lord it's none of my family," I said, "but how awful for someone's family. So the dead person is someone you think I know?"

Kanesha shrugged. "That's what I want you to tell me. Do you know a woman named Dixie Belle Compton?"

I suddenly felt sick to my stomach all over again. I had been right. Something terrible had happened to her after all.

It took me a moment to find my voice. "I've met her a couple of times," I said. "She was enrolled in the history course I'm taking at Athena. I saw her in class on Wednesday." I took a moment for a deep breath. "I saw her again yesterday when she came to my office to see me."

"What did she want?" Kanesha asked when I failed to continue right away.

"I'll fix you a glass of sweet tea," Azalea said. "Looks like you need it."

"Thank you." I caught Kanesha's expression, one that I interpreted as irritation. She did not like the idea of her mother's continuing to work as a housekeeper. Azalea was every bit as strong-minded as her daughter, and this was one area where the two women did not agree. I should have thought of that before I asked Azalea for the tea. I didn't like to be the cause, even an inadvertent one, of conflict between the two.

While Azalea poured the tea and set the glass in front of me, I started answering Kanesha's question. "She wanted to find a study partner for the course." I paused for a drink of tea. My throat felt dry. "She thought that I, as another 'mature student,' as she put it, might want to team up and work together."

"I see," Kanesha said, her eyes narrowed as she watched me drink more tea. "What was your answer?"

"That I didn't need a study partner because I was only auditing the course, not taking it for credit," I said. "She was disappointed with my answer, but she understood why I wasn't interested."

"Was that the last time you saw her?" Kanesha asked.

I nodded. "Yes. She wasn't in class this afternoon, and that surprised me. When I talked to her yesterday, she seemed really determined to do well in the class, despite some opposition . . ." I trailed off, realizing what I was saying.

Kanesha immediately picked up on it. "Opposition? What opposition?"

"From the professor who taught the course," I said. "Carey Warriner. He wanted her to drop the class. I don't know why." I hesitated, then decided I had no choice but to tell her about what I had overheard after class on Wednesday.

Kanesha's enigmatic expression rarely gave any cues, and her reception of what I had to relate was no exception. I feared that, because of my sharing what I'd heard, Carey

Warriner now occupied the lead position on the suspect list in Dixie Compton's death.

I ventured to ask a question. "Why did you come to me? What connection did you find?"

"Note in her handbag," Kanesha said. "Your name and the location of your office scribbled on a piece of paper torn from a notebook."

"I see," I replied. "Am I allowed to know what happened?"

"She was found dead around noon by her apartment manager," Kanesha said.

"Poor guy let himself into her unit to change air conditioner filters," Haskell explained. "That's how he came to find her."

"Poor woman." I shook my head. "I feel so bad for her."

"Thanks to you, at least," Kanesha said, "we have a solid lead on a potential person of interest in the case."

"You mean Professor Warriner," I said.

"Yes," Kanesha replied. "I was hoping that, as usual, you might know something helpful."

I wasn't sure how to take that remark. The tone had been bland, but with Kanesha, I was never really sure.

"Always glad to help," I said, raising my glass in salute to her and Haskell.

Kanesha pushed her chair back, and Haskell did the same. "Thanks, we appreciate the information. Now that you've given it, though, I hope you'll let that be the end of it." She jerked her head in the direction of the front door. "We've got more work to do." She bade her mother goodbye and nodded at me before she left the kitchen.

Haskell shrugged as if to say *You know how she is* before he followed her to the front door.

Kanesha had not shared any details of what had actually befallen Dixie Compton. I knew only that the poor woman had died under suspicious circumstances. That was awful.

"Are you all right?" Azalea asked. "You're looking mighty pale."

"Yes, I'm all right. A little shaken up by this," I said. "What a terrible thing. Did you happen to know Ms. Compton?"

Azalea shook her head. "I don't believe so. You only saw her twice?"

I nodded. "She was an attractive woman, in her mid to late thirties, I'd say."

"Terrible young for her to die like that." Azalea's lips moved in silent prayer, her eyes closed.

"Yes, it is." I downed the rest of my tea, rose from the table, and carried the glass to the sink. "I think I'll go to the den for a while, in case you need me for anything."

"All right," Azalea said.

I turned in the doorway. "Did Stewart say anything to you about dinner tonight? I'm thinking Haskell won't be here, now that there's a case to investigate."

"Stewart was planning to be here anyway," Azalea said. "That nice Dr. Bellamy said he wouldn't, though. He already had plans with a friend."

"Thanks." I left the kitchen and headed for the den. I wondered vaguely where Diesel and Ramses had gone. I found them tussling on the floor in the den. I watched them for a moment before I stretched out on the sofa, my shoes off, my head on a cushion against the armrest.

The news of Dixie Compton's suspicious death had knocked me off-balance, and I was still trying to recover my equilibrium. Given what I had overheard between her and Carey Warriner, I couldn't help but speculate. Did the history professor play any role in her death? As I recalled it, his tone when he asked the poor woman why she was taking his class was nasty. What had happened between the two of them to cause such obviously strong—perhaps even violent—feelings?

If Carey Warriner were in any way responsible for the woman's death, I knew Kanesha would be relentless in pursuing him. Her tenacity was one of the qualities that made her such an outstanding investigator. That, and her intelligence. Very little ever got by Kanesha Berry.

I resolved that this was one instance when I would not get involved in one of Kanesha's investigations. I had shared what little I knew that was pertinent, and that was the end of it as far as I was concerned. I shifted uneasily on the sofa.

Ramses chose that moment to jump onto my stomach. He weighed only about five pounds, but that weight yielded enough impact to make me groan in response. Diesel, thankfully, had learned early on not to do that. He had weighed eight or nine pounds when I found him, wet and bedraggled, shivering and hungry, in the shrubbery at the public library several years ago. Now he weighed in at around thirty-seven or thirty-eight pounds. If *he* landed on any of my body parts, he could cause some damage.

Ramses crawled forward to try to lick my face, but I held him firmly back, stroking him and rubbing his ears. Diesel's face appeared near mine as he took up a position on the floor beside me. He meowed loudly, either in complaint or remonstrance over the kitten's behavior. Which of the two, I wasn't sure. Ramses ignored him. I twisted my head to look Diesel in the eye.

"Yes, he hasn't learned not to do that," I said. "You are such a good boy, you know better, don't you?"

Those words seemed to appease him, and he warbled happily.

I rubbed Ramses for a few seconds more, then took

hold of him and set him gently on the floor. I swung my feet off the sofa and sat up. I realized that I had lain down on the sofa still wearing my jacket. By now it was probably creased in the back. I sighed. I needed to send it to the cleaners anyway.

"Come on, boys, let's go upstairs," I said. "I need to put my jacket away."

Diesel hurried out the door with Ramses in hot pursuit. I went after them in a much more leisurely fashion. Upstairs I shrugged out of the jacket and discovered that it was not as badly creased as I had feared. I hung it in the closet before I pulled off my shoes to exchange them for the slip-on sneakers I had recently taken to wearing around the house. All the while the two cats rolled around, wrestling, on the floor.

"That's good, Diesel," I said. "Wear him out." I watched them play for a couple of minutes before deciding to go back downstairs. I felt restless. I tried to put Dixie Compton out of my mind, but I couldn't. I kept remembering her in my office, asking for my help. She was beyond anyone's help now, I reflected sadly.

Back in the den I turned on the television, already set to one of those nostalgia stations. While I watched the antics of characters from a sitcom from forty years ago, I tried to keep my mind off the tragic death of a woman I had met only twice. I had trouble paying attention to the television screen. I had seen this particular episode more than once and knew what was going to happen in every scene.

Diesel and Ramses had not accompanied me. They might still be wrestling in my bedroom, or they could be chasing each other on the stairs. I suspected, however, that if Ramses had tired of playing he had gone to the kitchen to beg treats from Azalea. If he thought food was in the offing, Diesel would be right there with him.

"Hi, Charlie." Stewart's voice roused me from my thoughts. I turned to see him in the doorway. He advanced into the room a couple of paces. "Sorry to interrupt you, but do you happen to have your keys with you? I need the key to the liquor cabinet. If you don't have it, I can run upstairs to get mine."

I had started locking the liquor cabinet in the living room as soon as baby Charlie began to crawl. I fumbled in my pocket to extract my key ring. I handed it to Stewart. "Are you having a drink before dinner?" This was not a usual thing with Stewart.

"Not for me." Stewart took the keys and turned to leave the room. Over his shoulder he said, "For Dan Bellamy. He just found out his ex-sister-in-law has died." He disappeared into the hall.

I sat, stunned by Stewart's revelation. Was Dixie Compton Dan Bellamy's former sister-in-law?

TEN
||||||||||||||||||||||

Surely it was mere coincidence that Dan's former sister-in-law had died. That didn't mean *she* was Dixie Compton, but I couldn't shake the feeling that the two women were one and the same. Still dazed, I got up and left the room to find out more.

I found Stewart and Dan in the kitchen, along with Azalea, the two felines, and Dante. The poodle danced around in excitement, trying to entice one or both of the cats into playing with him. At the moment, however, neither one appeared to be interested. Diesel crouched under the table at the opposite end from where Dan and Stewart sat, and Ramses sat beside him.

Dan, obviously shaken, reached with an unsteady hand for the glass of brandy Stewart had poured and raised it to his lips. After sipping at the amber liquid twice, he up-ended the glass and drained it. Color flooded his face as the liquor warmed him, and he set down the glass.

"Thank you," he said to Stewart, who sat watching him, frowning.

"Would you like more?" Stewart asked.

Dan shook his head. "No, thank you. I'm feeling better." He essayed a weak smile and looked first at Stewart and Azalea, then at me. "Some unexpected bad news. I guess it hit me harder than I realized."

"Stewart said that your former sister-in-law died," I said. "I'm sorry for your loss."

"Thank you," Dan said. "I haven't seen much of her in several years, not after she and my brother, Ray, divorced. Still, it's a shock. She was only thirty-seven, I think. Maybe thirty-five, I can't remember." He shook his head again. "I can't quite wrap my head around it. The sheriff's deputy who contacted me said they're treating it as a suspicious death. I don't know why."

That clinched it. I pulled out the chair at my usual spot and sat. Azalea placed a glass of sweet tea in front of me, and I nodded my thanks. "Was your sister-in-law Dixie Compton?"

Dan looked at me oddly. "You knew her?"

"I met her twice in the past couple of days," I said. "She was enrolled in the course I'm taking in the history department at Athena, and I noticed her in class on Wednesday. Then she came by my office yesterday to ask if I'd be interested in being her study partner." At Dan's puzzled look, I hastened to explain. "She and I were the only older students in the class, and she thought she might need help with the class."

"What class are you taking?" Dan asked.

I winced as I felt tiny claws digging into my leg. Ramses climbed up and into my lap, and I rubbed his head. "Dr. Warriner's early medieval England course." Ramses settled down and tried to lick my hand. I discouraged him gently.

Maybe it was my imagination, but I thought I saw Dan's lips tighten briefly at the mention of the professor's name. "I had no idea she had enrolled at Athena," he said.

"She was taking two classes," I said. "The other one was Old English literature." I wanted to gauge his reaction at this news.

Dan's eyebrows rose. "Irene's course?"

"Yes, I believe so," I replied.

Dan shrugged. "I never knew she was interested in either history or literature."

"Why did the sheriff's department call you?" Stewart asked. "If you don't mind my asking, isn't that a bit odd?"

"I'm not sure why." Dan frowned. "Unless she had me listed somewhere as an emergency contact. From what I can remember, I don't think she had any family to speak of, except an ex-husband or two. As far as I know, Ray was the latest. He died on an oil rig offshore a couple years ago."

Along with Stewart, I briefly expressed my condolences over the death of his brother, and Dan nodded.

"She went by the name Compton," I said. "Was that her maiden name?"

Dan shook his head. "No, my brother's name. Ray was my half brother. His father died when he was about seven, and our mother married my father a year or two later. Ray was eleven years older than me." Suddenly he stood. "Thank you again for the brandy. If you'll excuse me, though, I need to go up to my room to get ready for dinner with a friend."

"Of course," I said. "Let us know if there's anything we can do for you."

Stewart nodded. "Again, we're sorry for your loss."

Dan smiled briefly and looked at the three of us. "I appreciate it." He left the room.

Diesel emerged from under the table then. He rubbed against my leg and meowed softly. I realized that he had not made any effort to comfort Dan, and that was unusual behavior. Perhaps it was because Dan was still so new to him, or there was something about Dan that put him off. I wondered what it could be.

Azalea spoke then, her tone thoughtful. "He was shocked, but he's not grieving."

Stewart nodded. "I thought the same thing. I don't believe he really cared for his sister-in-law that much."

I hadn't picked up on any of this. I'd not really given it much thought. Dan had seemed upset, and I hadn't taken time to analyze the nature of it.

"You're right," I said as I thought back over the conversation. "He seemed more shocked over the idea that her death was suspicious than grieved over her loss. There wasn't any hint of affection for her, now that you mention it."

"Wouldn't be the first time that an in-law didn't care for someone," Stewart said.

"No, it wouldn't," I said. "I'm really surprised to find out about Dan's connection to Dixie Compton. Melba didn't say anything about it to me, but she knew Ms. Compton."

Stewart laughed. "Melba doesn't always know everybody, although she'd like you to think she does."

"I think they're both from somewhere down on the coast," Azalea said. "Mr. Dan and that Ms. Compton, I mean."

"Really?" Stewart said. "How on earth do you know that? I've never heard Dan say anything about the coast." He shrugged. "But I don't think the subject has ever come up at the gym. That's where I know him from."

Azalea regarded him with one eyebrow raised. "I thought you went to that place to get you some exercise. Sounds to me like y'all are just sitting around gossiping instead."

Stewart grinned. "Some of us gossip while we're exercising, I'll have you know. We can talk and do biceps curls or squats at the same time."

Azalea didn't look convinced. She addressed me. "The professor and I talked for a little bit this morning after breakfast, and he happened to mention that he grew up down there, maybe around Bay St. Louis." She frowned. "Can't remember exactly where he said."

"If his brother worked offshore in the Gulf, then the brother and his wife would have lived down there somewhere, I suppose," I said. "How long has Dan Bellamy been at Athena, Stewart? Do you know?"

"Not really sure," Stewart replied. "He's been coming to the gym for the past two years, so at least that long." He shrugged. "I don't really know that much about the history department or its faculty, unless I've served on a committee with someone from there."

"Why're you so curious about the professor?" Azalea asked.

"You know me," I said, keeping my tone light. "Always curious about people."

Azalea's gaze narrowed in suspicion. "You'd best not be thinking that poor man had something to do with that woman's death. You should have seen him when he was talking on the phone. Lord help me, I thought he was sure going to faint."

Stewart said, "He did look stunned, Charlie. If he already knew about her death, then he's missed his calling. He should be on the stage or the screen."

"I don't recall saying, or even hinting, that I suspected

him of anything of the kind." I frowned at both of them. "Is it so wrong of me to want to know something about the background of a man who's going to be living in this house for two months or longer?"

"No, I guess not." Stewart had the grace to appear slightly abashed. Azalea's expression did not change, nor did she respond to my statement.

"Everything's ready for dinner," she said. "Stewart knows what to do. Time for me to be getting on home." She went to retrieve her bags, and Ramses trotted after her.

"Looks like someone wants to go home with you," Stewart observed.

Azalea glanced down at the kitten. "Wanting and getting aren't the same thing," she said. "You shoo, little Mr. Cat. I don't have time for you."

Ramses sat and meowed plaintively. He clearly wanted to go with her. Azalea's gaze softened minutely, and she shot me a quick glance.

I had to suppress a grin. "If you want to take him home for the weekend, you're welcome to him."

Azalea grimaced. "He's nothing but trouble, but I reckon he's company. All right, little mister." She opened her bag, held it down, and Ramses jumped right in. Seconds later his head appeared, stuck out of the bag. I would have sworn he was smiling. "If he gets to be driving me crazy, I'll bring him back before Monday."

"That's fine," I said, knowing perfectly well I wouldn't see Ramses again until Monday.

Stewart shot me a quick grin, then ducked his head so Azalea couldn't see his face.

Dante barked at Azalea. She stared down at him. "I am surely not going to take *you* anywhere. You get on back to Stewart."

Dante whimpered and scuttled backward until he reached his master. Stewart reached down and stroked his head. Now I was the one who had to hide a smile.

"See you on Monday," I called to the housekeeper as she left through the back door.

"He'll come back stuffed full of bacon and chicken," Stewart said. "She spoils him rotten."

"Being around Diesel the last few years has softened her up," I said. Hearing his name, Diesel chirped loudly. "Yes, you finally wore her down," I told him.

Stewart rose from his place at the table. "Are you ready to eat? I can start getting everything ready."

"I forgot to tell you, Helen Louise is coming," I said. "Plus she's bringing a chocolate cake." I glanced at my watch. "She should be here in about ten minutes."

"I'm glad she can make it," Stewart replied. "I'll go ahead and get things ready if you'll set the table."

Before I could do as Stewart asked, my cell phone rang. I pulled it from my pocket and saw that Helen Louise was calling.

"Hello, love," I said. "Everything okay?"

"I'm running a little behind," Helen Louise said. "I should be there around six fifteen. I'll tell you about it when I get there."

"Okay, see you then." I ended the call and laid my cell on the table. "That was Helen Louise. She's running late. She said she'd tell us about it when she gets here."

"Sounds like something must have happened at the bistro," Stewart said. "If she's coming from there and not from home, that is. I hope there's nothing seriously wrong." Dante danced around his feet, and he motioned for the poodle to move away. Dante stepped back and sat, still within reach of any goodies Stewart might drop.

"She didn't sound upset," I said, "and, yes, she's coming from the bistro." I explained that she had to bake the cake for tonight.

"Too bad Dan won't be here," Stewart said, "but there's more for us." He grinned.

Stewart had a weakness for chocolate, and for Helen Louise's chocolate cakes in particular. As did I. The only difference was, Stewart burned off the extra calories at the gym and could afford to eat multiple pieces.

While I set the table, Stewart put out a trivet and set the hot dish of Azalea's marvelous beef stew on it. "I'll leave the rolls warming in the oven until Helen Louise gets here. Ready for some sweet tea?"

"More than," I said.

He poured glasses for both of us and set the pitcher on the table. Then he rummaged in the fridge to find the cold chicken that Azalea had taken to preparing for us to give as treats to the animals. He set it on the counter to warm while we waited.

We sipped at our tea and chatted in desultory fashion about nothing of particular import until I heard a car in the driveway. "Helen Louise is here," I told Diesel, and he immediately trotted to the front door. I followed to open the door for her.

I swung the door open and stepped out onto the stoop. Helen Louise advanced along the walk from the driveway, and Diesel ran to meet her. He escorted her back to the door, and I stood aside to let her enter. Then I shut the door behind us and exchanged a quick kiss with her, taking care not to disturb the cake plate she carried.

"Everything is ready," I told her as we headed to the kitchen. Diesel walked right by her side. "Did something happen at the bistro this afternoon?"

Helen Louise set down the cake plate and greeted Stewart before she answered my question. "I'll say something happened." She slipped off her jacket, and I took it from her. "I thought I might have to call the police because two men looked like they were going to fight, right there in the middle of the bistro."

"Good grief," I said.

"Anyone we know?" Stewart asked, his avid curiosity evident in his expression. He loved tidbits of gossip.

Helen Louise glanced between us. "Yes, Carey Warriner and another man."

ELEVEN

|||||||||||||||||||||||||||||||||||||||||||||

"Warriner?" I said, shocked.

"Jeez," Stewart said at the same time.

"What were they going to fight over?" I asked, although I figured I knew the answer.

"Irene Warriner," Helen Louise said. "She was there with another man, and then her husband came in with another woman." She laughed suddenly. "Since they were each with other people of the opposite sex, I can't see what her husband got so het up about."

"Who was the other man?" I figured it was Dan Bellamy.

"I don't know him," Helen Louise said, "but he looks either French or Italian. Very handsome. Dark wavy hair, tall, with dark eyes. He's been in the bistro a couple of times, but I never managed to catch his name before." She grinned at me, but I ignored this bit of teasing.

Stewart and I exchanged glances. "Not Dan Bellamy," he said. "I wonder who this guy is."

"I did overhear a name at one point tonight that sounded like *d'Arcy*," Helen Louise said. "That was before I had to get between them to put a stop to such foolishness. You men are such silly creatures sometimes, acting like women are your personal property." She grimaced.

"Was Carey Warriner upset because his wife was out with another man?" I asked.

At the same time Stewart asked, "Who was the woman with Warriner?"

"One question at a time, if you please. And if you don't mind, I'm going to sit down. I've been on my feet most of the day."

I hurried to pull out a chair for her. "Sorry, love, we got carried away by curiosity. You tell us your way, and we'll be quiet." I shot a pointed look at Stewart, who grinned back at me. He and I resumed our seats.

"I'll answer Stewart first," Helen Louise said. "The woman with him was Barb Lamont. I know her slightly from church. I think she's an English professor."

Stewart nodded.

"Now, as to Carey Warriner," Helen Louise went on. "His wife and d'Arcy, if that's his name, arrived first and were seated at a table in the back corner. Warriner and Barb Lamont came in about ten minutes later. I don't think they spotted one another right away, but Warriner happened to sit down at a table about ten feet away, facing in their direction. I was at the register at the time. The next thing I knew, Warriner was on his feet in front of the other table, yelling at d'Arcy." She grimaced again. "He was using ugly words, throwing out accusations. He was spouting invective so fast I couldn't make out most of what he said. D'Arcy stood up and got right in Warriner's face. He started yelling, too, and I couldn't understand either one.

That was when I went over and got between them. Henry came to help, and the women tried to tug on them, too. It was a mess."

"You shouldn't put yourself between two men about to fight," I admonished her. "You could have been hurt if one of them had swung at the other one."

Helen Louise snorted. "I'd like to have seen them try. I'd have decked both of them if I'd had the chance. You forget those years I spent in France, training as a chef. I had to dissuade many a Frenchman from trying it on with me." She grinned suddenly. "I know I broke at least two arms while I was there."

Stewart and I laughed. Helen Louise, at six feet, was a formidable woman. I was barely an inch taller than she.

"All right, then," I said. "You could have handled them. Once you got them apart, what happened next?"

"I asked them all to leave," Helen Louise said. "Both women looked horribly embarrassed, and d'Arcy apologized profusely. He has the faintest accent, now that I think about it. Warriner still looked pugnacious, but both women grabbed an arm and pulled him out of the bistro. His wife looked ready to kill him, and poor Barb Lamont looked like she was ready to sink through the floor. D'Arcy slunk out after them."

Carey Warriner was obviously a hothead, if this incident was anything to judge by. There was also his unpleasant remark to poor Dixie Compton. Was there any connection between his temper and her suspicious death? The thought made me uncomfortable.

"That was the end of it," Helen Louise said. "It happened around four thirty, when a lot of customers drop by for coffee and croissants. Because of them I got a late start on the cake."

"I'm glad they didn't start hitting each other," I said.

"They'd better be glad they didn't, too," Helen Louise replied, a martial gleam in her eye. Before she went to France to train as a chef, she had been a lawyer, and a successful one. No one trod on her toes and got away with it.

"Enough of all that," Helen Louise said. "How about some of Azalea's beef stew? I'm famished."

"Sounds good to me," Stewart said. "Would you like sweet tea or wine with dinner?"

"Sweet tea," Helen Louise said. "Time to please my inner Southern belle."

Stewart poured her tea, and I began to dish out the stew. Stewart next took the rolls out of the oven and plated them before he joined us at the table.

I was determined to banish all thoughts of the Warriners and their domestic issues, as well as the death of poor Dixie Compton, from my mind while we chatted and enjoyed the meal. Stewart seemed to sense my resolve, because he didn't bring up the suspicious death, either. Instead, we talked of various domestic things, including plans for tomorrow. Helen Louise was working at the bistro until two, and then she planned to come by to spend time with me and the grandchildren.

While we ate, Stewart and I doled out bits of chicken to the two four-legged beggars who accosted us. Helen Louise occasionally joined in, and it wasn't long before the supply of chicken disappeared. When they realized no more was forthcoming, both Diesel and Dante settled down and napped.

Over coffee, we enjoyed Helen Louise's delicious chocolate cake, and I finally broached the matter of Dixie Compton's death. To begin with, for Helen Louise's benefit, I mentioned her being in my class with Warriner and having talked to her about being her study partner. Then I shared what I had learned about her death.

Helen Louise narrowed her eyes at that but surprisingly asked only one question: "So all you know is that she died under suspicious circumstances?"

"Yes, Kanesha wouldn't say anything else," I replied.

"I *might* be able to get more information out of Haskell," Stewart said. "Although if Kanesha is bound and determined not to let Charlie know anything, he won't tell me. He's loyal to her, and I admire him for it." He grinned. "Even when it frustrates the heck out of me because he doesn't tell me the good bits."

"Good for him." Though I couldn't help but be curious about what had really happened to Dixie Compton, I knew that when, and if, Kanesha concluded that she had been murdered, we would know. In a town this size, sooner or later most people got to know about such things pretty quickly.

"There is one more thing," I said. "To do with Dixie Compton and Carey Warriner."

"What?" Stewart asked. "You mean you've been holding out on us? What else do you know?"

"Give me a moment," I said, "and I'll tell you. It may not mean anything, but in light of what you told us, Helen Louise, it could have bearing on Dixie Compton's death." I related to them the incident between Warriner and Ms. Compton that I'd overheard two days ago.

When I finished, Stewart said, "Too bad you didn't stay and listen to the whole thing. If Warriner was that angry with her for signing up for the class, he could have threatened her."

"Possibly," I said. "I told Kanesha this, and now it's up to her to question Warriner."

Helen Louise nodded approvingly. "Sensible attitude. This is one you can stay out of, though I know you're itching to find out exactly how the poor woman died."

"Yes, but not for prurient reasons," I said.

"I know that," Helen Louise replied. "You met the woman, felt a little sorry for her, and now you feel a bit guilty because you turned down her request for help studying for the class. Am I right?"

Stewart chuckled. "She's got you pegged, Charlie."

I gave them a rueful smile. "That she does. Yes, I do feel a little guilty." I shrugged. "I can't explain it; it was simply a feeling I had while we were talking that she wanted something besides a study partner."

"I wonder if she was afraid something bad was going to happen to her," Stewart said, his expression thoughtful.

"I wonder what could have happened between her and Carey Warriner to have him accost her so angrily," Helen Louise said. "Given the scene in the bistro tonight, I have to wonder if he'd had an affair with her and had broken it off."

"And she showed up in his class in a stalking kind of way." Stewart nodded. "I can see that. Maybe she was angry he broke it off, and she didn't want it to end."

"Let's not turn this into some kind of *Fatal Attraction* scenario. She didn't seem enamored of Warriner when she came to my office," I said. "I grant you that an affair gone wrong between them is a quick and easy explanation for his reacting so angrily to her, and her being negative about him to me, but there must be other reasons. We don't know anything about their personal lives. Maybe he owed her money, for example, and wasn't intending to pay it back."

"So she showed up in his class as a reminder?" Helen Louise asked. "Possible, I suppose."

"There's one other thing," I said. "She had also enrolled in Irene Warriner's course on early medieval literature, Old English, I think. She told me so."

"I wonder if Warriner was aware of that," Stewart said.

"I have no idea," I replied.

"Maybe Ms. Compton was truly interested in both subjects and simply wanted to further her education," Helen Louise said. "It makes sense to take both courses together, to get a complete picture of early medieval English history and literature."

"It does," I said. "And you're right, she might have been interested in the subjects and wanted a degree in order to better herself."

"Warriner obviously had reason not to believe this, don't you think?" Stewart asked. "Otherwise he wouldn't have responded the way he did to her presence in his class."

"You know what I think?" Helen Louise said, and Stewart and I looked at her. "I think we're spending way too much time talking about people we don't really know. Make that *wasting* time," she amended. "I'm ready to talk about something else."

"You're right," I said. "This gets us nowhere. So what should we talk about instead?"

"You two are no fun," Stewart said in mock protest. "Speculation is such an entertaining game."

"Yes, it is," Helen Louise said, "but you can have too much of an entertaining game." She cocked an eyebrow at him.

"Yes, ma'am, Miz Brady, ma'am," Stewart said meekly.

"I'll bet you were a handful in elementary school," Helen Louise said with a grin.

"Naturally," Stewart replied.

"How about more coffee and cake?" I said.

"I thought you'd never ask." Stewart held out his plate.

We chatted a while longer while Stewart ate his second—or was it third?—piece of cake, then Helen Louise pleaded weariness and headed home. I walked her to the front door to bid her good night in private.

After a satisfying kiss, she pulled back and said, "You will stay out of this one, won't you, Charlie? I have a bad feeling about this, that there's something nasty at work."

"Have you suddenly turned into Sean?" I said lightly. My son deplored my habit of becoming involved in murders. "I can assure you I have no intentions of having anything to do with this, other than answering Kanesha's questions. After all, I know practically nothing."

"Good." Helen Louise bent to scratch Diesel's back, because he had, as always, accompanied us to the door. "You two have a good night, and I'll see you tomorrow." With that, she turned and headed to her car. I watched until she had safely backed up onto the street and driven away.

I had every intention of doing exactly what I told Helen Louise I would do, but good intentions didn't always hold.

TWELVE

I had always enjoyed weekends—family time for so many years. First, for my wife and me with our two children, and second, as a respite from the workweek. These days I looked forward to Saturdays because it meant time with the next generation, my two precious, adorable, incomparable grandchildren. Along with other members of the family, of course, but being a grandfather brought special joy.

Sean and Alex dropped off Rosie a little earlier than they'd originally planned, but I did not complain as it meant more time with my little girl. Alex hovered for several minutes while Sean patiently waited for her to decide she was ready to leave her daughter in my care. Alex had improved significantly in the past few weeks, but I still saw vestiges of her uncertainty over her abilities as a mother and hints of the depression that had worried us all. Finally she appeared calm and ready to go.

"Have a wonderful afternoon," I told them after kissing Alex's cheek. "Rosie and I will do fine, and don't forget, we have a backup nanny." I indicated Diesel, who stood by my legs, watching every move I made with Rosie.

"Helen Louise is coming over, too," Sean reminded his wife.

"Laura ought to be here with baby Charlie any minute," I said. "Relax and enjoy yourself. You've earned an afternoon off." I smiled at her.

"You're all so kind to me," Alex said. "You're right, Charlie, I do need a break." She glanced at Sean. "So does my poor husband, all the hours he's putting in to make up for my working only half-time at the moment."

"Not nearly as many hours as I had to put in every week when I worked for that corporate law firm in Houston," Sean said. "This is fun by comparison."

"Shoo, both of you," I said. "Get going."

"Yes, Dad." Sean took Alex gently by the arm and drew her toward the front door. "We should be back by five so you can make it to that thing at the bookstore."

"Thanks," I called after them. Moments later I heard the door open and shut.

Rosie yawned, and I took her to her crib in the living room and put her down for a nap. She had been fed not long before Sean and Alex brought her over, and she would sleep for a while now. Like her cousin Charlie, she was not a fretful baby now that her problems with colic had subsided. For that I frequently gave thanks. At my age I wasn't sure I was up to the task of dealing with one cranky infant, let alone two at the same time.

Diesel stretched out on the floor beside Rosie's crib, and I knew he would keep watch. At the first sign of any kind of distress he would let me know if I happened not to be nearby. I went into the kitchen to pour myself a glass of water. Back in the living room I settled into a comfortable chair with my current book and began to read.

Helen Louise arrived fifteen minutes later, followed quickly by Laura and baby Charlie. We put Charlie into his matching crib next to Rosie's and removed to the kitchen to talk. Diesel, the ever-faithful and alert baby monitor, remained in the living room. Before we left the room, however, I switched on the mechanical baby monitor as a backup to the feline one.

Laura amused us with stories of baby Charlie's crawling exploits and his attempts to pull himself up on various pieces of furniture. "I swear he's going to be walking any day now," she said. "He is so determined."

"He sounds a lot like you at that age," I said. "You learned to pull yourself up pretty early on. Sean did, too." I grinned at Helen Louise. "Both of them are strong willed and go after what they want."

Helen Louise and Laura exchanged a glance, then both of them fixed their gazes on me. "I think Sean and I came by it honestly, Dad," Laura said. "You have been known to be pretty strong willed yourself, you know."

"Not to say hardheaded," Helen Louise added.

"Who, me?" I said in mock astonishment. "No, not me."

"Yes, *you*," Laura retorted. "The second you sniff a mystery, off you go. You're Frank and Joe Hardy rolled into one."

"I think this is an argument I can't win," I said.

Helen Louise laughed and shook her head. "Don't even try, Frankie Joe."

I groaned at the moniker, but Laura giggled. "Oh, I like that. Frankie Joe. I'll have to tell Sean, Alex, and Frank about that. They'll love it."

"On one condition," I said. "Just don't tell Melba, or I'll never hear the end of it."

"Maybe," Laura said. "I'll think about it."

I decided that I'd better introduce a new subject before

the conversation went any further along these lines. "So what's the latest in the theater department?" That question never failed to get my daughter talking, and it did not fail now.

Laura regaled us with various tidbits about the odd behavior of several of her colleagues and some of the inner workings of the department until Diesel appeared in the doorway of the kitchen and meowed. Not a sound of distress or concern, simply an announcement, I decided. One or both of the babies must now be awake. I followed him back to the living room to find Charlie sitting up in his crib. The moment he saw me he raised his arms and made a garbled sound that I interpreted as either *up* or *out*. Rosie did not appear disturbed by this. She still slept.

I took Charlie out of the crib, and he started wriggling for me to put him down. I did so, wondering what he would do. Diesel watched him, alert for any sign of trouble. Charlie began crawling toward the door. Diesel and I followed him out into the hall, across it, and into the kitchen. Charlie made a beeline for his mother.

Laura scooped up her son, and he made known what he wanted by rooting around on her chest. "Excuse me," she said. "He's hungry." She resumed her seat, pulled up her blouse, and Charlie began to nurse. The first time this happened in my presence, I had been somewhat shocked by my daughter's apparent unconcern that others might be watching. Then I took myself to task. This was the most natural thing in the world. A beautiful thing, in fact, and I made no protest from then on when it occurred in front of me.

My cell phone rang, and I pulled it from my shirt pocket. "Kanesha," I said in some surprise to Helen Louise. What on earth did Kanesha want? I greeted her by name before saying, "What can I do for you?"

"If it's convenient," she said in her usual brisk tone, "I'd like to drop by for a few minutes to go over again what you told me about Dr. Warriner and Ms. Compton. Is this a convenient time?"

"Sure, come on by," I said.

"Right, be there in less than ten." She ended the call.

"What does she want?" Helen Louise asked.

Laura looked at me with a frown after I answered Helen Louise's question.

"Okay, Frankie Joe, what's up? Not another murder, surely?" she said.

"I don't know," I said. "A woman I met briefly has died under suspicious circumstances—those are Kanesha's words, not mine—and I happened to overhear something odd that someone said to her. It might have some bearing on her death, or it might not. That's all."

"Honestly, Dad," Laura said, "how do you do it? You end up being in the wrong place at the right time somehow."

"I'm sure Kanesha would agree with you," Helen Louise said. "It's a knack Charlie has."

"Or a jinx," I said gloomily. "Now, listen here, both of you, I don't want to hear either of you call me Frankie Joe in front of Kanesha, understand?"

They both nodded. "Good," I said. "I don't think she'd see the humor in it anyway."

"She might surprise you," Helen Louise said.

"I'd rather not take the risk," I replied.

We continued in this vein while Laura fed Charlie. The doorbell rang to signal Kanesha's arrival. I rose to answer it. "I think we'll go in the den. I don't want to disturb Rosie."

"I'll check on her," Helen Louise said and followed me out of the kitchen.

I opened the door to Kanesha and invited her in.

"Come on back to the den, if you don't mind," I said. "Laura's in the kitchen feeding Charlie, and Helen Louise is in the living room checking on Rosie."

"That's fine," Kanesha said as I closed the door. "How are the grandchildren? Mama gives me reports on them from time to time."

I figured the question was mostly her being polite so I didn't go into detail. "They're both thriving," I said. "Growing fast." We walked down the hall, and I turned on the light in the den. "Have a seat wherever you like."

Kanesha chose a straight-backed chair, and I took the sofa.

"Thanks for talking to me on short notice like this," she said. "I won't keep you too long from your family."

"It's not a problem. You have an investigation to run, and that's important," I replied.

She nodded as she pulled out her notebook. She flipped the pages until she found whatever she wanted to consult. After a brief glance at her notes, she looked at me. "You overheard angry remarks directed at Ms. Compton by Dr. Warriner."

I nodded.

"Would you please tell me again what you heard and the circumstances in which you heard it?" Kanesha said.

I launched into my story after a brief pause to marshal my thoughts. "Class had ended, and Warriner said he would like to talk to me. I approached him at the front of the room, and he said he wanted me to consider taking the course for credit, instead of auditing it. I said I would consider it, and he appeared satisfied with my answer. I headed for the door, and I almost collided with Dixie Compton. I thought she had been waiting there until I left. She brushed past me into the room, and before I had stepped away from the doorway, I heard Warriner ask her what the hell she was doing in his class."

"Those were his exact words?" Kanesha asked.

"He said, *What the hell are you doing in my class?*" I replied.

Kanesha nodded as she checked her notebook. "That tallies with what you said before. Now, how would you describe the tone of this question?"

"Nasty, savage," I said. "Shocked me, because it was completely unlike the persona he presented in class. He sounded furiously angry over it."

"Did you hear anything else? Her response, for example?"

I shook my head. "No, I got away from the door then. It wasn't any of my business, and I didn't want to hear any more of their confrontation."

"Are you certain about the tone of Warriner's voice when he asked her the question? Would you swear to it in court?"

Her questions and the harsh tone in which she delivered them took me aback. "Yes, to both. What's going on here?"

Kanesha snapped her notebook shut and regarded me with her trademark enigmatic expression. "I questioned Dr. Warriner about this incident without identifying the witness. He readily admitted that he talked to Ms. Compton after class. According to him, however, he said, in a friendly tone, *I wasn't expecting to see you in my class. This is a pleasant surprise.*"

"He's lying," I said flatly, suddenly angry.

"I agree," Kanesha said. "The question is, *why.*"

THIRTEEN

||||||||||||||||||||||||||||||||||||||||||||||

"I'd say he doesn't want anyone to know he was angry with her," I said. "At least he didn't deny outright that he knew her."

"Too clever for that," Kanesha said. "He knew we'd find evidence that they were acquainted."

"And have you?" I asked, despite the fact that I knew she might decline to answer.

"We have," she replied, but didn't supply any further details.

"Why did you think he was lying when he denied the tone and the words he used speaking to Ms. Compton?"

"I know you," Kanesha said. "You don't lie, so I figured he had to be."

I felt like I'd just won an Olympic gold medal. Kanesha rarely complimented me, and this one was definitely golden.

"Thank you," I managed to say. "I appreciate your trust in me."

"You've earned it," Kanesha replied coolly. "Which is

why I'm going to ask you something, although you know
it goes against the grain for me to do it."

I nodded and waited for her to continue.

"You know people on campus at the college," Kanesha
said. "You hear things." For a moment a smile flashed, then
was gone. "Particularly given your best friend on campus,
who seems to know everything about everybody."

"I can't disagree," I said, trying not to grin. "People talk
to Melba and tell her things, and sometimes she tells me."

"That's what I'm counting on," Kanesha replied. "I need
to know if there has been any talk about Dr. Warriner, anything that would suggest he's been having an affair, for
example."

"You must consider him a prime suspect in Ms. Compton's death," I said. Time to bargain for information, I decided. "Does this mean you believe she was murdered?"

Kanesha's gaze narrowed as she regarded me. "Yes, I
do. There are indications that she was struck by someone
before she died. She fell against the brick hearth, on a
sharp edge, and died from the impact to the back of her
head."

I tried not to picture the scene, but my imagination was
too creative. I winced. "How horrible."

"Back to Dr. Warriner," Kanesha said. "What can you
tell me?"

"You need to talk to Melba," I said. "She told me what
she heard from two of the department administrators she
knows. One in the history department, the other in the
English department. I'd rather you get the details from
her."

"I will," Kanesha said. "Is there anything else?"

I nodded unhappily. "Yes, there is, but I think Helen
Louise needs to tell you herself. It happened at the bistro
yesterday evening." I rose. "I'll send her in to talk to you."

"Thank you," Kanesha said.

I found Helen Louise in the living room, holding Rosie and rocking her in the rocking chair I had placed in the room for exactly that purpose. I paused to watch them for a moment. Helen Louise had never had children of her own, but Sean and Laura had accepted her readily as their potential stepmother. They already considered her a grandmother to their children, even though she and I hadn't married yet. Helen Louise had embraced the role happily and lovingly.

I knew Kanesha was waiting for Helen Louise, but I was reluctant to disturb the peaceful scene. Knowing that if I didn't, however, the chief deputy would, I forced myself forward into the room.

"Kanesha wants to talk to you," I said, keeping my voice low.

"It's okay," Helen Louise said. "Rosie's awake, so you don't have to whisper. I think she's ready to be fed."

I held out my arms for Rosie, and Helen Louise gave her to me. "She has a couple of bottles in the fridge. I'll get one ready for her while you talk to Kanesha."

Helen Louise rose from the chair. "Why does she want to talk to me?"

"You need to tell her about what happened at the bistro last night," I said as we walked to the door. Helen Louise preceded us into the hallway. I realized that Diesel wasn't with us. "Where's Diesel?"

"He went to check on Laura and Charlie." Helen Louise sighed. "I wonder what Kanesha will make of it all."

"I don't know, but it could be pertinent to Ms. Compton's murder," I said.

Helen Louise stopped short. "Murder?"

I nodded. "Kanesha told me."

Helen Louise shook her head and muttered something, but she walked off down the hall before I could ask her what she said. I had a good notion that I was probably better off not knowing.

Laura had finished feeding Charlie and was burping him while Diesel supervised anxiously. Laura reassured the cat that the baby was fine, and almost on cue, Charlie burped. She wiped his mouth before she rose from the chair with him.

"I'm going to put him down for another quick nap," she said. "He usually likes to doze a little while when he's finished a meal. I'll be back in a minute." She left the room. Diesel looked at her retreating back, then at me. He appeared torn. Should he go with Laura and Charlie, or should he stay and supervise me with Rosie? After a moment, he trotted after Laura. I think he knew she would put Charlie down for a nap, and he would be needed as guardian there. Between us, Laura and I ought to be able to take care of Rosie. Or so I imagined his reasoning went.

I retrieved one of Rosie's bottles from the fridge and put it in the bottle warmer. By the time it was ready, Laura had returned. I made myself comfortable in my usual spot at the table and began to feed my granddaughter. Laura watched, smiling.

"You make such a wonderful picture," she said. "I wish Mom could be here to see it."

I glanced at her and saw tears glistening on her lashes. "I know, sweetheart, but I always feel she's near when Charlie and Rosie are here. Aunt Dottie, too. They're both watching over us. All of us."

Laura nodded. "I hope so." She pulled a tissue from Charlie's diaper bag and dabbed at her eyes.

"I know she is," I said simply. "Nothing would keep

her from seeing her grandchildren and being their guardian angel."

"You're going to make me cry again," Laura said, using the tissue once more.

I shook my head. "Don't. She wants you to be as happy as she is." People outside the family might think I needed a psychiatric evaluation, but I didn't think much about that. I knew what I felt, not to mention the occasional whiffs of their separate perfumes I smelled in the house from time to time. Jackie's and Aunt Dottie's presences hadn't disappeared with their deaths, and I took great comfort in that. Nothing to do with haunting whatsoever. Simply love, strong and enduring.

Rosie sucked noisily at her bottle, and by the time she finished draining it, Helen Louise reappeared in the kitchen.

"Where's Kanesha?" I asked.

"I told her about Diesel keeping an eye on the babies, and she wanted to see for herself," Helen Louise replied. "But don't let her know I told you that." She glanced first at me, then at Laura. We both shook our heads.

"Thank you again, both of you," Kanesha said from the kitchen doorway. "I appreciate your information. I've got to go now, more people to talk to. I'll see myself out." She turned and disappeared into the hall, and moments later I heard the door open and shut.

"What did Kanesha think of the incident?" I asked Helen Louise.

She glanced at Laura, who correctly interpreted the look. Laura stood. "I'm going to recuse myself—isn't that the legal term?—from this discussion. If you don't mind me leaving Charlie with you for half an hour or so, I need to run to the store for a few things. It's a lot easier without him trying to grab at everything and squirming to get down so he can crawl."

"Sure," I said. "We'll be glad to keep him. No point in waking him up."

"Thanks." Laura grabbed her purse and headed out the back door. "See you in a bit."

Helen Louise asked, "How about some coffee or a glass of sweet tea?"

"Sweet tea is fine with me," I replied, "but if you'd rather have coffee, I'll have some, too."

"Coffee it is." She began to prepare the coffeemaker, and I waited until she had finished with that before I repeated my question. Helen Louise resumed her seat at the table before she answered. "She found it interesting. We both knew she would. I get the feeling that she's zeroing in on Warriner as her chief suspect. I'm sure she knows more about him and his relationship with the dead woman than she's willing to let on, at least with us."

"I think you're probably right," I said. "She told us only what she thinks is appropriate." I chuckled. "At least it's something."

"Things aren't looking good for your class this semester," Helen Louise said. "If the professor is charged with murder, that will be the end of it."

"Unless there's someone else on the faculty who can teach it," I said. "Or a graduate student, maybe. He could be completely innocent, though. I certainly hope he is, and not only because I want to take this class."

"Me, too, I suppose," Helen Louise said. "Although someone has to be guilty, if Kanesha is sure it's murder."

"She is," I said.

"Warriner seems to have a problem controlling his anger," Helen Louise said.

"He lashed out pretty quickly at d'Arcy, from what you told us," I said. "He might have lashed out just like that at Dixie Compton without meaning to kill her."

"If that's the case, wouldn't it be manslaughter?"

I shrugged. "I think so, but I'd have to ask Sean to be sure."

"You'd probably better not," Helen Louise said. "Once he gets wind of your connection to this case, he'll be unhappy about it."

"He'll have to be," I said. "I can't ignore what I heard, and you can't ignore what happened at the bistro. Both incidents may have direct bearing on a woman's death. Sean is reasonable, and he's not going to fuss at me over this."

"He'll have to fuss at both of us," Helen Louise said. "He's never actually fussed at me."

"You haven't given him cause," I said. "Whereas I, on the other hand, have given him plenty. Sometimes I feel like our roles have reversed, and now he's the father and I'm the child."

"He's probably exactly like you were at his age." She got up from the table. "Coffee's about ready." She went to the cabinet and pulled out two mugs, both emblazoned with the bistro's logo. She added two spoons of sugar to one mug, none to the other. She liked her coffee with a bit of cream, nothing more. I couldn't stand the taste without sugar and cream.

"He is a lot like me at that age," I said. "I don't remember fussing at my father much, though. I wouldn't have dared. Perhaps I might have later, if he'd lived long enough." My father passed away when I was thirty-one, and Sean was almost that now. My mother had outlived Dad by three years.

Helen Louise set a mug on the table in front of me. Rosie had fallen asleep in my arms. I rose. "I'm going to put her down again before Charlie wakes up."

Diesel looked up when I entered the living room. He

meowed softly when I laid my granddaughter in her crib and covered her with a blanket.

"You keep watch," I said softly, and he meowed again. I was thankful Ramses had gone home with Azalea for the weekend. He liked to jump into the cribs with the babies and lick their faces at every opportunity.

I resumed my seat and lifted my mug to my lips. My cell phone rang, and I set down the mug. A glance at the screen informed me that Melba was on the line. I mentioned this to Helen Louise before I answered.

I barely had time to greet her before Melba rushed into her speech. "I have a big bone to pick with you, Charlie Harris." She sounded peeved with me. "I swear I'm going to stop telling you *anything*."

FOURTEEN

||||||||||||||||||||||||||||||||||||||||||||||||

Melba's words startled me. "What have I done?" I asked,
puzzled. Helen Louise shot an inquiring look at me, and I
shrugged.

"You sent Kanesha Berry over here and didn't give me
a heads-up," Melba said. "She's on her way now. I just
happened to be at home when she called. Said she wants
to talk to me about things you said I could tell her about
stuff on campus."

"You've talked to her before about things you've heard
on campus," I pointed out reasonably. "Why are you so
riled up now?"

"I know I've told her things before," she said, "and I
don't mind telling her this time. I only wish you'd let me
know she was going to call me. She said you said she
should. Call me, that is." She snorted. "So the least you
could have done was to call me and tell me that."

"I'm sorry I didn't call you," I said in the most placatory tone I could muster, although I was slightly dazed by all the *you said*s and *she said*s. "I've been busy with company here at the house. Both babies are here, along with Helen Louise. Laura ran an errand, but she ought to be back soon for Charlie. I guess I didn't think about it."

"Well, I guess that's okay then," she said, sounding less peeved. "Spending time with those precious babies is more important. I'll forgive you. This time."

"Thank you," I said.

"There goes the doorbell," Melba said. "Talk to you later." She ended the call.

"What was all that about?" Helen Louise asked.

I explained, and Helen Louise laughed. "She likes to know everything the moment it happens."

"I probably should have called her, but I honestly didn't think about it," I said.

"I wouldn't worry about it too much," Helen Louise said after a sip of coffee. "She adores you like a brother, and she can't ever stay mad at you for long."

"I adore her, too," I said. "Like a sister. But an aggravating sister." I grinned and took a sip from my mug. "Delicious."

"What time are we supposed to meet her at the bookstore?" Helen Louise asked.

"A quarter past six," I said. "The event starts at six thirty. That should give us enough time to find seats before it starts."

"Do you think there'll be a large crowd?"

"I doubt it will be standing room only," I said, "even though I know Lucy Dunne is a popular writer. This was arranged without much time for advance notice, so I'm sure that will affect people who otherwise might have come. Not everyone can change their plans on short notice."

"I'm glad I'm free tonight," Helen Louise said. "This sounds like it could be interesting. The subject definitely is."

Helen Louise, like me, was a Jane Austen fan. She also loved Georgette Heyer, along with the Regency mysteries of the late Kate Ross, as well as those of current writers like Tracy Grant and C. S. Harris.

"I've read Dan Bellamy's book on the period," I said. "I think having the two of them in conversation is an excellent idea. Having both the historian's take on the period and the novelist's should be interesting."

Loud meows coming from the living room alerted us once again that Charlie was awake and no doubt attempting to climb out of his crib. I set my mug on the table and went to answer the summons. I wanted to intercept my grandson before he woke up Rosie.

As expected, Charlie had pulled himself up by the crib rail and stood looking down at Diesel. The moment he saw me, the baby lifted his arms and chanted the word I couldn't understand. I picked him up, but this time when he started wriggling, I resisted and carried him into the kitchen after a quick glance at Rosie.

When we reached the kitchen I found Laura had just returned. I put Charlie down, and he started crawling around. Laura watched him, smiling and shaking her head. Diesel kept up with the baby, apparently intent on seeing that Charlie didn't get into trouble.

"You see what I mean?" she said. "I swear that child could crawl to Memphis and back and still have energy left over." She looked at me. "Was he trying to get out of the crib?"

"He was," I said. "He may start walking early, if he can pull himself up this easily now."

"I'd better get him home and into his playpen," she

said. "He can crawl around in that, and the sides are too high for him to climb over. At least for now." She sighed.

"I'll help you get him and his things to the car." Helen Louise rose and picked up Charlie. He burbled at her, and his hands clutched at her hair. She winced when one hand managed to grab and pull it. "You are certainly energetic, *mon petit*." She gently disengaged his hand.

"I've tried to discourage that," Laura said, "but he's stubborn." She picked up his diaper bag. "Let's get him in the car seat before he manages to pull again." She came over to give me a kiss. "Bye, Dad." She turned to the cat. "Come on, Diesel, you're going with us."

"Thanks for looking after him," I said. "We'll drop by after the bookstore event to pick him up."

"My pleasure," Laura said. "He can help me keep an eye on Charlie."

"Good-bye, sweetheart. Give my best to Frank."

Laura flashed me a smile as she opened the back door for Helen Louise and Diesel. The women disappeared into the garage, Diesel on their heels, and Laura pulled the door shut behind her.

I resumed my seat at the table, listening for sounds coming from the living room. Rosie remained quiet, and I sipped more of my coffee. It had cooled by now. I got up to add more to the cup, along with a bit more sugar and cream, and when I tasted it, I found it more satisfying. I didn't care that much for cold coffee.

Helen Louise returned soon. "All safe and secure, but wiggling the whole time. He doesn't care for being strapped in." She laughed. "I hope Laura and Frank have the energy to keep up with your namesake. He's going to be a busy little bee when he starts walking." She picked up her mug and went to pour herself more coffee.

Until Sean and Alex returned to pick Rosie up, only a few minutes past the appointed time, Helen Louise and I took turns holding the baby when she woke and changing her diaper. Helen Louise fed her when she wailed to let us know she was hungry.

Once Sean, Alex, and Rosie departed, Helen Louise headed home to change for the evening's event. I needed to change as well, and I climbed the stairs slowly, thinking how odd it was not to have Diesel and Ramses with me.

At the appointed time, Helen Louise and I met Melba at the Athenaeum, where a crowd of about twenty-five had gathered. We made our way up the stairs to the second-floor gallery where Jordan Thompson hosted author events. The space held sixty-five chairs, Jordan had once told me, and only about ten of them were occupied. We chose three seats together four rows back from the front. I took the outside seat, and Helen Louise sat between me and Melba. I set my bag of books on the floor between Helen Louise and me. The crowd from the first floor began to trickle upward, and soon about forty seats were occupied.

A small platform, wide and deep enough to hold several chairs, stood at the back of the gallery. Currently it held two chairs, and as we watched, two people in costume emerged from a door to one side. Helen Louise and I exchanged smiles. Irene Warriner, in her Lucy Dunne persona, had chosen to wear Regency dress, and Dan Bellamy had done likewise.

They each cut an impressive figure. Helen Louise informed me in a whisper that Dan's trousers and coat looked molded to his physique and that said physique was quite muscular. I retorted that Lucy Dunne's gown was ravishing, and she looked like a diamond of the first water, using a phrase often encountered in Heyer's novels to signify a particularly beautiful woman.

We grinned at each other as Jordan Thompson approached the platform. Once satisfied that her guests had seated themselves, she turned to address the audience. She welcomed everyone to the event before giving both speakers a short but plaudit-laden introduction. After an announcement that books were available for sale downstairs and that both speakers would be happy to sign books and answer questions after their talk, she stepped aside and indicated that the speakers should begin.

Lucy Dunne spoke first. "Thank you all for turning out tonight for this presentation. Both Professor Bellamy and I appreciate it greatly, and we hope you will enjoy yourselves. As Ms. Thompson told you, Professor Bellamy, whom I shall henceforth refer to as Dan, is an expert in the history of this period. He's going to tell you a little about it."

"Thank you, Lucy," Dan said. "Thanks to the work of Jane Austen and its undying popularity, the Regency period has captured the imagination not only of readers but of movie and television fans for many years. Some of these productions are more accurate than others, but they have all, for the most part, been entertaining. In my experience, each person has a favorite actor in the major roles, such as Jennifer Ehle and Colin Firth as Elizabeth and Darcy, or Alan Rickman as Colonel Brandon. What lies behind these characters, of course, is a real historical period, and I will tell you a bit about it now."

For the next five minutes, Dan gave the audience interesting and entertaining facts about the Regency. Already familiar with all this, thanks to his excellent book, I let my attention wander. I cast my glance over the attendees as discreetly as possible. I spotted Carey Warriner a few rows behind us at the other side of the room. An attractive woman occupied the chair next to him. Was this Barbara

Lamont? I speculated that it could well be, though after the incident yesterday, I marveled that he would bring her to his wife's event.

Lucy Dunne reclaimed my attention. Dan Bellamy had finished his spiel, and she began to talk about her own interest in the period and what drew her to it for her fiction, rather than her own area of literary specialty, Anglo-Saxon and early medieval English literature. Primary among these reasons was reader interest, she admitted, and that was a consideration every writer had to address. But the main reason she enjoyed writing about the period was her love of Austen and Heyer.

I noticed many approving nods from attendees, primarily women, although a few men indicated agreement as well.

Lucy finished this part, and Dan began to ask her questions. She answered them with ease and fluency, and he occasionally joined in, his manner pleasant and conversational. They obviously felt comfortable with each other and respected each other's knowledge. The audience appeared rapt, and that was a tribute to the presenters.

Questions from the audience followed for about ten minutes. To one slightly indignant woman, unhappy that a character in her favorite Dunne novel had not inherited a dukedom, Lucy patiently explained that, as a second son, he could not inherit, as long as the heir or the heir's sons were alive to inherit. Despite the fact that the heir in this case was a despicable character, Lucy said, she could not change the laws of inheritance to reward her hero. He would have to be happy with his beautiful wife and her inheritance from her grandfather.

"Well, that stinks," the woman said, not sounding mollified by historical fact.

Lucy answered a few more questions, while Dan answered two others. Jordan came forward to bring the program to an end. She announced that the authors would be happy to sign books and that there were plenty of copies for purchase downstairs where the authors would sign.

"If you all would please remain seated until the authors have a chance to get to the stairs first, I'd really appreciate it. This will give them time to get to the signing table. Thank you."

Everyone complied with this request while Lucy and Dan stepped off the platform and moved to the stairs. Then, at a signal from Jordan, members of the audience stood and began to follow the authors. I noticed that Carey Warriner hurried to get to the stairs and pushed his way through the crowd to get to the front. The woman who had been sitting beside him did not accompany him, so perhaps they were not together, I thought.

Helen Louise, Melba, and I chatted for a moment while we waited for the group at the head of the stairs to thin out. Then we proceeded to follow the rest of the group down the stairs. I realized I had forgotten my bag of books and turned back to retrieve them. I told Helen Louise that I would join them in a moment.

I strode back to where we had been sitting, picked up the cloth book bag, and turned to rejoin my companions. I heard a piercing scream and sounds of an altercation suddenly coming from downstairs. I hurried to the rails to look down from the gallery to see what was going on.

FIFTEEN

||||||||||||||||||||||||||||||||||||

At first, in the confusion of people milling about down-stairs, I couldn't see anything. A clump of people stood by a range of shelves that ran perpendicular to the edge of the gallery near the front of the store. Whatever was go-ing on seemed to be happening there, but because of the angle from where I stood and the tall shelves, I couldn't see anything.

I hurried to the stairs to find that Melba and Helen Louise had reached the bottom of the flight. I went down as quickly as I could to join them.

"What's going on?" I asked in an undertone.

"I'm not completely sure," Helen Louise said. "It started before we reached the bottom of the stairs, and we can't see anything."

Suddenly a voice rang out over the hubbub. "Stop it this minute, Carey. Right now." That voice, I decided, be-longed to Irene Warriner.

All the chatter ceased, and now I could hear the sounds

of a scuffle. "I'm going to kill the bastard," a voice cried out. Carey Warriner, I thought. Whom had he attacked? Dan Bellamy?

Then I heard Jordan Thompson's voice telling them to stop. Jordan had a healthy set of lungs and knew how to use them. She emitted an earsplitting shriek, and suddenly all sounds of scuffle ceased. Jordan spoke again. "The police are on the way, and I'm going to press charges against both of you for disturbing the peace. I've never seen such a ridiculous demonstration of male stupidity in my life."

Frustrated that I still couldn't see the combatants, I tried to edge through the crowd but to no avail. People were pressed too tightly together. I heard a siren, and a police car pulled up in front of the bookstore. Two officers I recognized entered the front doors and quickly found Jordan.

To the surprise of everyone, music flooded the store through the speaker system. I dimly recognized the tune as that of a reel, and I figured Jordan must have planned this to play during the signing part of the event. The music served to mask the sounds of the police dealing with Carey Warriner and his opponent, whoever he might be.

As we watched, fascinated, Irene Warriner and Dan Bellamy, their clothing apparently undisturbed, emerged from the area behind the shelf range. Irene looked pale but determined, and Dan had a firm hold on her arm. They headed for the signing area at the back of the ground floor, and some of the crowd began to follow them. One of Jordan's staff members was urging people to follow the authors, and several people did so.

I was surprised that Irene Warriner did not seem bothered by the fact that her husband was about to be arrested for disturbing the peace. Then, on reflection, I thought maybe she was tired of his behavior and hoped that this might force him to consider curbing his temper in future. Tough love, I supposed.

"The poor woman," Helen Louise whispered to me. "How horribly embarrassing for her."

Melba overheard this. "If I were her, I'd kick his can to the curb. Imagine a grown man—a professor—acting like this, attacking someone in a store full of people."

"He definitely has a problem," I said. I wondered privately, however, if his jealousy had just cause or whether it was all in his imagination. If he were a philanderer, as it appeared he might be, then his behavior toward his wife was all the more ironic.

"I'm going to buy some books," Melba announced. "I think she needs to hear how much people like her writing." She moved through the crowd to find books for sale.

"Good for her," I said. "I'm going to get in line to have my books signed. Do you want to come with me?"

"What?" Helen Louise appeared distracted. "No, you go ahead. I see someone I want to talk to. Catch up with you after you're done." She moved away, and I wondered whom she had spotted. I made my way to the line that had formed in front of the signing table and waited my turn.

I listened to the people ahead of me in the line. I hoped no one would be gauche enough to talk to Irene Warriner about the altercation. I realized, however, that many of those attending the event might not know that the man involved was her husband. I hoped for her sake that they didn't. How embarrassing for her.

The line moved slowly, because everyone seemed to have things to say to her and to Dan. He signed only a few books, while Irene/Lucy stayed busy scribbling in tome after tome. Dan appeared not to be bothered by this. I did notice that he had attracted the attention of two pretty young women who lingered at the table to chat with him.

They were still with him when I reached the front of the line, so I didn't greet him as I normally would have.

"I thoroughly enjoyed your presentation," I told Irene. "I'm happy to have the opportunity to have copies of your books signed." I began handing them to one of Jordan's staff members, who opened them to the title page for signature.

"Thank you so much," Irene said. "I appreciate your support and encouragement."

She sounded perfectly sincere, but I could sense that she was a bit distracted. Perhaps she was wondering what was happening with her husband. I also thought I detected signs of strain in her expression, and no wonder. She must have been worn out by now.

"Thank you," I said when she had signed the last of my books. "I look forward to the next one."

She smiled and nodded, already looking toward the person behind me in line. As I walked along the line I saw Melba about five people back. She motioned for me to stop.

"What's up?" I asked.

"Helen Louise has gone to the bistro," she said. "She wants us to join her there. She has Barbara Lamont with her."

"Okay," I said. "See you there."

The police officers had apparently departed with the two men, because the patrol car was gone when I stepped out of the bookstore. I walked to the bistro, wondering again whether Barbara Lamont was the woman who had accompanied Carey Warriner to the event.

When I walked into the bistro, I looked for Helen Louise and spotted her, as I had expected, at our usual table. The woman with her was indeed the one I had seen tonight sitting next to Carey Warriner in the audience. As I approached them, I could see she appeared distraught.

Helen Louise glanced up at my approach and smiled in welcome. "Hello, love, did you get all your books signed?"

I pulled out a chair. "I did. Melba was in line when I left." I glanced at Barbara Lamont. "We've not met before. I'm Charlie Harris."

She nodded, a faint smile flashing for a moment. "I'm Barbara Lamont, a friend of Helen Louise's from church. I've heard about you and your cat. It's a pleasure to finally meet you."

"Thank you, it's nice to meet you, too." I smiled and waited for Helen Louise to enlighten me. I didn't want to embarrass myself or Barbara Lamont by saying the wrong thing.

"Have some wine." Helen Louise lifted a bottle and poured some of the vintage into a glass. "Barb, how about a bit more?"

"Thank you," Barbara said. "I think I will." She slid her glass toward her hostess.

Helen Louise added wine to the glass and then looked at me with a smile. "Barb was just telling me that she's a bridge player. I had no idea. I haven't played in years."

"I haven't, either," I said. "Back in Houston, my wife and I used to play regularly with friends. I'm not sure I'd remember how after all this time." I sipped my wine.

"I'm sure it would come back to you pretty quickly. A good bridge player never forgets." Barbara stared into her wineglass for a moment, then addressed me directly. "I was telling Helen Louise that I play regularly with Irene and Carey Warriner. Dan Bellamy is sometimes a fourth; other times we play with a professor from the music department. I'm not sure if you know him. His name is Armand d'Arcy. His specialty is Renaissance and early modern music."

I exchanged a quick glance with Helen Louise. At last, we knew who the mystery Mr. d'Arcy was. I didn't say anything, however, because Barbara suddenly seemed diffident.

"You might as well know," she said in a rush, "that Armand was at the bookstore tonight, and it was he that Carey attacked." She took a shaky breath. "I don't know what's wrong with Carey. Lately he's been acting so peculiar. He's become so possessive of Irene, and, well, I guess Helen Louise told you what happened here."

I nodded. "Yes, she did. It must have been horribly embarrassing for you."

"It's awful," Barbara whispered before taking a sip of her wine. "We were all pretty good friends, I thought, but the past few weeks, Carey has begun to change, and I don't know why."

"Perhaps he's ill," Helen Louise suggested gently.

"You mean mentally ill?" Barbara asked.

"Possibly," Helen Louise said. "If his personality has undergone such a radical change, there could be an organic cause."

"I don't know," Barbara said. "He hasn't confided in me, and neither has Irene." She paused. "Look, I know what people have been saying behind my back. I have not been having an affair with Carey. We've had a few meals together, but only as friends. I've been going through a rough patch with my career, and he's been advising me. That's all."

"I understand," I said. "Are you going through the tenure process?"

Barbara nodded. "I am, and it's nerve-racking. Normally I would talk to Irene, but with her teaching schedule and her writing deadlines, she doesn't often have time to talk. But Carey has been available, and he's been really helpful. Until recently."

"Had he ever behaved violently before?" Helen Louise asked.

"Not to my knowledge," Barbara said. "I've known

him and Irene ever since I came to Athena four years ago. Irene and I became friends right away."

"Do you think Carey Warriner has any reason to be jealous of Irene?" I asked.

Barbara shook her head. "She adores him, but I know she's been frightened by the change in him. Armand has helped her with the musical background for her books, and Dan Bellamy has advised her on history from time to time. That's all there is to it."

"But Carey doesn't believe so," Helen Louise said.

"No, not recently." Barbara reached for her wineglass and drained it. Suddenly she pushed back her chair and stood. "Thank you for the wine, and the shoulder, Helen Louise. I needed to talk, and I appreciate you listening. I need to get home, though."

"Would you like us to see you home?" Helen Louise asked. I understood her concern. Barbara still appeared a bit shaken by the night's events.

"No, I'm fine," Barbara insisted. "Please don't worry. Good night." She picked up her purse and hurried out of the bistro.

"I feel like I should have insisted on taking her home," Helen Louise said.

"She seemed pretty adamant that she was fine," I said. "I think she'll be okay. She needs some time alone now. Do you think she's in love with Carey Warriner?"

Helen Louise nodded, her expression troubled. "Yes, I'm pretty sure she is. What made you think so?"

I frowned. "I'm not really sure. Maybe it was the way she said his name. I don't know, I simply had the feeling that she is."

"Same here." Helen Louise sighed. "What a mess."

"Double triangle," I said, pushing my wineglass forward for a bit more.

"Would you care to explain that?" Helen Louise poured the last of the bottle into my glass.

"Irene, Carey, and Armand. Carey, Irene, and Barbara. Two interlocking love triangles," I said.

"You don't know that Armand is in love with Irene," Helen Louise said. "We think Barbara is in love with Carey, but we don't know that for certain. Maybe Barbara is in love with Armand, and vice versa."

"That would simplify matters, I suppose," I said. "But I think we're right about Barbara being in love with Carey Warriner."

"I feel sorry for her," Helen Louise said. "It never pays to fall in love with a married man."

"If he keeps up this behavior," I said, "he might not be married for much longer."

As it turned out, he wasn't.

SIXTEEN

||||||||||||||||||||||||||||||||||||||||||

Dan Bellamy hadn't returned by the time I was ready for bed that night. Probably just as well, I thought. I wasn't up to dealing with any awkwardness either one of us might feel over what had happened at the bookstore. Time enough to deal with that after a good night's sleep.

I had picked up Diesel on the way home, after a late meal at the bistro with Helen Louise and Melba. Now he sat on the floor keeping a close watch on me while I fried strips of bacon for my breakfast. "There will be a few bites for you," I assured him, but he remained vigilant.

I put the bacon aside to drain and prepared my eggs. I decided on fried this morning, a bit of a change because Azalea almost always served them scrambled. I popped several slices of wheat bread in the toaster and went back to tending my eggs.

A few minutes later, a full cup of coffee by my plate, I sat down to breakfast. I doled out pieces of bacon to Diesel, who wasn't about to let me forget that he was on the point of starvation. He always was first thing in the morning.

"I don't know how you make it through the night," I told him. "The pangs of hunger must be terrible."

He meowed in agreement and tapped my thigh with one large paw.

I heard the front door open while I was cleaning up after myself in the kitchen. I saw by the kitchen clock that it was 7:33. I wondered who was coming in this early, then figured it must be Stewart coming home from the gym.

To my surprise, I saw Haskell in uniform, along with Dan Bellamy, still in Regency costume, stride wearily into the kitchen. Dan almost stumbled to the table, pulled out a chair, and dropped into it.

"Morning, Charlie," Haskell said. "Any coffee available?"

"Yes, nearly a full pot."

Haskell went to the cabinet and extracted two mugs. He poured coffee in both and handed one to Dan, who accepted it in a rather dazed fashion. He looked utterly exhausted.

"Dan, what's happened? I thought you had come in long before now," I said in concern.

He stared at me, then at Haskell.

"Rough night," Haskell said.

"Carey's dead," Dan said, his voice hoarse.

I nearly dropped the plate I was drying. I set it down, my hands shaky. "What happened?"

Dan shook his head and sipped his coffee.

Haskell pulled out a chair and eased into it. "Guess I'd better explain." He nodded to indicate Dan. "The professor here was at the police station late last night with Mr. Warriner and Mr. d'Arcy. Ms. Thompson agreed to drop the charges if Warriner agreed to pay for any damages. He did, so the PD released both men around one o'clock this morning."

"Irene was so upset," Dan said. "She talked Jordan into dropping the charges. I drove her and Carey home in their car, but Carey walked out of the house after about five minutes. I stayed with Irene for a few minutes, and then I went out to look for him. I drove around for an hour or more. Never found him, so I went back to Irene."

"We got a call from the PD around three thirty," Haskell said. "Someone reported a man lying on his lawn. Said he thought the man was dead drunk." He sipped his coffee. "He was dead all right, but not drunk. Stab wound to the chest."

"Went with Irene to identify him." Dan made a sudden retching sound, but he controlled himself. He shuddered. "Horrible. She collapsed in hysterics. Had to take her to the ER, she wouldn't calm down. I was there until Haskell came to give me a ride here."

"Is she still in the hospital?" I felt so sorry for Irene Warriner. No wonder the poor woman broke down.

Dan nodded. "Keeping her for observation. They had to sedate her. She was still sleeping when I left." He suddenly pushed back his chair and stood. "I think I need to go to bed. Too exhausted to think about it anymore." He stumbled again, but Haskell was there to catch him.

"Come on," Haskell said. "I'll get you upstairs." He glanced over his shoulder at me. "I'll be back down in a minute."

Diesel, obviously disturbed, had gone under the table when Dan and Haskell arrived. Now he came out and rubbed against my leg. I rubbed his head to comfort him. I was shaken as well. The situation had become horribly worse. I had to wonder whether Armand d'Arcy had attacked Warriner. Had Warriner gone to confront him again, with the result that he ended up dead?

I continued to speculate over what could have happened until Haskell rejoined me several minutes later. He had taken time to change out of his uniform into blue jeans and a T-shirt. He, too, looked weary.

"Would you like breakfast?" I asked. "I'll be happy to fix it for you. You look done in."

"I am," Haskell said. "Stewart will be down in a minute to cook for both of us. Have a seat and relax." He picked up his mug and drained it. Diesel went to him and rubbed against his leg. Haskell smiled down at the cat and patted his head.

"Can you talk about it?" I asked after a brief silence.

"Not much I can tell you," he said. "Kanesha's already working on it, but she sent me home with Bellamy."

"Is he a suspect?" I asked.

Haskell shrugged. "Your guess is as good as mine. Until I know more, I couldn't say. Why don't you tell me what happened at the bookstore last night? Bellamy wasn't in any condition to tell much by the time I picked him up and brought him home."

I filled Haskell in with what I knew, and Stewart and Dante appeared in the kitchen halfway through my recital.

"Good morning, Charlie," Stewart said. "I'm going to put Dante out in the backyard for a few minutes while I get started on breakfast." He led the poodle out of the kitchen. When he returned I told him I'd let Dante in when he was ready.

"Thanks." Stewart refilled Haskell's cup and offered to refill mine. I accepted. He then poured himself a cup before going to the fridge to pull out yogurt and fruit. I sometimes wondered whether Haskell enjoyed these breakfasts as much as Stewart did, but I'd never heard him complain.

Stewart set bowls on the table, along with the large container of yogurt and the already prepared fruit. He retrieved spoons and granola from the cabinets and joined us at the table. Haskell began to serve himself, and Stewart waited until he finished to prepare his own bowl. "Would you like any toast?" he asked.

"Wouldn't mind a couple pieces," Haskell said.

Stewart got up to put bread in the toaster. Butter and jam were already on the table from my own breakfast.

"So tell me what happened at the bookstore last night," Stewart said. "I caught only the tail end of it."

I launched into my story again, and by the time I finished, Haskell's toast was ready. He buttered both pieces and slathered them with Azalea's homemade apricot jam.

"I'll go let Dante in," I said.

Stewart thanked me again. Diesel, hoping for a piece of toast, lingered behind. When I exited the kitchen, Stewart was pressing his partner for details of the murder.

I stood on the back porch a minute and watched Dante busily investigating the yard. When I thought he had finished his business, I opened the screen door and called him to me. He came readily, and he pranced alongside me, happy as always, on the way back to the kitchen.

Dante greeted his friend Diesel joyfully, and Diesel allowed the poodle to lick his face a couple of times. Then he meowed a warning, and Dante subsided. He knew what that meant.

"Who do you think killed Carey Warriner?" Stewart asked me.

I shrugged. "I would say the prime suspect must be Armand d'Arcy. He was apparently the man that Warriner attacked last night at the bookstore. Warriner also went after him at the bistro on Friday, if you'll remember."

"I could see where d'Arcy might have had enough of him by the second attack last night," Stewart said. "That doesn't excuse murder, naturally, but maybe they started fighting again and things got out of hand."

"You could say that." Haskell spooned more granola and yogurt into his mouth.

"Helen Louise said she thought d'Arcy spoke with a bit of a French accent," Stewart said. "With a name like that, he must be French, and they're known for crimes of passion."

"The hot-blooded Continental type?" I asked.

Stewart nodded. "Not like us rather cold-blooded Anglo-Saxons."

I laughed at that. "Your surname is Delacorte. I believe that's French, isn't it?"

"Yes, it is," Stewart said airily, "but anything French was long ago diluted by many generations of phlegmatic Anglo-Saxons."

"If you say so," I replied, still amused.

"The interesting thing about this is whether Carey Warriner was a murderer himself," Stewart said.

"You mean Dixie Compton," I said. "Good point."

"If he was her killer, maybe someone killed him to avenge her death. Somebody we don't know about yet." He paused. "Though I suppose it's possible that d'Arcy knew her. Maybe he was in love with her, even."

"You should be writing fiction," Haskell said.

"I'm sure Kanesha will sort out Dixie Compton's death, and she'll do the same for Carey Warriner's. If the two are related, she'll uncover the link," I said.

"Hasn't failed to solve a murder yet," Haskell said. "With or without help." He shot me an amused look.

"I don't imagine I'm going to be much help on this one," I said. "I really don't know any of the people involved."

"That hasn't stopped you before," Stewart said with a grin.

"Actually, Kanesha did tell me she'd appreciate it if I keep my ears open on campus for any tidbits I might hear that could be pertinent to Dixie Compton's death," I said somewhat defensively.

"Keeping your ears open and actively looking for information aren't quite the same thing." Stewart spooned more yogurt and granola into his bowl.

"No, they're not," I said. "But if I find myself in a position to ask a question and get an answer that helps, I'm not going to pass up the opportunity."

"Are you going to talk to Bellamy about all this?" Haskell asked.

I shook my head. "Not outright. If he wants to talk to me, I'll certainly listen. But I'm not going to sit him down and subject him to an interrogation. He's a guest in my home. Well, a paying guest," I amended.

Haskell pushed back his chair. "I'm going up to try to catch a couple hours' sleep. Have to be back at the department by eleven. See y'all later."

Stewart watched him go, frowning. He spoke in a low voice. "I hate it when he has to put in these strange hours. I worry about him not getting enough rest sometimes. Do you think he looked exhausted?"

"He looked pretty tired," I said, "but he's tough. He'll be fine." Privately I, too, worried about Haskell occasionally, but I wasn't going to let Stewart know that. He didn't need any encouragement to worry even more.

Stewart sighed. "I hope you're right. He'll be eligible for retirement in three years, but I don't know whether he'll retire. He loves his job."

"He always seems to, although I know sometimes it gets him down," I said, and Stewart nodded.

"Okay, enough of that," he said suddenly. "What's on your agenda today?"

"I had planned to do some reading for my class," I said, "but there's no point now. I'm sure the class will be canceled after what happened."

"Maybe," Stewart said, "although if there's anyone in the department who can handle it, they'll keep it going unless they can accommodate the students in other courses this semester. Warriner might have had a grad student who could take it over."

"I guess I'll find out tomorrow," I said. "I'll go by the history department in the morning and see what's going on." As I said that, a further idea occurred to me. While I was in the department office, I would talk to Melba's friend—whose name I had blanked on—and try to find out a few things about Warriner's background and relationships with his fellow history professors and instructors.

I felt a twinge of excitement. I might dig up information that would help Kanesha solve both murders.

SEVENTEEN

|||||||||||||||||||||||||||||||||||||||||||||||||||||||||||||||||||

Diesel and I headed to work the next morning without having seen Dan Bellamy. He had appeared briefly yesterday in the afternoon, but only to tell me he would be out the rest of the day and wasn't sure what time he might return. I didn't try to question him, other than to ask him how he was doing. To this he replied with a tersely polite, "I'm fine."

At breakfast I had informed Azalea of the situation and told her I had no idea whether he was in his room this morning.

"If he comes down, or if he comes in from somewhere else," she said, not seemingly perturbed by this interruption in routine, "I'll fix him breakfast if he wants it."

We left her and Ramses in the kitchen, and I heard Azalea singing as we left by the front door. We encountered a couple of neighbors during our walk who bade us good morning but didn't stop to chat.

Melba sat at the desk in her office, and we stopped by to say hello. She was all agog with the news of Carey Warriner's death. I wasn't surprised that she already knew. The story had leaked somehow, and it had made its way to her. When I asked her how she had heard, she said simply, "From Viccy Kemp, the history department administrator. Remember, I told you about her."

I nodded. "That you did."

"She called me this morning because she knows you're enrolled in Warriner's class," Melba said. "She told me what little she knew." She eyed me speculatively. "I figure you're bound to know more, so let's hear it."

"I really don't know much," I told her, "but I'm willing to tell you what I do know. First, though, I want to go upstairs to my office and put away my things."

"You go on upstairs," Melba said, "and I'll bring you a cup of coffee. Should be finished brewing by now."

"It's a deal," I said. "Come on, Diesel."

Two minutes later, I had barely hung up my jacket, unhooked Diesel's leash, and turned on my computer when Melba appeared in the doorway with two cups of coffee. She set one on the desk in front of me and made herself comfortable in the nearby chair.

"All right," she said. "Tell me everything, from the point where I said good-bye to you and Helen Louise at the bistro Saturday night."

"If you insist," I said, feeling mischievous. "After I took Helen Louise home, I drove to Laura and Frank's house to pick up Diesel. I chatted with them for a couple of minutes. I didn't tell them about what happened at the bookstore, though. It was getting late by that point, and I was tired and ready for bed."

Melba held up her hand. "Very funny. You know what I meant."

"Well, you did say *everything*," I replied with a grin. "All right, I'll cut to the chase."

I told her that Dan Bellamy came home yesterday morning with Haskell and what I had learned from the two of them.

"Still dressed in his costume," Melba said. "I have to say he looked mighty fine in that getup. Too bad men don't dress like that these days. Much more interesting and colorful than the suits I see the bigwigs on campus wearing."

"More colorful, yes, but on the elaborate side, don't you think? How would you like to go around dressed the way Irene Warriner was Saturday night?"

Melba shrugged. "I see your point. So, do you think Dan Bellamy had anything to do with Carey Warriner's death?"

"If he did, I have no idea what his motive could be. As far as I can tell, he's not in love with Irene Warriner."

"Not that I could see that night," Melba said. "They came across as friends. What about Dixie Belle?" She shook her head. "I knew she'd come to a bad end."

"What do you mean, what about her?" I ignored the comment about the *bad end*.

"Did Warriner kill her?" she said. "And then maybe someone killed him as revenge for her death."

"You should talk to Stewart," I said. "That was one of his theories yesterday." I shrugged. "I don't have any idea. I think Warriner was looking like the chief suspect in Dixie Compton's death, but now that he's been murdered, who knows? Kanesha hasn't taken me into her confidence."

"Didn't Haskell know anything?" Melba asked.

"If he did, he wasn't sharing it with me," I said. "He's not going to tell me or Stewart anything Kanesha doesn't want anyone outside the sheriff's department to know. You ought to know that by now."

"I do know that," Melba retorted. "But he might have told you something that Kanesha was okay with."

"He didn't, other than the fact that Warriner apparently died from a stab wound to the chest."

Melba shook her head. "Sad to think of that gorgeous man lying on a mortuary slab."

"I hate to think about anyone lying there," I said.

"Have you talked to Dan Bellamy?"

"No, I haven't," I said. "I've seen him only briefly since he came home yesterday morning. He didn't appear to be in any mood to talk about it with me, so I didn't try."

"That's that, then." Melba rose. "Hope somebody comes across with more of the skinny soon."

"Hold on," I said as she headed for the door. She stopped and turned to look at me. "When you talked to your friend Viccy this morning, did she happen to say anything about Warriner's classes? Is someone going to take over the class I'm auditing?"

Melba shook her head. "I don't know. I didn't think to ask, and she didn't say anything about it."

"Okay, thanks," I said. "I think I'll walk over there in a little while and try to find out something."

"They may not have had time to make a decision yet," Melba said. "Anyway, they'll probably e-mail students about it. Plus, there will be some kind of press release on the way from the president's office."

"True." I hadn't thought about that. "I might go over anyway. I think I'll take Diesel with me."

Melba snorted but forbore to comment further. I didn't think I deceived her for a second. She knew me too well. She left my office, and I heard her hurrying down the stairs moments later.

I spent a few minutes checking e-mail in case anything urgent had come in over the weekend. I occasionally received last-minute requests from groups on campus, particularly from the public relations staff, wanting pictures of various people or buildings on campus from many years ago. Nothing this morning, I was happy to see, so I wouldn't have to scurry around trying to dig things up.

That done, I decided now was as good a time as any to go to the history department office and find out what was going on with Warriner's classes. If I was lucky enough to catch Viccy Kemp in a quiet moment, I might be able to find out something about Carey Warriner's own history.

"Come on, Diesel," I said. "We're going for a walk to visit someone."

The cat climbed down from his window perch and stood still while I reattached his leash. I put on my jacket, and we went downstairs and out the building's back door that gave on to a small parking lot. The eight o'clock classes were in session, and we saw only a few people walking on campus in the cool morning air. The sun shone, I was thankful to see. Had the day been a rainy one, I might not have made the effort to see Viccy Kemp, no matter how curious I was.

A five-minute walk brought us to the building that housed the history department, along with English and classics. The history office was on the second floor, and Diesel and I climbed the stairs. The hall was empty when we emerged on the second floor. A short walk down one corridor brought us to the office I sought, and we stopped in the doorway.

At first I thought the office was empty because there was no sign of any activity. Then a woman bustled out of a back room, and I recognized Viccy Kemp. I was delighted to find her apparently alone in the office. She headed straight for a desk upon which she began to sort some papers.

I called out, "Good morning," and she looked up, frowning. When she spotted Diesel beside me, the frown vanished and was replaced with a broad smile.

"Good morning," she said. "This must be the famous Diesel that Melba is always talking about."

We approached her desk, and I said, "Yes, this is Diesel. You remember me, then. Charlie Harris."

Ms. Kemp nodded. "I do, and I imagine you're here to ask about your class." She shook her head. "Isn't it horrible? Poor Dr. Warriner. I can't believe it really happened. Such a nice man, and so handsome." She looked down at the cat. "You're mighty handsome, too." Diesel meowed in acknowledgment, and she smiled.

"Yes, it's terrible," I said. "I had only two classes with him last week, but I was so impressed by his abilities as a lecturer. He was one of the best I ever heard."

Ms. Kemp sighed. "Students loved his classes, even though he made them work hard. He had high standards, and a couple of his former students went on to grad school at some big-name universities."

"That's great." I knew that Athena graduates in general had high acceptance rates into graduate programs at top universities around the country, but I wasn't going to quibble with her.

"I've met the other Dr. Warriner a couple of times recently," I said. "Such a tragic loss for her."

Ms. Kemp's eyes welled with tears, and she reached for a tissue from a box on her desk. "Excuse me," she said as she wiped her eyes. "Yes, it is. They were devoted to each other."

I looked at her slightly askance. This wasn't what she told Melba, but I suppose in death she had closed ranks, so to speak, and wouldn't say anything negative about Warriner.

"She's such a sweet person," Ms. Kemp went on. "My friend Jeanette works in the English department, and she's always telling me how kind and thoughtful Mrs. Warriner is. And her a famous romance writer, too." She shook her head. "Such a sad story."

"I'm sure Dr. Warriner's family will be devastated by this," I said, hoping she would pick up on my cue.

"Oh, I'm sure they will," Ms. Kemp said, sniffling. "He came from a pretty well-to-do family in Georgia. They must have money, his people. He always gave such nice presents for Christmas and birthdays." She thrust out her wrist. "See this watch? He gave it to me last Christmas."

"Very nice," I said. It was a beautiful watch, but I had no idea of the cost. The face was too small for me to be able to read the brand, and Ms. Kemp didn't tell me what it was.

"It's hard to imagine why anyone would want to attack him like that," I said, offering another cue.

"Jealousy," she said. "Just plain jealous. Other men couldn't stand the fact that he was so handsome and nice and charming. Such a gentleman."

"I can see that," I said, trying not to sound doubtful. "He was a very attractive man, like a movie star."

"He sure was," Ms. Kemp said, sniffling again.

I heard footsteps behind me, and someone entered the room. I turned to see who it was and got a shock.

"Good morning, Mr. Harris," Kanesha Berry said. "Ms. Kemp, if you have a few minutes, I need to talk to you." She identified herself, and Viccy Kemp turned pale.

"Good morning, Chief Deputy Berry," I said. "Diesel and I were just about to leave. I came over to find out the status of the course I was taking with Dr. Warriner."

Viccy Kemp looked blank for a moment, then appeared to recover. "Oh yes, well, no class today. They haven't made a final decision yet, but you'll get an e-mail sometime today."

"Thank you," I said. "I appreciate it. Come on, Diesel, let's go back to the office."

Kanesha fixed me with one of her severe expressions, but I merely smiled and wished her good day. Diesel and I headed into the hallway and made our way out of the building.

Viccy Kemp had been talkative, and that had made my attempts at digging up information pretty easy. On the whole, however, I wasn't sure that I had learned anything useful. I might have, if Kanesha had not appeared on the scene when she did. That was unfortunate, but I couldn't do anything about it. I wondered how forthcoming Ms. Kemp would be with Kanesha, though. Chatting with another employee about recent tragic events was one thing, but answering questions put to you by a stern investigator was quite something else.

EIGHTEEN

‖‖‖

I wasn't all that surprised when, nearly an hour after I had encountered her in the history department, Kanesha Berry walked into my office. I generally left the door open while I worked, and it wasn't unusual for people to come in unannounced. It wasn't standard practice for Kanesha, because she usually called or texted before she came to talk to me.

"Good morning again," I said. "I thought I might be seeing you." I indicated the chair before my desk. "Please take a seat."

Kanesha did, and then she fixed me with her gimlet stare for a moment. "Mind telling me what you were talking to Ms. Kemp about when I arrived earlier?"

"I told you, I went to find out about my class," I said. "Given that the professor was murdered over the weekend, I didn't know whether to show up for it today. It meets Mondays, Wednesdays, and Fridays. Or rather, it did." I nodded at my computer. "I received an e-mail about ten minutes ago informing us that the course has been canceled."

"Let me rephrase my question," Kanesha said. "What *else* were you talking about with Ms. Kemp this morning?"

"We were commiserating over the death of a professor," I said truthfully. "She told me what a nice man he was and how he came from a well-to-do family. He apparently was in the habit of giving out nice Christmas and birthday presents. Did she show you her watch?"

I didn't mean to come across as facetious, but I was beginning to fear that I was. Kanesha's gaze narrowed as she continued to regard me sternly.

"Honestly, that's all it was," I said. "She obviously wanted someone to talk to, and I happened to be there. Yes, I did go there in hopes that she would talk to me about Warriner, but she didn't need any prompting from me." From behind me in the window, Diesel meowed loudly.

Kanesha's eyes flicked toward the window and then back again. "All right," she said in a grudging tone. "Sounds like you came up empty-handed."

"Pretty much," I said. "Now, hold on a minute. You're the one who said you wanted me to keep an ear out and let you know what I might hear around campus."

"I did," Kanesha said, "but I didn't expect you to interview people."

"I won't be doing that," I said, "but I can't be much help to you if I sit in my office all the time and don't talk to anyone."

"All right," Kanesha said. "You've got a point." She rose. "You need to be careful. Two people have died already. I don't want to end up investigating your murder."

"You won't," I said, "so you can rest easy on my account. Before you go, however, I do have one question."

"What is it?"

"Do you still think Carey Warriner killed Dixie Compton?"

"I think it's pretty likely he did, but I'm not considering it a proven fact. There's still too much I don't know, and Warriner's murder complicates it." She left the office before I could think of a follow-up.

Instead of getting to work as I should have, I thought about Dixie Compton's murder. If Carey Warriner had killed her, what was his motive? Was he hoping to cover up an affair they had been having? That seemed an extreme answer to the problem of keeping his wife from finding out.

How much did Irene Warriner know, if anything, about her husband's alleged infidelity? Or infidelities? Barbara Lamont claimed that she was a good friend of both the Warriners, but I was halfway convinced she had been in love with Carey Warriner. Had she become involved in an affair with him? If she had, perhaps Dixie Compton had found out and threatened to expose everything to Irene Warriner out of jealousy. I remembered what Melba had reported from her lunch with her friends Viccy and Jeanette. Viccy had told Melba that Carey Warriner had a roving eye. In the wake of his murder, however, Ms. Kemp might have decided that it was better not to talk about his alleged extramarital goings-on. She hadn't said anything of the kind to me this morning, and she'd had the opportunity.

Another thought occurred to me. What if Irene Warriner had killed Dixie Compton and had implicated her husband? Then, when he embarrassed her twice in public with his outrageous displays of jealousy, maybe she had decided she'd had enough. Maybe she had killed him, sending Dan Bellamy on a wild-goose chase to find him while she got rid of the body.

That sounded far-fetched, but it could have happened that way. Irene Warriner could even have confessed to Dan Bellamy that she had murdered her husband and then asked him to help her dispose of the body. Under the guise of searching for the allegedly missing Warriner, he instead found a place to dump the body. A man might go to such lengths for a woman he loved, but I didn't think Dan Bellamy was in love with Irene Warriner.

I had little to go on, because I'd seen them together only twice. But a man in love, unless he has superhuman control, betrays himself in small ways when he is with the object of his passion. I hadn't seen any of those small giveaways when Dan was with Irene Warriner. I might have missed a tender look, a sudden touch, or a stolen caress, but I didn't think so.

Then there was his former sister-in-law, Dixie Compton. Why would he have wanted to murder her? He had seemed genuinely stunned by the news of her death. He hadn't appeared to be mourning her particularly, but when he talked about her, he hadn't given the impression that they had been all that close. She had been his half brother's wife.

The still-unknown factor in this, at least for me, was Armand d'Arcy. I decided to check to see if the music department had pictures of their faculty on their website. I turned to my computer, and it took me only about five clicks to find Mr. d'Arcy. There was indeed a picture of him, and if the picture did him justice, he was a handsome man, with the sort of dark, brooding looks that made for romantic heroes in books and films. Black hair slicked down, a little long and curling at the back, a strong aquiline nose, and an enigmatic smile. Yes, he was attractive.

But was he attractive enough to tempt Irene Warriner to cast aside her marriage vows?

Carey Warriner had obviously thought so, otherwise, I had to assume, he wouldn't have behaved so violently in public toward this man. But why this one man? Was there something in particular about d'Arcy that elicited this behavior in Warriner? Or had he always been this possessive where his wife was concerned? I had a feeling Viccy Kemp might be able to tell me. What reason could I use for going back to talk to her again? Or could I find someone else who knew Carey Warriner fairly well?

I wanted to meet Armand d'Arcy myself. Helen Louise had seen him, but not in a situation in which she could judge whether Irene Warriner was involved with him. Would he now hover around the widow to offer comfort? And would he be welcome? I decided that when Dan Bellamy was ready to talk about the whole matter with me, I would try, as tactfully as possible, to find answers to at least some of my questions. If he couldn't answer them, I would have to look elsewhere.

Melba.

Of course. Why hadn't I already thought of her? Melba knew both Viccy Kemp and the woman Jeanette—I was getting really bad at remembering complete names these days—from the English department. I was sure Melba would be more than willing to get the two women to lunch with her and discreetly try to find out what they knew. Maybe I could be there as well. I'd have to think about this a bit more before I broached the idea to Melba.

A ping from my computer alerted me to the fact that I had an incoming message. Time to pay attention to actual work. I turned to the computer and focused on my job.

I managed to work steadily until lunchtime, with only a couple of brief, abortive lapses into speculation about the murders. Melba wasn't in her office when we came down. I would have to talk to her later about my idea to approach her friends for more information.

Diesel and I walked home, and we found Azalea and Ramses in the kitchen as usual. After greeting them, I asked Azalea whether she had seen Dan Bellamy this morning.

"Yes, he came down about nine," she said. "I fixed him a little something for breakfast. He wasn't looking too good. Real pale and tired, like he wasn't sleeping much. I didn't say anything, though."

"Did he talk at all about what's happened?"

"Just to say that he's real sorry for Mrs. Warriner," Azalea replied. "Says she's a good friend, and he wants to do what he can to help her. Told me he thought he'd be here for dinner tonight."

"Good, I'd really like to talk to him," I said.

"Lunch is ready whenever you want it." Azalea nodded at the stove.

"I'll run and wash my hands and be right back," I said.

Diesel was busy fending off Ramses's playful attacks, and I had to chuckle at the kitten's antics and his seemingly boundless energy.

When I returned from the first-floor washroom, I found my food at my place at the table. For today's lunch Azalea had prepared baked chicken, mashed potatoes, and salad. Added to that were Azalea's homemade yeast rolls and Thousand Island dressing. I settled in for a satisfying meal.

Diesel and Ramses took up spots on either side of my chair, both of them hopeful for chicken. I doled out three tidbits each as I ate. I noticed that Ramses was getting rather plump. He needed to be on a diet. I really would have to force myself to talk to Azalea about overfeeding him. She had left the kitchen to do some chore elsewhere while I ate, but I resolved I would broach the subject with her when she returned.

"That's all you're getting," I told the cats. Ramses tried to climb my leg but I dissuaded him. Then he jumped into my lap. I put him down and told him firmly not to do that. He still hadn't learned what the word *no* meant, but not from lack of hearing it from me.

Azalea had not returned to the kitchen by the time I finished my lunch. I needed to get back to work, so I decided to postpone my talk with her about Ramses and his food intake. I would do it this afternoon when I came home again, provided there were no distractions.

I went out into the hallway to the foot of the stairs and called out her name. No response. I moved up several steps and tried again, raising my voice. This time I heard a response. She appeared at the head of the stairs after a moment.

"Just letting you know that Diesel and I are heading back to the library," I said.

She nodded, and I left her to resume whatever she'd been doing.

Back in the kitchen I found Ramses on the table licking my plate. I should have known better than to have left anything on the table. I picked him up, held him so that his face was close to mine, and said, "Bad Ramses, bad kitten. No."

He licked the tip of my nose, incorrigible as ever. I sighed and put him on the floor. I put my dishes in the sink and ran water over them so that if Ramses managed to get to them, he'd have nothing but water to lick.

"Come on, Diesel, back to work." Ramses tried to follow us out the door, but I prevented that. I hoped he would go find Azalea once we were gone. Surely she would come check on him now that she knew we were leaving.

We found Melba in her office this time, and I walked in with Diesel. "Good afternoon," I said. "Good lunch?" Diesel ran up to her.

Melba nodded. "Tolerable. How about you?" She patted Diesel's head and cooed to him.

"Excellent, thanks to Azalea," I said.

Melba snorted. "You're spoiled rotten. I wish I had someone cooking for me the way she does for you."

"I have tried to tell her many times I'd be happy with a sandwich for lunch," I said. "She simply ignores that and cooks for me. I feel like I have to go home most days to eat, or I'd be in trouble."

"You're afraid of her." Melba laughed.

"Darn tootin', I am," I said ruefully. "I've learned not to get crossways of strong women. It just doesn't pay."

"That's good to know," Melba said, a wicked glint in her eye.

"Don't go getting ideas," I retorted. "Look, I want to talk to you about something to do with these murders."

"It's about time," Melba said unexpectedly. "Do I get to play Nancy Drew now?"

NINETEEN

|||||||||||||||||||||||||||||||||||||||||||||||||||||||||||

I had to laugh at a sudden vision of Melba tooling around in her blue roadster, magnifying glass at the ready, looking for a mystery to solve.

"What's so funny?" she demanded.

"You as Nancy Drew." I described the picture she had conjured up in my mind with her words, and she grinned.

"I always did want that roadster," she said. "I could have done without that sappy Bess, always more interested in food than in adventure. George was fun, though."

"She was," I agreed. "Yes, I want you to do a little investigating. You have to be discreet, and so do I. I talked to Viccy Kemp this morning, but I didn't really find out anything useful. Now that Warriner is dead, she isn't talking about his running around on his wife. At least, not to me. I want you to find out whether what she told you before is simply gossip or whether there was anything to the rumors."

Melba nodded. "I can do that. What else?"

"Your other friend, Jeanette. What's her last name?" I asked.

"Larson," Melba said.

"Right, Larson. I'll try to remember that. I want you to talk to her also, maybe the two of them together. See if you can find out anything about Irene Warriner and whether she was really running around on her husband. I think Armand d'Arcy is the most likely candidate."

"Who?" Melba asked.

"He's the other man she's been seen with," I said. "Music professor. Look him up on the department website."

"Hang on." Melba turned to her computer and a few seconds later she whistled. "I'd run around with him any day. Talk about romantic." She stared intently at the picture. "I've seen him a couple times around town. Never knew who he was before."

"He's the one Warriner went after in the bistro and at the book signing Saturday night," I said.

"I'll be more than happy to investigate him," Melba said.

"Don't get carried away because he's handsome," I said. "Remember that he could be a murderer. What if he killed Carey Warriner so Irene would be free to marry again?"

"Good point," Melba said. "Maybe I'll wait until we know who the murderer is before I try to cozy up to him."

"That would be a better plan," I said wryly. "Now, back to your friends. When do you think you can get together with them again? Soon, I hope."

Melba said, "Normally, we get together for lunch about once a month, and we've already done that this month." She thought for a moment. "We take turns paying for lunch. It's my turn next. I'm sure if I invite them to lunch at a nice place tomorrow, instead of in the student union grill where we usually meet, they'll jump at the chance."

"Would that make them suspicious?" I asked.

"What if they are?" Melba said. "It's not going to stop them from talking, believe you me. Those girls like to gossip, and I'm sure I can get what you need to know from them."

"What about the bistro?" I asked.

Melba shook her head. "It's nice enough, but the tables are all pretty close together. I think I'd do better to ask them to the Farrington House restaurant. The atmosphere is quieter there, not so busy."

"Good point," I said. "So tomorrow?"

"I'll e-mail them right now," Melba said. "I'll tell them it's a special occasion."

"Excellent," I said, and Diesel meowed. Melba laughed as she tapped at the keys.

"There, it's done," she said. "Are you free for lunch tomorrow?"

"I can be. Why? To join the three of you?" I asked. "Wouldn't that inhibit them from gossiping?"

"It probably would. I want you to be there, but not at the table with us," Melba said. "You know the dining room as well as I do. Remember that one section where the booths are divided by ledges with plants on them?"

"Yes, I do," I said. "So the plan is, I get there ahead of you and get seated in the next booth, and I'll be able to listen in on what you talk about."

"Exactly," Melba said. "I know the hostess there, and as soon as I hear back from Jeanette and Viccy, I'll get in touch with Marlene and get her to hold those tables for us."

"Sounds like a plan." I looked down at Diesel. "He's not going to be happy with being left at home tomorrow morning, though."

Melba stroked his head. "It's all for a good cause, isn't it, you handsome boy? You won't mind, just this once, will you?"

Although I was certain that for once Diesel really didn't understand what we were talking about, he replied to Melba's words with a happy-sounding chirp and meow.

Melba's computer pinged, and she glanced at the screen. She opened the message. "Jeanette. She says she'd love to. Oh, and there's Viccy. Same from her. So we're all set."

"Thanks for setting this up," I said. "What time?"

"Why don't you get there around noon," Melba said, "and I'll time it so we get there a few minutes later. I'll tell Marlene to be on the lookout for you."

I nodded. "Come on, Diesel, let's get upstairs to work. See you later."

Melba nodded, in the act of reaching for the phone on her desk. I figured she was probably calling her friend Marlene. Diesel and I left her office and climbed the stairs.

I managed to keep my mind on my work that afternoon, and I felt happy with what I'd accomplished by the time I was ready to go home for the day.

When I unlocked the front door, I heard a kitten yowling. I knew what that meant. Azalea had probably gone to the grocery store, and when she had to leave the house, she put Ramses in his crate. He did not like the crate, but there was no telling what kind of mischief he would get into if left on his own, freely roaming the house. Azalea didn't like having to put him in the crate, but I had persuaded her that it was for his safety.

Diesel hurried to the kitchen ahead of me, anxious to check on his little playmate. After I hung up my jacket on the coatrack in the hallway, I followed Diesel and found him sitting in front of the crate. Ramses had ceased his racket when he saw the bigger cat. When he saw me, though, he started crying again. I let him out, and he tried to swarm up my leg.

I grabbed him before those little needle claws could dig into my flesh. I held him up close to my face, and as he usually did, he tried to lick my nose. I held him a little farther away. "It's for your own good," I said. "I know you don't understand that, but you'll just have to get used to it." I set him down, and he jumped at Diesel. The bigger cat swatted him down, and Ramses backed off.

"Do you always talk to your cats?"

I turned to see Dan Bellamy in the doorway to the kitchen. I offered him an embarrassed smile. "Yes, I'm afraid I do. I know some people think it's strange, but it's a habit you get into."

Dan shrugged. "We never had pets around when I was growing up. We couldn't afford to feed them, my father said." Ramses ran to him and sat looking up at him.

"That's too bad," I said. "They can be wonderful companions."

"These two sure seem to be." Dan picked up Ramses and stroked his head. "This little fellow sure is friendly. What's his name again?"

"Ramses," I said, and Dan laughed.

"Ramses the Great," he said. "Ambitious name for a small cat."

"He doesn't think he's small," I said.

"Compared to Diesel, he looks like a dwarf." Dan put Ramses on the floor again, and the kitten commenced to rubbing himself against Dan's legs.

"Diesel is large, even for his breed." I told him a bit more about Maine Coons. While I talked, I covertly examined him for signs of distress. He no longer looked tired, and I presumed he had managed to catch up on his sleep. He appeared to have recovered from his initial horror over the death of Carey Warriner. I wondered if I could get him to talk.

"Would you like something to drink?" I asked. "There's usually sweet tea in the fridge, or I could make some coffee."

"Coffee would be good, if you really don't mind," Dan said.

"Not at all. Have a seat, and I'll get a pot going. How many cups do you think you'd like?"

"Two ought to do me fine," Dan said as he took a place at the table.

I decided to go ahead and make a full pot. Stewart would probably be home soon, and he often had a cup or two in the afternoon. When I finished with the coffee-maker, I went to the fridge and looked inside. Not spotting anything of edible interest for an afternoon snack, I checked the counter and found a covered cake plate. Lifting the lid, I discovered a fresh pound cake. I leaned forward to sniff it. Lemon, my favorite.

"There's fresh lemon pound cake," I said. "Would you like some? Azalea made it."

"That sounds good," Dan said. "Thank you."

I got out a couple of dessert plates and cut pieces of cake for both of us. When I put his on the table in front of him, I noticed that Ramses had climbed into his lap and was curled up, napping.

"If he bothers you," I said, indicating the kitten, "put him down. He's incorrigible."

Dan shook his head. "He's fine. He's not bothering me. First time I've had an animal take to me. It's a nice change."

Miranda James

Not for the first time I realized that Diesel hadn't really taken to Dan. I wasn't sure why. Usually that meant the big cat didn't like someone, but he hadn't exhibited the signs he usually did in such cases. He didn't seem to be bothered by Dan's presence. Perhaps he had sensed that Dan wasn't as comfortable around pets the way most of the people he encountered were. Ramses obviously had no such problem.

"Coffee's about ready," I said as I took forks from the drawer. "How do you take it?" I handed him a fork and a napkin.

"Black is fine," Dan said.

I nodded and didn't speak again until we were both seated with our coffee and cake. "I don't want to be intrusive, but I do want you to know that I've been concerned about you. You've had some terrible shocks the last few days."

Dan shrugged. "I'm okay. It's all a bit overwhelming, but I guess I'm handling it okay." He forked a piece of cake into his mouth and began to chew. After he swallowed, he said, "This is delicious."

"Azalea's desserts are always delicious," I said. "I haven't had a chance to tell you, because of everything that's happened, but I really enjoyed the presentation the other night at the bookstore."

"Thank you," Dan replied. "Irene and I put several hours' work into it, and I think it went well. At least until the end." He grimaced. "I couldn't believe Carey behaved the way he did. I don't know what got into him."

"From what I gather," I said slowly, "I think he was under the impression that his wife was seeing another man."

"You mean Armand?" Dan said, his tone noncommittal.

150

I nodded. "There was another incident involving him and Warriner."

"Really?" Dan looked surprised. "Irene never said anything about it to me."

"It happened the previous evening at the bistro." I gave him a brief description of the confrontation.

Dan shook his head when I finished. "Carey must have been suffering some kind of mania. As far as I know, Irene wasn't having an affair with Armand." He paused, as if suddenly struck by something. "But maybe it wasn't so far-fetched an idea after all."

"What do you mean?" I asked, trying not to betray my excitement at his statement.

"Nothing I can really put my finger on," Dan said. "I happened to see Irene and Armand together last week. Irene had told me she was consulting Armand about the musical background to the book she's currently working on, and at first I thought they were simply meeting to talk about that." He paused. "But there was something about the way they looked at each other." He shook his head. "I think I'm probably imagining it now."

"Maybe so," I said blandly.

Dan had another bite of his cake and a sip of coffee. "If I tell you something, will you promise it won't go any further?"

I felt uncomfortable responding in the affirmative, but I figured unless I did so, he wouldn't say anything more. So I said, "Of course. What is it?"

He put down his fork and gazed earnestly at me. "You know yesterday morning, I said that I took Irene home and then went out to look for Carey?"

I nodded.

"The thing is, I was gone for over an hour while I tried

151

to find him. When I got back to her house, she was acting a little strange. I can't really explain it." He paused. "Something just seemed a little off about her. It made me wonder if she hadn't killed Carey herself."

TWENTY

||||||||||||||||||||||||||||||||||||||||||||||||||||

Although I had already considered the scenario in which Irene Warriner had murdered her husband, and possibly Dixie Compton as well, I still felt a thrill of shock at Dan's statement.

"Why do you think she would have murdered him?" I asked.

"She was so angry with him," Dan said. "Now that you've told me about what happened Friday, I can see that his attack on Armand after the talk on Saturday might have pushed her over the edge." He hesitated. "You see, she had hinted to me before that Carey was inclined to be possessive, but honestly, I hadn't seen any signs of it. At least, not until recently."

"Strong women don't care much for possessive attitudes in men." I knew Helen Louise fit into that category, and I admired her for it.

"I guess they don't," Dan said. "Irene is a strong woman, so I can see where it would have bothered her a lot. But to go to the lengths of killing him because of it." He shook his head. "I don't know. That's pretty extreme."

"Have you ever known her to show signs of a volatile temper?" I asked.

"No, not that I can recall," Dan said. "Until Saturday night, that is. She really shocked me on the drive home. She was ranting and swearing that she hoped he spent time in jail. She was horribly embarrassed by the whole thing. Who wouldn't be?"

"I'm sure she found it mortifying," I said. "I really have struggled to reconcile his behavior with the behavior I saw in the classroom. He was utterly charming and a terrific lecturer."

"He had a gift," Dan said, "one that I certainly envied. He felt entirely comfortable in front of the classroom, but I've always struggled with it."

"Perhaps you'd rather not talk about this, but do you think Carey Warriner killed your former sister-in-law?" I asked.

"I think he must have," Dan said. "I think he had been having an affair with her. I don't know for sure, but he was exactly the type of man Dixie would go after." He sounded bitter. "She ran around on my brother while they were married but Ray was so besotted with her, he was blind to what she was doing."

"She was a very attractive woman," I said, taken aback by his sudden anger at the dead woman.

"I suppose so," Dan said. "I never saw it myself. She always looked cheap and hard to me. If Ray had listened to me, he never would have married her. Instead, he wouldn't have much to do with me after that."

"I'm sorry," I said. "Was he your only brother?"

"My only sibling," Dan said. "And by that time, my only family."

No wonder he had felt so strongly about his former in-law. Though a wiser man would have put up with her for the sake of his relationship with his brother, I thought.

"Are you going to say anything to Chief Deputy Berry about your suspicions?" I asked.

Dan toyed with the remains of his cake, poking it about on the plate with his fork. "I don't know," he said. "If I'm completely off base, I could get Irene in a lot of trouble, and I'd hate to lose her as a friend." He dropped the fork, and it clattered against the plate. "What would you do?"

"It's a tough decision," I said. "I understand your reluctance, but if you really have doubts about Irene Warriner's innocence in the matter, you should confide in Kanesha. She is completely trustworthy."

"Sounds like you know her pretty well," Dan said. "Especially if you call her Kanesha."

"I do," I said. "You may not have realized this, but Azalea is Kanesha's mother."

That startled him. "I had no idea."

"Kanesha isn't happy about it," I said. "She doesn't think her mother should be working as a housekeeper, but Azalea has her own opinions. The thing is, I've known Kanesha for a number of years, and I've actually been involved in several murder investigations in the past."

"Have you?" Dan looked surprised.

"Yes, I have," I said. "Through no fault of my own. I've got an enormous amount of respect for Kanesha and her integrity. If Irene Warriner is not guilty of murder, then you have nothing to worry about. Kanesha isn't going to railroad her on anyone's say-so."

Dan picked up his fork and resumed eating what was left of his piece of cake. After he swallowed a bite, he said, "Thanks for your advice. I'll have to think about it awhile longer before I make up my mind about what's best to do."

"I promise I won't say anything to Kanesha," I said.

"Thank you," Dan said.

I wouldn't talk, unless I found a compelling reason to. If I became certain myself that Irene Warriner had killed her husband, I would tell Kanesha for sure.

"Have you told Kanesha that you think Carey Warriner killed Dixie Compton?"

"Not yet," Dan said. "I suppose I should. The thing is, I don't really have any evidence that they were having an affair."

"If they were, I'm sure Kanesha will find out," I said. "The first question after that will no doubt be whether Irene Warriner was aware of it."

"The whole thing's such a horrible mess," Dan said.

"Murder always is," I said. "It disrupts lives in ways that people don't always understand."

"I suppose you're right," he replied. "Right now it's like a nightmare you can't wake up from." He pushed back abruptly from the table and removed the sleeping kitten from his lap. "If you don't mind, I think I'll take my second cup up to my room with me."

Ramses sat on the floor by the chair, yawning, then began to stretch.

"That's fine," I said. "If you don't mind bringing the cup back the next time you come down, it would be a help."

"Sure." He refilled his cup. "Thanks for listening." He left the kitchen.

Had I not been vigilant, Ramses would have followed him. I was ready for him, though, and I grabbed him before he could get out of the room. "You stay here," I said, face-to-face, my nose out of reach. "Dan seems to like

156

you, but I don't know that he wants you as a companion at the moment."

Azalea returned a few minutes later, and Ramses forgot all about trying to escape the kitchen to find his new friend. I helped Azalea bring in the groceries from her car, but she wouldn't let me assist in putting them away.

"I want to know where they are," she said. "Last time you put things up, it took me a while to find them. You go on and do something else."

"Okay," I said, although the time to which she referred was at least four years ago. "Dan and I had some of the lemon pound cake. He said it was delicious. I knew it would be."

Azalea nodded as she extracted an iceberg lettuce from a bag. "Glad to hear it."

I poured myself more coffee and cut another sliver of cake and ate it at the table while Azalea continued what she was doing. I felt ill-mannered sitting there and not helping, but I had been told not to, and I obeyed.

I replayed my conversation with Dan, and I realized I should perhaps have pushed a little harder on the subject of Armand d'Arcy. In the meantime, I wondered what I could do to encounter the man. I would like to be able to take his measure for myself and not rely on hearsay.

How to do it? He was a music professor, and I didn't know anyone in his department that I could ask about him.

Then it hit me. He was a professor. He taught classes. I could try to audit a class with him. Now that my class with Warriner had been canceled, I had the time.

"I'm going to the den for a few minutes," I announced to Azalea. Diesel followed me out of the kitchen and down the hall. I picked up my laptop and switched it on, making myself comfortable on the sofa. Diesel stretched out lengthways on the remaining space, his head against my thigh the way he liked it.

When the laptop was ready, I opened the browser and found the college's spring semester classes. It took me a minute to find the music department amid the other courses in the School of Arts and Sciences. When I did, however, I became excited. D'Arcy was teaching medieval and Renaissance music this semester on Tuesdays and Thursdays from 9:40 until 11:05. Perfect timing. If I could get into the class tomorrow, I'd have plenty of time to make it to the Farrington House restaurant for my lunch appointment.

I looked up the number of the music department and punched it in on my cell phone. When someone answered, I asked about availability in d'Arcy's course. The voice replied that it would check. I couldn't decide whether the voice belonged to a woman or a man. The pitch was indeterminate.

After an agonizing two minutes—so it seemed—the voice came back on the line and said that there were still spaces available in the class.

"That's great," I said. "I was auditing another course, but it got canceled, and this one sounds really interesting." I gave the person my name and said that I would come by the office in the morning to get more information before class started.

After that call ended, I went online to the registrar's office section of the college website, logged in to my account, and formally dropped Warriner's course. I found d'Arcy's course and registered for it. It was marked as *pending approval*. I thought that meant the instructor had to approve it, but maybe the voice with which I had spoken could do it. I would sort it out tomorrow morning if need be.

I felt pleased with myself for figuring out a way to meet

d'Arcy as part of a group. As far as I was aware, he had no idea who I was, but word had made it around in some quarters about Diesel, if not about my amateur sleuthing.

My cell phone rang, and I recognized the number. My friend Miss An'gel Ducote, one of the grandes dames of Athena society, along with her younger sister, Miss Dickce, was calling.

"Good afternoon, Miss An'gel," I said. "How are you?"

"Hello, Charlie. A bit frazzled, if you must know," came the tart reply. "Sister and I have just left an emergency meeting of the board at Athena, and we would like to talk to you about it. Are you at home now?"

"Yes, ma'am, I am. Please feel free to come by, or if it would be easier, I can meet you somewhere else."

"We'll come there," Miss An'gel said. "We're only a few blocks away." She ended the call.

"Our friends Miss An'gel and Miss Dickce are coming," I told the recumbent cat. Diesel perked up right away. He recognized the names. "Come on, let's go tell Azalea."

Azalea had finished putting away groceries and was now preparing to cook dinner. I told her that the Ducote sisters were coming for a visit.

"That coffee's pretty fresh, isn't it?" she asked, eyeing the pot.

"It is," I said.

"I'll bring in coffee and lemon pound cake," Azalea said, turning away from the stove. "You know they both have a sweet tooth."

I nodded. "I'll take them into the living room."

When I reached the front door, I heard a loud screech of brakes and knew that the sisters had arrived. I grinned. Miss Dickce usually drove, and her philosophy was that you never could get anywhere fast enough. Miss An'gel had nerves of steel, I reckoned. I opened the door, and sure enough, their car stood parked, slightly askew, in front of the house.

Diesel and I met them halfway down the walk. "What a pleasure it is to see you," I told them, offering Miss An'gel, then Miss Dickce, a quick peck on the cheek.

"Sorry for descending on you at such short notice," Miss An'gel said, "but Sister and I agreed that you are the person we need in this matter."

I walked between them up the walk to the house, and Diesel scampered ahead.

"What matter are you talking about?" I asked, though I had already figured out what it probably was.

"These murders," Miss Dickce said. "You have to help Kanesha solve them."

TWENTY-ONE

I opened the front door, and Diesel and I ushered the Ducote sisters into the house. "Let's go into the living room," I suggested. "Azalea's going to bring us coffee and lemon pound cake."

"One of Azalea's heavenly cakes." Miss Dickce sighed. "Wonderful."

"Why don't we go in the kitchen?" Miss An'gel stopped in her tracks. "Surely you know us well enough by now not to stand on ceremony. Come on, Sister."

I didn't try to argue. One *didn't* argue with Miss An'gel, in the same way one didn't argue with Azalea.

If Azalea were at all disconcerted by the sisters' sudden appearance in the kitchen, she didn't let on. "Good afternoon, Miss An'gel, Miss Dickce, how are y'all doing?"

"Fine as frog hair," Miss Dickce said in cheerful tones, oblivious to the pained look Miss An'gel gave her for using such a phrase. "How are you doing, Azalea?"

"Fine," Azalea said. "I was going to bring coffee and

pound cake to the living room for you." Her tone held a slight reproof.

Miss An'gel said, "That's very kind of you, but we thought we'd rather have it in here. Sister and I have such fond memories of this room, visiting with you and Dottie over the years, Azalea."

"Miss Dottie sure did love it when y'all came to call," Azalea said.

I pulled out a chair for Miss An'gel, and then one for Miss Dickce. After they were comfortably seated, I took my usual place. Diesel busied himself going back and forth between the sisters for attention. Ramses, oddly enough, seemed skittish of our visitors. He didn't appear to remember them from the last time they visited.

Miss Dickce coaxed him out of his shyness, though, and soon he was ensconced on her lap. Miss An'gel frowned at her. "I don't know how you do it," she said. "I can never get Endora to sit in my lap." Endora was the Abyssinian cat they had adopted.

"That's because she knows you prefer Peanut," Dickce said. "That dog adores you."

"Labradoodles are reckoned to be quite clever," Miss An'gel said tartly.

Before the sisters got into full bickering mode, Azalea set dessert plates and forks in front of them, followed by coffee. They immediately focused on sampling the cake, and it was easy to see that they both found it delicious.

"Don't you dare tell Clementine this," Miss Dickce said, "but your lemon pound cake is better than hers."

Clementine was the Ducotes' housekeeper and had been with them for many years.

"Thank you kindly, Miss Dickce," Azalea said, "but that's her recipe."

"Even so," Miss Dickce replied with a smile.

I did not interrupt their enjoyment of the coffee and pound cake by asking them to come to the point for their visit. One didn't rush ladies like these.

Miss Dickce finished her piece several bites ahead of her sister, and I caught her casting wistful glances at the cake plate.

"I believe Miss Dickce would like another slice, Azalea," I said.

"I do believe I would," Miss Dickce said.

"Sister," Miss An'gel said, her tone stern. "Really."

Miss Dickce rolled her eyes. "Really, Sister. You're going to do all the talking the way you always do, so I might as well enjoy another piece of cake while you talk." She held out her plate, and Azalea provided a second slice. Miss Dickce grinned in triumph at her sister.

I had to work hard to keep from laughing. In the end I coughed a little, but I didn't think I fooled anyone.

Having finished her cake, Miss An'gel got straight to the point. "There was an emergency board meeting to discuss the murder of a distinguished professor, as well as that of a student," Miss An'gel said. "Now, Azalea, you know how highly we regard Kanesha and her abilities."

Azalea nodded. "Yes, ma'am, I do."

"But we also know that she has in the past benefitted from help in certain quarters," Miss An'gel continued, "especially in matters related to Athena College." She looked straight at me.

"Kanesha has already told me she would be grateful for any information I happen to come across," I said. "I was able to tell her about one incident that she wouldn't otherwise have known about, but that's really about it so far."

"Excellent," Miss An'gel said, and Miss Dickce nodded in agreement as she had another bite of pound cake.

"But she did not ask you to take a more active role, did she?"

"No, she usually doesn't," I said.

"Understandably so, I suppose," Miss An'gel said. "The sheriff can be persnickety about things. Officially he is not aware of how much you have helped his department in the past, but off the record, although he does completely not approve, he is happy with the success rate of murder investigations."

"Good to know," I said. "I'm happy for Kanesha to get the credit, because she deserves it. I don't want to be in the limelight. She actually solves the cases; I simply provide corroborating information. She gets the evidence."

Azalea snorted. "That girl is too prideful sometimes. I've told her the good Lord only knows how many times that she can't expect to carry everything on her shoulders. The hardest lesson she ever learned is that it's not weakness to ask for help when you need it." She regarded me with something approaching a smile. "You helped her learn that lesson."

I had never heard such a compliment from Azalea before, and I felt my face flush. "Thank you," I said.

Miss An'gel and Miss Dickce beamed at me. Miss Dickce said, "Sister and I know you'll do your best to help Kanesha the way you always have."

"I've already made plans to try and dig up some information that could be helpful," I said.

Miss An'gel said, "You let me or Sister know if you need anything."

"While you're here," I replied, "I might as well ask you whether you're acquainted with any of the persons who could be involved in this."

"Of course," Miss An'gel said. "We met the unfortunate young professor a couple of times at college events. Such a charismatic and attractive man."

"I'll say," Miss Dickce said. "Young Henry Fonda, Cary Grant, and Gary Cooper all rolled into one."

I grinned at her enthusiasm.

Miss An'gel shot a repressive glance at her sister. "You certainly fawned over him when we chatted with him on one occasion."

Miss Dickce glared back. "As I recall, you were in no hurry to let him go, Sister. You hung on his every word."

Miss An'gel sniffed. "He was a charming, interesting young man. We knew of his family, Charlie. I once had business dealings with his late grandfather over some property in Atlanta."

"I heard from someone that he came from a well-to-do family in Georgia," I said.

"That is correct," Miss An'gel said, "though I would describe them as considerably more than well-to-do. His grandfather was one of the richest men in Georgia, and I believe young Warriner was the only grandson." She shook her head. "So sad for the family. Were his grandfather still living, I imagine the shock of this might have killed him."

"Do you know if he had any sisters?" I asked.

Miss An'gel frowned. "I don't recall. Dickce?"

Miss Dickce shook her head. "I don't remember hearing about any. I think he was an only child. There are a couple of cousins, maybe." She looked doubtful.

"Definitely a tragedy for his family," I said. "Can you tell me anything else about him?"

Miss An'gel considered for a moment. "I do believe he mentioned that his father died a few years ago, but his mother is alive and in Atlanta or one of the suburbs."

"Yes, I remember that," Miss Dickce said. "I think he said she had remarried recently."

"That's about it," Miss An'gel said. "We also met his wife, a lovely young woman. I've heard that she is highly regarded in the English department, and her students are quite taken with her."

"I've met her a couple of times," I said. "We attended the event at the bookstore Saturday night when she did a presentation along with a history professor, Daniel Bellamy, on the Regency period. Were you aware that she writes historical fiction under a pseudonym?"

"As I recall, you recommended her books to us a couple of years ago," Miss An'gel said. "We've both enjoyed them, and we regretted not being able to attend that event."

"We met her on those same occasions when we talked with her husband," Miss Dickce said. "An attractive young woman, I thought, well-spoken with nice manners."

Miss An'gel nodded. "Yes, an apt description. We don't know anything about her background, however. The subject of her family never came up."

"No, it didn't," Miss Dickce said before she forked the last bite of her second slice of cake into her mouth.

"This is dreadful for her, poor girl," Miss An'gel said. "They seemed like a perfect couple. They obviously adored each other. Wouldn't you agree, Sister?"

Miss Dickce stared wistfully at the lemon pound cake on the counter. Her sister's question brought her attention back to the conversation. "Yes, I would."

I hesitated over my next question but decided I might as well ask it. "Did Warriner seem at all possessive toward his wife?"

Miss An'gel shook her head. "Not that I can recall. He was solicitous of her, bringing her a fresh glass of wine on one occasion."

"Didn't see anything of that nature," Miss Dickce said.

I frowned. "From what I've heard, he had certainly become quite jealous of her friendship with another professor. You may have heard about the incident at the bookstore that ended with his being taken to jail."

Miss An'gel looked startled. "Heavens, no, what happened?"

I gave them a précis of the situation at the bookstore, as well as a description of what happened at Helen Louise's bistro. They both appeared shocked by the incidents.

"And you say that the other man involved was a music professor at Athena?" Miss Dickce asked.

"Yes, ma'am," I said. "His name is Armand d'Arcy. Do you know him?"

The sisters exchanged a glance, and then they shook their heads. "No, I don't know him, though the name sounds vaguely familiar."

"I'm going to see if I can audit his class," I said. "His specialty is Renaissance and early modern music."

"Clever idea," Miss Dickce said. "That sounds so interesting."

"I agree," Miss An'gel said. "I'm sure you'll be able to assess his character by the way he behaves toward students in his class."

"I guess I'll find out," I said. "I'm going to the music department in the morning. I've enrolled online, but that still has to be approved."

"If there are any problems about your getting into the class, you let me know," Miss An'gel said.

"Thank you, I will, though I'm not anticipating any issues," I said. "What about the first murder victim? Dixie Belle Compton. Did you ever meet her or know anything about her?"

"Only by reputation," Miss Dickce said, her voice sounding strained.

"And that wasn't good," Miss An'gel added. "A friend of ours lost his head over her, and it cost him a marriage and a lot of money."

TWENTY-TWO

‖‖

Given what I'd already heard from Melba about the late Dixie Belle Compton, I wasn't totally shocked by Miss An'gel's revelation. Having confirmation of Melba's statement did make it all the more real and sordid.

"I heard something similar from Melba," I said, "but without any details or names."

The sisters exchanged a glance. As I watched, I thought I saw Miss Dickce nod slightly. Miss An'gel turned to me. "We know you will treat what we're about to tell you with discretion, Charlie, since it involves an old friend of ours. We don't think he is involved in the murders, but perhaps knowing about this will help you understand the character of Ms. Compton better."

"I appreciate your willingness to confide in me," I said. "Knowing more about Ms. Compton's background will help, I'm sure."

"Our friend Herman Blakely apparently first met Ms. Compton at one of the casinos on the Gulf Coast," Miss

An'gel said. "She worked there in some capacity. Perhaps a hostess of some sort. He had a penchant for that kind of place. He loved to gamble but he never let it get out of control. He liked his money too much."

"I think Herman went to them to cheat on his wife," Miss Dickce said flatly. "Sister is too nice to say it outright, but I'm not. He found a willing partner in Ms. Compton."

"I can't argue with Dickce," Miss An'gel said, "because I fear she is correct. Herman had a weakness for attractive women, and most of the time Agnes, his wife, overlooked that."

"Until Ms. Compton came along," Miss Dickce said. "She followed him back to Athena after they got together at the casino. He seemed besotted with her."

"Herman Blakely," I said. "Isn't he a prominent surgeon?"

Miss An'gel nodded. "A fine one, but I'm afraid his reputation suffered in the wake of his dalliance with Ms. Compton."

"Agnes was out for blood," Miss Dickce said. "Herman had never brought one of his floozies home, so to speak, but he put this woman in an apartment and spent a couple of nights a week with her."

"This all came out in the divorce proceedings," Miss An'gel said. "Poor Agnes was out for blood, as Sister said, and she didn't care who knew it. I can't really blame her. Herman practically flaunted the woman and embarrassed Agnes dreadfully."

I didn't know either the surgeon or his former wife, but my sympathies definitely lay with Agnes Blakely. I didn't approve of infidelity.

"The upshot of it was a nasty divorce," Miss Dickce said. "Agnes took him to the cleaners, and I'm glad she did. What a fool that man is. He allegedly tried to buy off

Ms. Compton when things got really ugly with Agnes, but Ms. Compton wouldn't play."

"I think she fancied herself as the next Mrs. Herman Blakely," Miss An'gel said, "but Herman learned his lesson. He had spent an enormous amount on Ms. Compton, giving her jewelry and an expensive car, along with a bank account. Between that and the settlement on Agnes, he could barely afford gas to head out of town."

"So he left Athena?" I asked.

Miss Dickce giggled. "He sure did, for a couple of months. Then he came slinking back. I almost felt sorry for him, but really, he brought it all on himself."

"Sounds to me like he could have had a grievance against Dixie Compton," I said. "Despite his own culpability, he could have blamed her for all his troubles."

"And wanted her dead," Miss An'gel said. "I suppose that's possible, but I really don't think he did it."

"What about Mrs. Blakely?" I asked.

Miss Dickce snorted. "Agnes wouldn't have soiled her hands, believe me."

"I will keep all that in mind," I said. "I'm sure Kanesha knows all this, too."

"I would think so," Miss An'gel replied. She glared at her sister. "Are you finally done eating?"

Miss Dickce wiped her mouth with her napkin and laid it beside her empty plate. "I am, thank you so kindly for asking. Does this mean that you're ready to go now?" Her demure tone did not match the mischievous gleam in her eyes, and I wondered what Miss An'gel would have to say to her once they were in their car again.

"I believe we have told Charlie everything we know." Miss An'gel stood. "Thank you again for the cake and coffee, Charlie. And thank you, Azalea. This was what we needed after a dreary board meeting. Come along, Sister. I know Charlie has things to do." Azalea smiled to acknowledge her words.

Both sisters took final farewells of Diesel and Ramses as I escorted them to the front door.

Miss An'gel's parting words to me went straight to the point. "We're counting on you, Charlie. I know you won't let us down."

"No, ma'am." I watched their progress down the walk for a moment, Ramses tucked under one arm to keep him from bolting after Miss Dickce, his new best friend. I had seen her sneak him a couple of small bits of pound cake when she thought no one was looking.

I shut the door before Miss Dickce took off down the street. I wasn't sure my nerves could stand it. Every time they left I expected to hear a loud crash, but thankfully so far, it hadn't happened.

I put Ramses down, and he trotted off to the kitchen, probably in hopes that he would find Azalea still there. Diesel stayed with me, and we went down the hall.

Laptop once again in place, Diesel on the sofa with me, I decided to e-mail Melba and tell her about my plan to audit Armand d'Arcy's class on Tuesdays and Thursdays. The subject did interest me, but I wasn't sure I would continue with the class after the murders were solved. I wasn't particularly musical and hoped that there would be no singing required.

I was about to send the message to Melba when another thought struck me. The Ducotes had told me about their friends' messy divorce because of Dixie Compton. Melba had said there were two such cases. I wondered who was involved in the other one. Could that case have any bearing on the murders?

After adding a few sentences to the message, asking for further information on Dixie Compton's marriage-wrecking career, I hit send. I set aside the laptop to consider what I had learned from my visit with the redoubtable Ducotes.

I hadn't given much thought to Viccy Kemp's statement that Carey Warriner came from a well-to-do family. With the corroboration of the sisters, however, that information took on a whole new significance. The Warriners were apparently rich, and as the only grandson, Carey Warriner might have inherited a substantial sum from his grandfather and his father.

Who would most likely be his chief beneficiary? His wife, naturally. A wife who might have become incensed over his recent bizarre behavior and decided to rid herself of her husband. Her potentially rich husband.

That theory certainly bore consideration.

How did Dixie Compton fit into this scenario?

According to the Ducotes, Ms. Compton had made out pretty well in her affair with Dr. Blakely. Jewels, a fancy car, an apartment, and a bank account—not shabby if she had managed to hold on to it. If the tale Melba had to tell yielded similar information, I thought it worth considering that Ms. Compton had a history of bilking wealthy men. An old, old game, but one that could pay very well indeed.

Had she tried the same game with Carey Warriner? Seduced him into an affair, hoping for expensive gifts, but perhaps he hadn't been willing to play by her rules. He ended the affair, and she decided to put the pressure on by showing up in his and his wife's classrooms. Had Irene Warriner had any knowledge of the affair? That could be a key point. If she had known, she might have decided to solve the problem by getting rid of Dixie Compton once and for all. Then, in disgust over her husband's betrayal and his increasingly erratic, possessive behavior, to rid herself of him as well. Outcome, a wealthy widow who could retire from teaching and devote herself to writing, if she so chose.

I didn't want to think of Irene Warriner as a double murderer, but I had to admit that the scenario was plausible.

Also plausible was the notion of two murderers. Carey Warriner got rid of Dixie Compton before she could cause a scandal that led to divorce. Then, perhaps out of guilt over his betrayal of his wife, he suddenly became jealous of her friendships with d'Arcy and Dan Bellamy. He might have attacked her, and she could have killed him in self-defense.

If that were the case, I speculated, Dan Bellamy might have helped her dispose of the body by taking it from the Warriners' house and dumping it on some unsuspecting man's lawn.

I couldn't rule Herman Blakely completely out of the picture, however, despite the Ducote sisters' faith in their friend. Or Agnes Blakely, for that matter, although I couldn't see what motive she might have for killing Carey Warriner. Herman, though, could have been jealous that Dixie Compton had transferred her so-called affections to Warriner, killed Ms. Compton in a rage, then her alleged lover.

That scenario had its appeal, as did the others I had come up with. But were any of them anywhere close to the truth?

I wished I could discuss all this with Kanesha. I figured she had probably already come up with the same scenarios and perhaps others besides. She was privy to inside information that I wasn't, and that was frustrating.

Not much I could do about that, I knew. Instead I decided to focus on writing down the variations I had come up with. I retrieved my laptop and started typing.

The task took me about twenty minutes, and when I read over what I had written I wondered whether there were possibilities I hadn't considered. For one thing, I had no idea how—or if—Armand d'Arcy figured into any of this. Or, come to think of it, Dan Bellamy. Both men had been spending time with Irene Warriner recently. Time easily explained by shared interests, in the case of Irene and Dan Bellamy, and asking for help with the musical background, in the case of Irene and Armand d'Arcy.

Maybe that was all there was to it in both cases. All perfectly innocent, with no connection to the murders, other than Carey Warriner's episodes of raging jealousy against d'Arcy. What about Dan Bellamy? I wondered. Had Warriner exhibited any similar behaviors toward Dan? Dan hadn't mentioned any, but then he might think it best not to bring up the subject. I reasoned, however, if Carey Warriner had suspected Dan of any designs on Irene, he would have displayed those feelings at the event Dan and Irene shared at the bookstore. Instead, Warriner had attacked d'Arcy.

A thought niggled at the back of my consciousness. Something—or someone—I hadn't included. But who? Or what?

Then it came to me. Barbara Lamont. Helen Louise and I both thought she exhibited signs of being in love with Carey Warriner. If she were indeed in love with Warriner, how could she be involved in the murders?

For the same reasons as Irene Warriner, more or less, I thought. She could have found out about Dixie Compton and decided to remove her from her path to the man she wanted. With Compton out of the way, though, there was still the matter of Irene. But perhaps Warriner had rejected Barbara Lamont in a way that infuriated her. She could have struck out, killing him in a fit of rage.

I added these thoughts to my document and saved it. Now I debated whether to share it with Kanesha. Would she consider this helpful? Or would she think I was trying to push myself into a bigger role in her investigation?

I knew it would be a mistake to underestimate Kanesha's intelligence, but I couldn't be sure of what details she knew about some of these people. For example, did she know anything about Barbara Lamont? Granted, Helen Louise and I didn't know for sure that she had been in love with Carey Warriner, but the possibility was there. Every plausible possibility had to be considered.

What about Dan Bellamy? I had already considered the fact that he could have murdered Carey Warriner, or he could have helped Irene dispose of the body. If he were the murderer, though, what was his motive?

I hadn't observed any signs of his being in love with Irene Warriner. During the interactions I witnessed, he had treated her as a friend, a colleague, nothing more. He had appeared badly shaken by the news of his former sister-in-law's death, and I thought that exonerated him in this murder. What motive could he have had, other than resentment against her for the estrangement from his brother?

He hadn't appeared to know much about her recent life, although that could have been a deliberate deception on his part. If he had known, perhaps he was disgusted by her activities. He could have confronted her, argued with her, and struck out in a rage, not meaning to kill her. That was plausible.

What about Carey Warriner? That was the sticking point. Why kill Carey Warriner?

I stared at the screen of the laptop for several minutes while I tried to come up with plausible motives. I finally gave up in irritation and shut down the laptop. I set it aside.

That was one decision made. I wouldn't share my theories with Kanesha for now. If she came to mc and asked for my thoughts on the case, I would feel free to give her the sum of my speculations. Until then, I had other things to consider, more facts, I hoped, to uncover.

Restless now, I couldn't decide what to do. My gaze settled on the stack of Lucy Dunne books on my desk. I got up and pulled one, *The Marquis and the Murderer*, and began to read the first chapter. The eponymous marquis, the hero of the tale, entered the scene a few pages in, and the heroine's description of him signaled her immediate attraction. She mentioned his darkish blond hair, curls flopping over his brow, and his deep blue eyes. As she watched him, he casually brushed the curls back with one hand.

My meeting with Dan Bellamy in my office came immediately to mind. The marquis sounded a lot like him. No wonder Dan had seemed familiar. Irene had modeled her hero on him, at least physically.

Curious, I picked up another book and another, skimming them until I had found descriptions of the heroes in each. Three others Irene had described in similar fashion. Surely this was no coincidence. Was Irene in love with Dan Bellamy?

TWENTY-THREE

||||||||||||||||||||||||||||||||||||||||||||||||||||||||||||||||||||||||||||||

Dan Bellamy hadn't come in by the time I went to bed, and that left me feeling a bit frustrated. I wanted to talk to him, although I felt diffident about prying into his relationship with Irene Warriner. After rereading some of the intensely emotional scenes in the Dunne books between her heroines and the heroes who, I was now convinced, were modeled on Dan, I had concluded that Irene had strong feelings for Dan. They might amount to no more than lust, to put it crudely, projections of her fantasies about physical contact with an attractive man other than her husband.

Dan surely must have read one or two of the Dunne books, if not all of them. Had he read one in which the hero matched his own physical description? I didn't know Dan well enough to compare his personality to that of the men in the books. He could have read them and been totally unaware of the likeness, I supposed. If Irene were truly in love with him—or in lust—from what I had observed on two occasions it must be one-sided. Dan had evinced no signs of a similar attraction while they were together.

If Irene wanted to replace her husband with Dan, that gave her a strong motive to get rid of Carey Warriner. A divorce would no doubt have been messy, but she wouldn't end up in prison for life—or worse—with a divorce. Why did he have to be killed?

Money.

Carey's wealthy family. Irene might not have received much from a divorce settlement. At least, not nearly as much as she would potentially inherit as a grieving widow.

Was Irene Warriner that coldly calculating? That ruthless?

My thoughts returned to Dan. Perhaps he was aware of Irene's attraction to him. Perhaps he even returned her feelings. I wouldn't be able to tell unless I could observe them interact again.

What about Dixie Belle Compton? How did she fit into this?

The more I thought about the whole situation, the more I started to think that she might be the key to solving the case. Why did she have to die? What threat did she pose? And to whom?

I might be trying to follow a red herring, but knowing more about the woman's past could lead to information relevant to the present. I wanted to talk to Dan about her. If Kanesha had uncovered more of the woman's background, she had not shared that information with me. There were far too many unanswered questions in this investigation, and as usual I was working at least half-blind. Kanesha wanted any information I stumbled across on campus but left me in the dark to do it.

I woke up the next morning still feeling frustrated. I

felt tired. From what I could recall of my dreams, I had
been on a fruitless search for something and not ever finding it. Before I came completely awake, I felt a small body
land on my chest, and then a cold nose against my cheek.

"Good morning, Ramses." I rubbed his head, and he
purred in satisfaction. A rumble near my ear reminded me
that another feline wanted attention. "Good morning to
you, too, Diesel." I felt the brush of whiskers against my
ear as Diesel laid his head on my pillow and stretched out
alongside me.

We lay there for several minutes, and I began to relax.
Nothing like a bit of feline therapy to improve one's
mood, I reflected. I thought briefly about my agenda for
today, a day when I didn't have to be at work. I needed to
go to the music department office and finish signing up to
audit Armand d'Arcy's course. Then I had to be at the
Farrington Hotel restaurant for lunch so I could listen
while Melba persuaded her friends Viccy and Jeanette to
talk about their respective departments. I hoped all this
effort yielded useful information.

There was no sign of Dan at breakfast, and I resigned
myself to having to wait to talk to him. I didn't really look
forward to the task, but I felt that I had to try. I might be
able to find out something he wouldn't tell Kanesha, but I
figured he might be wary of letting anything slip. Devious
means, therefore, might yield information I couldn't get
otherwise, information that could lead to the truth. I was
being a snoop, and eavesdropping on conversations wasn't
a nice thing to do, but cold-blooded murder was far worse.
That was how I justified my behavior to myself. Specious
reasoning, perhaps, but there you had it.

At breakfast I told Azalea I had errands to run and
needed to leave Diesel at home with her and Ramses. She
simply nodded to acknowledge my statement. I thanked

her and headed upstairs to get ready for the day. Diesel and Ramses remained with Azalea, no doubt hoping bacon might mysteriously appear in her hands.

Armand d'Arcy's class started at 9:40, and I decided that arriving at the music department around nine should give me plenty of time to take care of completing my registration. When I checked online earlier in the morning, my request was still marked as pending. I hoped there wouldn't be an impediment to my joining the class.

A light rain had set in about twenty minutes before I planned to leave for campus, and I decided to drive and park in my usual spot. The music school occupied a building half a block down the side street past the library, and I wouldn't mind a short walk in the rain. Better than walking all the way from home, anyway.

My lower pants legs got damp, as did my shoes, but not unpleasantly so. They would dry quickly once I was inside. I pushed open the door of the music school and furled my umbrella. I gave it a quick couple of shakes to get rid of some of the water, then went inside to find the department office. I hadn't been inside this building for many years, and I had only a hazy memory of where the office was.

I found the office suite number listed on a board in the foyer, and I ambled down the hall in search of the number. As I neared the doorway I thought I recognized a voice coming from inside the office.

When I entered the outer room, I found my suspicions confirmed. I had been right. Miss Dickce Ducote stood there, talking to one of the office personnel. The young man behind the desk glanced my way when I entered, and Miss Dickce turned to see who had arrived. I smiled at her, pretty sure I knew why she was here.

"Why, if it isn't Charlie Harris." She beamed at me.

"What a pleasant coincidence. I wonder if you're here for the same reason I am."

"And what would that reason be, Miss Dickce?" I asked, trying to keep a straight face.

"I'm signing up to take a course on early music," Miss Dickce replied, her eyes twinkling. "I've heard good things about the professor, and you know how interested I am in music. I thought this would be the best way to indulge my craving for knowledge."

"This certainly is a coincidence," I said blandly. "I'm here for that exact same reason. Isn't that interesting?" I smiled at the young man behind the desk, who was eyeing us both and grinning. No telling what he was thinking.

"This nice young man was telling me that there's still time to join the class." Miss Dickce turned the full wattage of her smile upon the assistant, and I saw him redden slightly. According to the nameplate on his desk, he was Arthur Glanville.

"That's excellent news," I said. "Good morning, Mr. Glanville. I put in a request yesterday online, but this morning it was still pending. Is there any further information you need? I'm hoping to audit the class. I don't need to take it for credit."

"I told him the same thing," Miss Dickce said. "Won't this be fun? We can audit the class together."

"I just need to check with Dr. d'Arcy," Glanville said, his voice a reedy tenor. "If you don't mind waiting, I believe he's in his office." He reached for the phone and punched in a number. After a brief pause, he identified himself and explained that he had two people in the office interested in auditing his course. He listened for a moment, said "Okay," and replaced the receiver.

"He's coming to the office," Glanville said. "He'll be

here in a moment." He indicated a small row of chairs against the wall. "Have a seat if you like."

"Thank you," Miss Dickce said.

I led her to the chairs, and we sat to await the professor. "I didn't expect to see you here this morning," I said in an undertone, hoping that Glanville couldn't understand what I was saying.

Miss Dickce grinned. "I'm sure you didn't," she whispered back. "But I thought it would be fun. I am interested in music, you know, and of course I wouldn't mind helping the investigation, either."

I gazed fondly at her. "Does Miss An'gel know about this?"

Miss Dickce tossed her head. "She doesn't. Not yet, anyway. I'll tell her after I find out whether we can get into the class."

I didn't think Miss An'gel would be too happy that her sister had decided on a course of action without consulting her, but that was between the two of them. Having Miss Dickce in the class with me could be fun, unless she took it into her head to start asking the wrong kind of questions or somehow tipped her hand to let d'Arcy know the real reason behind our interest in him.

Moments later a tall, dark man entered the office. When he spotted us, he walked over and regarded us without smiling.

"Good morning. Are you the persons who wish to join my early-music class?" His voice had the lilt of a native French speaker, and I wondered how a Frenchman had ended up in Athena, Mississippi, teaching music history.

Miss Dickce extended her hand, smiling up at him. "Yes, we do. I am Dickce Ducote. I've heard great things about you, Professor d'Arcy, and music is my great love, you see. I often sit in on courses here."

D'Arcy had taken her hand and pressed it lightly. He evinced no sign of recognition at the Ducote name. He turned to me. "You, too, are interested in music?"

I nodded. "Yes, I'm not musical myself. I mean, I can't play any instruments, but I love music and history. Your course seems like the best way to know more about both."

"I see." He regarded us, still unsmiling. "You are both registered as students here?" He sounded as if he found that doubtful.

Miss Dickce laughed. "Heavens, no. I was a student here, eons ago. My sister and I, An'gel Ducote, are members of the board of trustees of the college, and we both take a great interest in the school. We've both audited classes on occasion." She paused to let the effect of her words sink in, and I could see a subtle change in d'Arcy's posture. It at once became less stiff and forbidding, now more relaxed and seemingly open.

"I am also a graduate of Athena," I said. "I'm currently an employee as well. I'm a librarian, the archivist for the rare book collection. My name is Charlie Harris."

I might have imagined it, but I thought there was a flicker of recognition in his gaze when I mentioned my name.

"I see," d'Arcy said, his tone a bit more cordial. "I am happy to welcome you both to my class. You both wish to audit, I presume?"

Miss Dickce and I nodded.

"That is fine," d'Arcy said. "You will be able to attend the class this morning, I trust. This is the second meeting of the class, so you have not missed much." He bowed his head quickly and turned as if to depart.

"Pardon me, Professor," Miss Dickce said, "but I must ask. Your charming accent. You are French, of course."

D'Arcy turned back, with what looked like a forced smile. "*Mais oui, mademoiselle*. French Canadian, from Quebec."

"A beautiful city," Miss Dickce said.

"*Merci*," d'Arcy replied. "I will see you in class." He left the room.

Miss Dickce and I smiled at each other. "You pulled rank on him," I whispered.

"I thought he might refuse to let us in the class if I didn't," Miss Dickce said. "I hate doing it, but sometimes you have to."

"I'm thinking that if you hadn't been here," I said, "he would have refused to let me in."

Miss Dickce patted my hand. "Then I'm glad to be of some use." She stood, and when she spoke, she used her normal tone. "Let's see what else Mr. Glanville needs us to do so we can get to class on time." She walked over to the desk, smiling at the young man, and I joined her.

Finalizing our presence in the course took only a few minutes. When we finished I checked the time and saw that we had a little over fifteen minutes before the class started. "Shall we go ahead and find the room?" I suggested.

"I know where it is," Miss Dickce said. "Follow me."

We walked to an elevator and took it to the third floor. A few doors down we found the room, and when I glanced inside it, I remembered having a class in it as an undergraduate. It was a small amphitheater in style, and we stood at the base. "Music Appreciation 101," I murmured.

The room appeared to be empty upon first glance, and I ushered Miss Dickce in. To my surprise, however, I saw that one person had arrived ahead of us. She occupied a seat toward the back of the amphitheater. I was even more surprised when I realized who she was.

Irene Warriner.

TWENTY-FOUR

|||||||||||||||||||||||||||||||||||||||||||||||||||||||||||||||||||||||||||||||||||||||

Miss Dickce and I exchanged startled glances. She had seen and recognized Irene Warriner also. Irene Warriner, however, did not appear to have seen us yet, her gaze focused on her phone.

"Good morning," I called out to her. For a moment, I thought she hadn't heard me, but then she raised her head. Seeing us, she appeared puzzled, as if she recognized us but wasn't certain who we were.

"Good morning," she said in a polite tone, but immediately went back to staring at her phone.

I shrugged, and Miss Dickce and I found seats about halfway up. Irene Warriner sat several rows behind us, slightly to the left. I had to admit to being a little shocked at seeing her here. Not that I expected her to be at home, wearing sackcloth and ashes, bewailing her loss, but given the circumstances of her husband's death, I thought she might have felt inclined to withdraw from the public eye. I shrugged. Sitting in a college classroom wasn't exactly the same thing, but I knew if I were grieving, I wouldn't be going to a lecture so soon after my spouse's murder.

"Don't you think it's strange that she's here?" Miss Dickce asked in an undertone, obviously as taken aback as I was.

"Yes, I do," I said. "Maybe it's her way of coping with her grief. Some people can't stand being alone, no matter what."

"I suppose you're right," Miss Dickce replied. "I still think it's peculiar of her." She frowned, and I risked a quick glance over my shoulder. Irene Warriner still appeared to be absorbed in whatever she was reading or looking at on her phone. I hoped she hadn't been able to make out any of our conversation.

Time to change the subject in case she could understand what we were saying.

"Did you bring a notebook?" I asked Miss Dickce.

She tapped her large handbag. "I have one in here. I don't take a lot of notes. I only jot down things I want to follow up on, on my own."

"That's probably what I should do," I replied, "rather than wearing my hand out trying to write down everything. After all, I'm not an undergrad who needs to take a test these days."

Miss Dickce giggled. "Neither am I." She leaned closer to whisper. "Don't you dare let the professor know, but my bachelor's degree was in music performance."

"Really? I had no idea. What was your instrument?" I had never heard Miss Dickce speak about her degree.

"Voice," Miss Dickce said, somewhat wistfully. "I wanted to be another Maria Callas." She giggled again. "We heard her at the Met in New York when I was a teenager, and I thought she was the most amazing singer. I was good, but not in that league, sadly."

"Do you still sing?" I asked.

"In the choir at our church," she said. "I can still hold a long note, and on pitch," she added proudly.

"That's wonderful," I said. "I don't have much of a singing voice myself."

We lapsed into silence as other students began to appear and found seats around us. I continued to think about Irene Warriner's presence in the room. I supposed it stemmed from her wanting to know more about music for background in a book she was working on. Perhaps focusing on writing was her way of coping with the death of her husband. That was probably it, I decided.

I realized that my sense of propriety had been somewhat offended by seeing her here, out in public as it were, so soon after the murder. Presumptuous on my part, I thought ruefully, but given my Southern upbringing, not an unnatural reaction.

Armand d'Arcy entered the classroom, and slowly the chatter around Miss Dickce and me trailed off. A bell rang, and d'Arcy surveyed the now-quiet group. "Good morning, *mesdames et messieurs*. Today we will discuss early medieval liturgical, or sacred, music. The music of the church, and perhaps the best-known form of this music today, is what is called the Gregorian chant. These chants were sung during the Mass." He paused, then nodded to a young man seated several rows below Miss Dickce and me who had raised his hand. "Yes, you have a question?"

"Yes, sir," the young man said, his voice hesitant. "When you talk about the church, are you talking about the Catholic church?" When amused tittering from other students greeted his question, he seemed to shrink into his seat.

D'Arcy frowned. "There is no need for amusement among you. You may ask any question and need not fear ridicule from me." He paused again, and I could almost feel the embarrassment in the room. "To answer your question, sir, yes, it is the Catholic church." He smiled suddenly. "It was the only game in town in the early Middle Ages, other than Judaism and, of course, Islam."

"Thank you," the young man said.

"Catholicism, synonymous with Christianity in this period, was older than Islam, the beginnings of which are said to lie in the early seventh century of the Common Era. Judaism is older than either. This course focuses mainly on the Western music tradition. One of my colleagues who is an expert on Eastern music offers a course for those who are interested.

"Now, let us go back to Gregorian chant, which, as I said, was sung during the Mass." He walked over to a console on one side of the room. "First, we will listen to some chant." He pressed buttons, and a few seconds later, music issued from the speaker system.

We listened to several different chants during the ensuing ten minutes. I had always found Gregorian chant almost hypnotic in its cadences, and when I closed my eyes, I imagined I was in the choir with the monks as they sang. I could see Brother Cadfael, the monk-detective in Ellis Peters's wonderful medieval mysteries, as he joined his brethren in song.

When d'Arcy cut off the music, he dimmed the lights at the front of the room and turned on the large screen on the wall. He opened his presentation, and for the next quarter hour he told us about early musical notation and went into considerable technical detail. I had pulled out my own notebook and jotted down a few things. So far Miss Dickce seemed not to have heard anything she didn't already know, because the page of her notebook remained blank.

D'Arcy was a capable lecturer. He did not have the flair

of delivery of the late Carey Warriner, but his passion for his subject was obvious. From the monophonic chants we moved on to other forms of early medieval music, such as secular songs, and more technical detail about the development of polyphonic music and notation. By the time the bell rang at 11:10 to end the class, I felt overwhelmed by the amount of information packed into the class period. If every meeting contained this much detail, I was happy that I wasn't taking this course for a grade. All this aside, however, I thoroughly enjoyed the lecture, so much so that I nearly forgot my original purpose in signing up for the course.

Miss Dickce and I waited until most of the students had trickled out of the room. D'Arcy stood at the console, doing something with the controls. When Miss Dickce and I made our way to him, he had apparently finished. He glanced at us and smiled briefly.

"That was so interesting, Professor d'Arcy," Miss Dickce said. "I don't believe I've ever heard Gregorian chant explained so thoroughly. It's so beautiful."

"Yes, it certainly is," I said. "I have a new appreciation for it now that I have learned so much more about it."

"I take it that you will both continue to attend my lectures?" d'Arcy said, one eyebrow slightly raised.

"I will do my best," Miss Dickce said. "I may have to rearrange my schedule a few times, but I most definitely don't want to miss a word."

D'Arcy inclined his head. "That is truly flattering, Miss Ducote. I imagine that you are a very busy lady." He glanced past us, his eyes glowing briefly at whoever had come up behind us. "You must excuse me now, I must talk to my colleague."

"Of course," I said, and Miss Dickce and I turned to withdraw.

Irene Warriner stood a few steps behind us, her eyes downcast. As we moved by, she looked up, and this time recognition dawned. Her expression grave, she said, "Good morning, Miss Ducote, Mr. Harris. I'm sorry I didn't realize earlier who you were when you first came in."

"That's quite all right, my dear," Miss Dickce said, her tone full of sympathy. "My sister and I want to offer our deepest sympathies on the death of your husband. He was such a vital, talented young man with so many more successes ahead of him."

"Thank you," Irene whispered, suddenly overcome with emotion, it seemed. She closed her eyes and took a deep breath. When her eyes opened again, she said, "This is such a nightmare. I can't really believe it happened."

Armand d'Arcy moved quickly to her side and slid his arm around her in a gesture of comfort. "*Ma chère* Irène," he murmured. "Do not upset yourself so."

I found his use of the French version of her name oddly intimate, and I shifted uneasily.

"Thank you, Armand," she said, her body stiff in his embrace. "I'm all right."

D'Arcy frowned and let his arm fall away from her. He did not step away, but Irene Warriner moved uneasily aside.

"I'm really sorry for your loss," I said to cover the awkward pause that ensued. "I had signed up for your husband's course, and I thought he was truly a gifted speaker."

"Thank you," she said softly, and I thought I saw tears glistening in her eyes.

"We mustn't keep you any longer," Miss Dickce said, kindly but firmly. She addressed d'Arcy. "We will see you again on Thursday." With that she headed briskly out of the room, leaving me to trail along in her wake.

Miss Dickce came to a halt a few yards down the hall. I almost stumbled into her but I caught myself in time. She appeared not to notice.

"Well, what did you think?" she asked, her voice low.

"About what?" I responded, slightly puzzled.

"Irene Warriner and d'Arcy," Miss Dickce said. "Are they madly in love with each other?"

"I'd say he definitely has tender feelings for her," I said. "She seemed uneasy with the close contact, though. She also seemed to be grieving her husband, unless she was putting on an act for our benefit."

"He's in love with her, I'd say." Miss Dickce nodded. "The tone of voice in which he called her his *dear Irene* left me in no doubt." Her expression clouded. "I'm less sure of her, though. She did shy away from him, but I'm not entirely convinced that his embrace was unwelcome." She paused for a moment. "I wonder if she only wanted us to think it was."

"You don't think her appearance of grief was authentic?"

Miss Dickce shrugged. "I'm just not sure. I can't put my finger on the reason." She sighed. "I'm probably only imagining it, but I thought she might be putting it on for our benefit."

"I see." I had found Irene Warriner's display convincing. What had I missed that Miss Dickce had picked up on? I would have to think more about it later. I checked my watch. I had plenty of time to get to the Farrington House restaurant for my next task for the day.

"Miss Dickce," I said, struck by sudden inspiration, "do you have any plans for lunch today?"

She wrinkled her nose. "A garden club meeting. The board is lunching together."

"That's too bad," I said.

"Do you have a better offer?" Miss Dickce smiled. "I could be tempted."

I laughed. "Yes, how would you like to join me at the Farrington House restaurant for a little more sleuthing?"

Her eyes sparkled. "Of course. I'll text An'gel and tell her that something has come up, and she'll have to go without me." She rummaged in her handbag and pulled out her phone.

I waited while she sent Miss An'gel her message. Moments later her phone rang. Miss Dickce rolled her eyes. "I told her not to call." She answered. "Yes, Sister, what is it?" she said in tones of deep resignation.

She listened for a moment. "I'll explain later. I'm with Charlie Harris. We're going to have lunch. You'll just have to go to the board lunch without me." She ended the call and stuck the phone back in her handbag. She linked her arm through mine and said, "Let's go. Now tell me all about it."

TWENTY-FIVE

||||||||||||||||||||||||||||||||||||||||||||||||||||||||||||||||

I escorted Miss Dickce to her car and waited until she had driven off. Then I made my way back to my car and headed to the Farrington House hotel on the square. We met in the bar, as arranged. We had time for a drink before we needed to find our table. I found Miss Dickce ensconced in a booth, and I slid into it opposite her.

"What would you like to drink?" Miss Dickce shot me a roguish look. "How about a Long Island iced tea?"

I chuckled. "That's a bit strong for me, usually, but if you're having one, I will, too."

Miss Dickce giggled as the waiter approached. She gave him our order, and he went to the bar to place it.

"Tell me more about the purpose of this lunch," Miss Dickce said.

"Melba has invited two of her friends to lunch here, and we're going to be sitting in the next alcove while she tries to get them to talk about their departments," I said.

"One of them is the administrator in the history department, the other in English."

Miss Dickce nodded her approval. "Excellent idea. If there's anything to find out, Melba will get it out of them. And I'd be willing to bet good money that they will know something useful." She giggled again. "Some of the departments here are hotbeds of scandal. I could certainly tell you a few tales that would shock you. But I can't. All confidential board business." She looked sad.

"It's okay," I hastened to assure her. "I'd just as soon not know, frankly. I remember a few things that happened when I was an undergrad." I shook my head. "Like the time one of the coaches of the basketball team ran off with a physics professor's college-freshman daughter."

"Oh my, yes, that was quite a scandal," Miss Dickce said. "At least they ended up married. Still are, as far as I know, with several children." She thought for a moment. "Goodness, the oldest must be around thirty by now."

"Probably so," I said, not wanting to think about how long ago I'd been a student at Athena. Some days it felt far longer ago than thirty-odd years; other days it was like yesterday.

The waiter appeared with our drinks and set them down with a flourish. "Would you like anything else?" he asked.

"No, thank you," Miss Dickce said.

He nodded and withdrew.

We both sipped at our drinks, and I winced slightly at the strength of the alcoholic mixture. I'd have to eat something pretty soon, or I'd be light-headed from the alcohol.

"Tell me," I said, setting down my drink, "why do you think Irene Warriner might have been insincere in her grief?"

Miss Dickce sipped at her drink before she replied. "I

really can't tell you," she said slowly. "Simply a feeling I had. If I think about it more later, I might be able to put my finger on it."

"Okay," I said. "If you do figure it out, please let me know. I'll be doing the same thing."

As if in silent agreement we chatted for the next quarter hour about matters totally unrelated to the murders. Miss Dickce regaled me with some humorous tales from garden club meetings, and I sipped discreetly—and slowly—from my Long Island iced tea. I could definitely feel the alcohol beginning to have an effect.

Miss Dickce seemed completely the same, despite the fact that she had already consumed at least half of her drink. I had to admire her head for alcohol.

I checked my watch and had to blink a few times to bring the time into focus. "Time for us to head to our table, I think."

Miss Dickce drained her drink, set the glass on the table, and slid out of the booth. "I'll settle up at the bar," she said, leaving me to extricate myself from the booth—a task that suddenly seemed more difficult than usual.

When I managed to get out and stand up, I put my hand on the back of the booth to steady myself. I shook my head several times in an attempt to clear it. A few deep breaths later, I felt steady enough to walk from the bar into the restaurant. Miss Dickce rejoined me, taking my arm and leading me purposefully out of the bar.

While we waited for the hostess, I glanced around the dining room. About half the tables were occupied. I knew the restaurant here was a popular choice for business lunches, and today seemed no exception, to judge by the number of men and women in business attire.

The hostess appeared in front of us. "Miss Dickce,"

she said with a broad smile. "What a great surprise." She glanced at me. "Are you okay, sir?"

I nodded, hoping that the room wouldn't suddenly move. I must have had more of that Long Island iced tea than I realized. Or it was far more potent, one or the other.

"Marlene, my dear friend Charlie invited me to join him for lunch," Miss Dickce said. "How are the little ones?"

From the ensuing conversation I gathered that Marlene had a small menagerie of dogs and cats, and she happily gave a report on their well-being to Miss Dickce, who listened with evident interest.

Finally Marlene broke off and looked at me again. "I think I know you. Charlie Harris, right? Melba's friend."

"Yes, guilty as charged," I said.

Marlene grinned. "Then y'all come with me. Your table is ready." She led us to the last booth along the wall, and the top of the divider between it and the next booth contained a thick cluster of plants. Perfect.

I assisted Miss Dickce—or more likely I held on to her so as not to lose my balance—and she took her place. I managed to get into the booth, my back to the next booth so I could hear what went on. My head was beginning to clear a bit. I told myself that the next time I dined anywhere with Miss Dickce, I would not be drinking any Long Island iced tea with her.

"Your server will be with you in a moment," Marlene said. "In the meantime I'll bring your water." She laid a menu on the table in front of each of us.

"I think you'd better get some black coffee for Charlie," Miss Dickce said, her tone wry.

"Will do," Marlene said, and disappeared. She came quickly back with water and coffee for me.

Ordinarily I don't like black coffee, preferring it with

cream and sugar, but I managed to drink about half the cup. Thankfully for my mouth and tongue, it wasn't hot, just warm enough.

"You'll feel better soon," Miss Dickce said with a grin.

"Thank you," I replied. "Normally about the most I ever have is a glass or two of wine. That stuff is lethal." I began to feel a bit steadier.

Miss Dickce waved that away. "You drank it on an empty stomach. Of course it affected you."

"It didn't seem to affect you," I said, trying not to sound censorious.

She giggled. "I've got nearly thirty years' experience on you. Not that I'm a heavy drinker, but I do like a good stiff drink on occasion."

Our server appeared, and Miss Dickce placed her order without ever having opened the menu. She asked for the Tuesday lunch special, and I said that would be fine with me, although I had no idea what it was. It turned out to be a grilled chicken breast with melted Parmesan, steamed broccoli, mashed potatoes, and freshly baked rolls. I ordered sweet tea to go with my meal, and Miss Dickce did the same.

"Here they come," Miss Dickce said in an undertone. She scooted down in the booth until she was next to the wall, and I did the same.

The three women were talking about something one of them had spotted in one of the boutique shops on the square. Turned out to be a handbag that Melba said was ridiculously expensive. They continued to discuss whether Melba should buy it as they seated themselves in the booth.

I recognized Viccy Kemp's voice, so it was easy to identify the voice that belonged to Jeanette Larson. I could hear them pretty well. They were making no attempt to lower their voices. They continued to chat about such things until the server came to take their orders, and after the server departed, Melba took charge of the conversation and steered it in the direction of the murders.

"The mood on campus seems pretty dark to me right now," Melba said. "Do y'all feel it, too? It bothers me to think that there's a murderer running around campus."

"I certainly do," Viccy Kemp said. "Everyone in the history department is jumpy. I'm afraid to be in the office by myself." She gave a shaky laugh. "I told my boss that I wouldn't stay in there on my own until they catch whoever killed poor Dr. Warriner."

"What did he say to that?" Jeanette Larson asked. "The English department is just about as bad, since it was our Dr. Warriner's husband. Nobody really seems to know what to say to her."

"What *do* you say to a woman whose husband was killed?" Viccy asked. "Anyway, my boss told me he understood, and he's instructed everyone in the office to do things in pairs. Thank goodness there are five of us, so someone's always around when I need to visit the ladies' room or go to the supply closet down the hall."

"What about your department?" Melba asked.

Jeanette replied, "It's not quite that bad for us, though a couple of people have been saying that the killer might come after our Dr. Warriner next."

"Why would anyone want to kill her?" Melba asked. "She seems like such a nice woman."

"She is," Jeanette replied. "The person who first said that to me seems to think some deranged student has a vendetta against the Warriners."

"Our Dr. Warriner was pretty tough on students," Viccy said. "He had high standards for them and wouldn't put up with lazy students. I know of three at least who screamed at him because they wanted him to change their grades."

"Did he do it?" Melba asked.

Viccy snorted with laughter. "He sure didn't. I over-heard him talking to one of them, and he told the girl he didn't care who her daddy was, if she didn't do the work required she deserved the grade she got."

"Good for him," Jeanette said. "Sounds like a student of ours. Was it Tiffany Jo Robertson, by any chance?"

"No," Viccy said, "not her, but I know who you're talking about. Just because her father's a big-name doctor she thinks everyone should kowtow to her. She had trouble with one of the other professors over grades. She's lazy and not very bright."

"Do you think this Tiffany girl would attack some-one?" Melba asked.

Jeanette snorted. "And break one of her expensive fake fingernails? Not on your life. I swear that girl looks like she's made up to play a streetwalker in a low-budget movie. If her mama only knew how she goes around on campus, that girl would get the spanking she deserves and a good scrubbing with lye soap."

As amusing as this was, it wasn't bringing forth any useful information. Miss Dickce and I exchanged glances of exasperation. *Come on, Melba*, I thought. *Get them back on task.*

"Somehow, I don't think a student is responsible," Melba said slowly. "And remember, there was a student who was murdered before Dr. Warriner."

"That's right." Jeanette sniffed. "Dixie Belle Compton. Talk about a painted woman."

I hadn't thought Ms. Compton looked like a *painted woman*, but obviously Jeanette had different standards.

"She wasn't that bad," Viccy replied in tones of protest. "I saw her a couple of times in our office. She wore a little too much foundation, but I figured she was probably covering up some kind of skin condition."

Miss Dickce and I looked up to see our server at the table with our food. While the server was setting our plates and our drinks in front of us, chatting all the while, I missed out on what was going on in the next booth. By the time the server departed, after having to be reassured twice that we didn't need anything else at the moment, Miss Dickce and I had lost nearly two minutes' worth of conversation.

". . . no idea why anyone would want to kill *her*," Jeanette said, "unless she broke up a marriage or two."

"Well, she did do that." Melba commenced to tell them a story similar to the one that Miss Dickce had shared with me about her friend. Miss Dickce grimaced as she listened to Melba.

"That's terrible," Viccy said. "Not a nice woman, but I still don't think she deserved to be killed." She paused. "But I wonder if she was working on Dr. Warriner, trying to break him up with Mrs. Warriner."

Someone gasped, and I wasn't sure whether it was Melba or Jeanette.

"Lord have mercy," Melba said. "Are you serious?"

"Yes," Viccy snapped. "Otherwise why would I say it? Seriously, I saw this woman coming out of his office a few times before the semester started, and at that point I didn't know who she was. Then when she registered for his class, I found out."

"Maybe she was just talking to him about the class," Melba said. "She was an older student. Maybe she needed some reassurance."

"She was getting more than reassurance," Viccy said. "Judging by the sounds I heard coming from his office one afternoon."

TWENTY-SIX

▐▌▏▏▏

Miss Dickce's horrified expression no doubt mirrored my own. If Viccy Kemp was right, then Carey Warriner *had* been cheating on his wife with Dixie Belle Compton.

"Are you serious?" Melba said in a slightly scoffing tone. "Surely the professor would have known better than to do something like that right there in his office where anyone could overhear what was going on."

Viccy sounded huffy when she replied. "You don't work in a department with professors and students, honey. Let me tell you, this isn't the first time I've heard something like that going on."

"It happens in my department, too," Jeanette said. "Especially with older male professors and their female students." Her disgust was palpable in her voice.

"How did you happen to overhear these trysts, I guess you'd call them?" Melba asked.

"Our supply closet is a couple of doors down from his office, that's how," Viccy said.

"You must visit that closet pretty often," Melba said.

"Someone is always running out of something and going in there and helping themselves," Viccy said. "Even though they're supposed to come to the office first, so I have to check on things every other day to see what I need to order."

"Isn't it locked?" Jeanette said. "Ours is, and I'm the one with the key."

"Our department head has a key, and so do a couple other senior professors," Viccy said, obviously annoyed by this. "I've complained I don't know how many times, but they don't pay any attention. Then the department head gripes at me about the supply budget."

"That's not really fair," Jeanette said. "I'm glad our situation is different."

I had to suppress a groan. I'd already heard enough about supply closets to do me for the next ten years.

Melba took charge again. "Did the professor know you'd overheard any of this? Did you say anything to him about it?"

"Well, not in so many words," Viccy said, drawing her answer out. "I made a reference or two to strange noises I'd heard in the hall, but he just blew me off. He did kind of avoid me as much as possible the last couple weeks, though."

"Was he acting strange at all?" Melba said. "Men who are cheating on their wives usually do. They all give themselves away eventually."

"Actually, yes, now that you mention it," Viccy said. "The couple of weeks or so before he was killed, he seemed different somehow. I didn't mention this to anyone except that sheriff's deputy who interviewed me, but he was going around kind of tight-lipped and closed off, if you know what I mean. Not as friendly as he used to be."

"Did that start before you heard him having it off with this woman in his office?" Melba asked.

Viccy dropped her voice when she replied, and Miss Dickce leaned forward over the table as we both strained to hear.

"Come to think of it, yes it did," Viccy said. "About the only person I saw him talking to recently was Dr. Bellamy. He's such a nice man and so good-looking." She sounded wistful. "Not married, either. I've tried flirting with him, but he doesn't seem to get it."

"Maybe he's gay," Jeanette suggested.

"He's not," Viccy said.

"How do you know?" Melba asked. "Did he tell you?"

"Do you think I would've tried flirting with him if he told me he was gay?" Viccy asked, sounding irritable.

I nodded. Stewart would have said something to me if Dan Bellamy were gay. Miss Dickce understood my gesture.

"Then he's just not interested in you," Melba said. "Maybe he doesn't think workplace flirtations are proper."

"I suppose so," Viccy said. "You're probably right."

"So Dr. Warriner had been talking to Dr. Bellamy lately," Melba said. "A lot? Or just now and then?"

"A lot, from what I could see," Viccy said. "I saw them leaving the building together several times, and they seemed to be involved in pretty intense conversations. Dr. Warriner looked upset about something, and Dr. Bellamy seemed to be trying to calm him down. I don't know *what* was going on."

Jeanette said, "Maybe this Dr. Bellamy was trying to talk him into stopping his affair with that woman."

"That's possible," Viccy said. "It might have worked, too, because I didn't see her for almost a week before classes started. Before that it was like almost every day, usually in the afternoon."

"The one I feel sorry for is Warriner's wife," Melba said. "You think she's a nice person, right?"

Jeanette responded promptly. "Yes, she is. And she certainly deserved better than a cheating husband. She's so pretty, in an old-fashioned kind of way. Always dresses so nice, too. I wish I had her taste in clothes." She laughed suddenly. "I guess when you're that rich you can afford the best. Her clothes always look so expensive."

"Elegant, yet simple," Melba suggested.

"Yes, exactly," Jeanette said.

"It was our Dr. Warriner's family who has all the money," Viccy said. "They say his parents, or maybe his grandparents, own half of downtown Atlanta."

"They must be pretty rich then," Melba said.

"Dr. Warriner never put on any airs, though," Viccy said. "I have to give him credit for that." She sighed. "When you grow up with that kind of money, maybe you don't think about it."

"I'd sure like to be that rich," Melba said.

"Wouldn't we all," Jeanette replied.

For the next couple of minutes, all we heard was the sound of the women eating. Then Melba started up the conversation again.

"I guess Mrs. Warriner is going to be pretty rich now," she said. "She'll have all kinds of men swarming around her. Rich widows are very attractive, even if they have faces like a brick henhouse."

"Maybe you need to start telling people you're a rich widow, Viccy," Jeanette said, with more than a touch of malice. "You'd get some guys interested in you real quick that way." She laughed.

Viccy didn't answer that, and after an awkward pause, Jeanette continued on a more ordinary note. "I guess Mrs. Warriner will inherit, unless his family made her sign some kind of prenup, that is."

"With rich people, you never can tell," Melba said. "I hope for her sake she gets a lot out of the deal."

"She's already had one man hanging around her," Jeanette said. "That gorgeous man from the music department, Dr. d'Arcy. So handsome, and so French."

"Does he have an accent?" Melba asked.

"He does," Jeanette said, "and he sounds so romantic when he talks. I think our Dr. Warriner has been talking to him about research for one of her books, you know, the novels she writes."

"He's in the music department, you said?" Melba asked.

"Yes, I think he teaches ancient music or something like that," Jeanette said. "Anyway, he's been coming by the department to talk to her for several weeks lately."

Miss Dickce and I exchanged knowing glances.

"Do you think he's in love with her?" Viccy asked. "Maybe they've been having an affair, and that's why our Dr. Warriner started having one with that woman."

"She's not that kind of woman," Jeanette said. "Anyway, I never heard anything weird coming from her office when he was with her."

"Did you walk by just to check it out?" Melba asked slyly.

"No, I did not," Jeanette said hotly. "If you must know, I have to pass her office on the way to the ladies' room, and, well, I have to go pretty often. I drink a lot of water during the day so I stay full. I like to snack, but if I drink water, I don't."

"Okay, so Mrs. Warriner isn't having an affair," Melba

said. "But did you know that Dr. Warriner had attacked this d'Arcy a couple of times?"

"No," Viccy and Jeannette said in unison, obviously astonished. "How do you know that?" Viccy asked.

"I have my sources," Melba said. "Right there in public, both times. The second time the police came and took them to jail. They both got released, and sometime later that night, or in the morning, I guess, Dr. Warriner was killed."

"I had no idea," Jeanette said. "Do they think Dr. d'Arcy killed him?"

"He's as good a suspect as any," Melba said.

"What if Mrs. Warriner did it? Maybe she found out about his affair with that woman," Viccy said.

"She could have done it, too, I guess," Melba said. "After all, she's probably going to be a rich woman now."

"I don't believe it," Jeanette said. "I tell you, she's not like that."

"I'm sure she'd appreciate your loyalty," Melba said. "You may end up on the witness stand, you never know."

"That would be horrible," Jeanette said, although her tone sounded more excited than horrified.

"I guess I could end up there, too," Viccy said, sounding equally titillated.

"You've both talked to the sheriff's department, right?" Melba asked.

"I have, a couple of times now," Viccy said. "That Deputy Berry is pretty intense, let me tell you."

"She's smart and dedicated to solving cases," Melba observed.

"More power to her," Viccy said. "Jeanette, she talked to you at least once, right?"

"Yeah," Jeanette said. "She scares me a little. Looks at

you like she's expecting you to confess something any minute."

"Guilty conscience?" Melba said jestingly.

"No more than you," Jeanette retorted.

"Then *you* are a living angel, like me," Melba said sweetly. They all laughed at that, and Miss Dickce and I both had a hard time not joining in. I almost spit out a bite of chicken, in fact.

"Seriously," Melba said, "Kanesha Berry is first-rate. I've known her for years. Her mother is my friend Charlie's housekeeper, you know."

"I didn't know that," Viccy said, "but I've heard about your friend Charlie, with that great big cat."

"Me, too," Jeanette said. "I've also heard he's kind of like Jessica Fletcher from that TV show, where dead bodies turn up all the time." She giggled. "Better be careful, Melba, you could be next."

I winced, and Miss Dickce shot me a look full of sympathy.

"Ha-ha," Melba said, the two syllables dripping with sarcasm. "Yes, Charlie has been around a couple of murders, but they had nothing to do with him. Well, not much, anyway. He's a smart guy, and he's been a help to Kanesha, I can tell you that."

"You mean he solves her cases for her?" Viccy asked. "Like that Lord Peter Wimsey did because the police weren't smart enough?"

"I don't know who the heck this Lord Peter guy is," Melba said, "but it's nothing like that. Kanesha is smart as a whip, and Charlie stumbles across information sometimes. He's a nice guy. He can't help it if people tell him things."

"If you say so," Viccy said. "Lord Peter is this rich, handsome detective in England. An amateur. My mother loved those books, and she made me read them when I was a teenager. They were pretty good, actually." She sighed. "I guess I've wanted to meet a guy like that."

"Better move to England, then," Jeanette said, then giggled. "No lords around here that I know of."

The conversation had rapidly descended into the realm of nonsense. I figured Melba had gotten pretty much everything she could from her friends. Miss Dickce and I had finished our meals, and Miss Dickce had started to check her watch. She probably had somewhere she needed to be this afternoon.

"We should all be so lucky," Melba said. "I guess that's what Dixie Belle Compton was trying to do, hook herself a rich husband in Dr. Warriner."

"I don't think it would have been legal," Viccy said.

"What do you mean, *legal*?" Jeanette asked.

"I think she was married to some guy," Viccy said. "I overheard her say something to one of the other women in the office about her husband helping pay for her to go back to school."

Miss Dickce and I stared at each other. A husband?

TWENTY-SEVEN

||||||||||||||||||||||||||||||||||||||||||||||||||||||||||||||||||||||||||||

Viccy Kemp's revelation stunned me. This was the first I'd heard that Dixie Belle Compton had a husband. Miss Dickce appeared to be surprised as well.

After I'd had a moment to consider it I wondered if it were true. Maybe Dixie Compton had made up the husband for reasons of her own. I'm not sure what they would have been, but she could have done it, just the same.

Either way, this information bore investigation. I wondered if Viccy Kemp had shared this with Kanesha.

Melba must have wondered the same thing, because she asked Viccy.

"I don't think I did," Viccy said. "Do you think I should?"

"Of course you should." Melba sounded a bit impatient with her friend. "Don't you see? If she had a husband, and he found out about the affair, he could have killed both of them."

"Oh my Lord," Viccy said, "I never thought of that."

"Melba's right," Jeanette said. "You need to tell them. He could be aiming for someone else, you never know. I've read that once men kill, it's hard for them to stop."

"Goodness, what on earth have you been reading?" Melba asked.

"True crime," Jeanette said, sounding defensive.

"No wonder," Melba said. "They don't write those books about boring murders. Surely you realize that."

One of them must have caught sight of the clock because they started talking about having to get back to their offices. "Y'all go on," Melba told her friends. "This is on me, remember. I'll take care of the check, and y'all can get back on time. I'm not in a hurry like you are."

"Thanks, Melba," they both said in turn.

"You call Kanesha Berry," Melba reminded Viccy, who promised that she would as soon as she got back to the office.

Moments later, Melba came to our booth and started in surprise at seeing Miss Dickce. Then she slid in beside me. "I didn't expect to see you here, Miss Dickce."

I explained that Miss Dickce had signed up for the same class and that I'd invited her to lunch. Melba laughed. "Team effort, I guess. Could you hear everything?"

"Most of it," I said.

Miss Dickce nodded. "That was quite a bombshell about the husband. I had no idea she was still married to anyone."

"I'm not so sure she was," Melba said, "despite what Viccy heard her say. Still, it could be true, and if it is, there's a husband out there who could be a killer."

"Will your friend follow up and call Kanesha?" Miss Dickce asked.

"She'd better," Melba said, sounding determined. "Or I'll call Kanesha myself. Other than the bit about a husband, did you learn anything else important?" She looked at me for an answer.

"One thing we heard basically confirmed a suspicion that Miss Dickce and I have," I replied. "About Irene Warriner and the music professor, d'Arcy."

"That he's in love with her?" Melba asked.

"Yes," Miss Dickce said. "Mrs. Warriner was in the class this morning, too, and afterward she came up to us while Charlie and I were talking to Dr. d'Arcy. I thought his behavior toward her gave him away. He's very much in love with her."

"Then that should put him high on the suspect list," Melba said. "Especially since Dr. Warriner attacked him twice in public." She frowned. "That seems so bizarre to me."

"I know," I said. "It really seems out of character. I wonder what was going on with him, to get him to that state of mind."

"Jealousy," Miss Dickce said. "Remember *Othello*. Jealousy can fester for a long time and then erupt in violence."

"We had to read that in sophomore English at Athena," Melba said. "Creepy play, if you ask me. But I see your point."

Othello was indeed a creepy play in some ways, a terrible example of jealousy, corrosive and destroying, causing a man to murder his wife, his innocent wife. If Carey Warriner had been eaten up with jealousy over d'Arcy's attentions to Irene, had he ever threatened his wife with violence? If he had, that would add a new dimension to the case.

Surely Kanesha had already thought of that and had questioned Irene Warriner about it. I wished I knew how, or whether, Irene had responded to any such questions.

That same corrosive jealousy could be the motive for another husband to have committed two murders. If Dixie Belle Compton was married at the time of her murder, then her husband obviously had to be a prime suspect.

I wished I could talk to Kanesha and find answers to some of these questions. At this point there were too many possibilities, and it was hard to know where to focus to dig for more information.

Miss Dickce brought me back to attention by saying that she had better be going. "I've tried Sister's patience long enough," she said. "She'll be ready to hang me from the roof when I get home for leaving her to face the garden club board all alone." She grinned. "Thank you for lunch, Charlie. It was fascinating."

"My pleasure," I said. "If you think of anything or run across any pertinent information"—she and Miss An'gel had all kinds of influential connections—"let me know."

"I certainly will," she said as she slid out of the booth. "Melba, thanks for a most entertaining, if not entirely edifying, lunch."

Melba laughed and bade Miss Dickce good-bye. As my guest walked away, Melba turned to me. "Do you have any idea who the killer is, Charlie?"

"No, not yet," I said. "Too many possibilities and not enough solid information. I'm beginning to think I should give up and leave everything to Kanesha. She has to know a lot more about what's going on than we do."

"I should hope so," Melba said. She shrugged. "But that doesn't mean you can't find out something before she does, something that wouldn't occur to her, like you've done in the past. After all, you're a lot more familiar with the academic world than she is."

"Does that mean you think the answer to all this lies in the academic world, as you call it?"

"Stands to reason, don't you think?" Melba cocked her head at me. "What's the connection between the two murder victims? Professor and student. Other than Dixie Compton's alleged husband, everyone else involved is an Athena faculty member. So I'd say the answer is just as likely to come out of the academic world."

"I see your point," I said. "But I'd sure like to know about this alleged husband, as you called him."

"Why don't you ask Kanesha?" Melba slid out of the booth. "I've got to get back to the office. Are you going home?"

"Maybe. I don't know yet. Thanks for everything," I said.

"Glad to help." She grinned. "I'm part of the team, aren't I?" With that she turned and walked out of the restaurant, leaving me chuckling.

The server came by to ask if I wanted anything else, and I told her I was ready for the check. She pulled it out of her apron and handed it to me. I looked at the total, then pulled out my wallet and handed her enough cash to cover the tab and a good-sized tip. "I'm going to finish my tea," I told her after she thanked me. "Then I'll be leaving."

I sat in the booth for a few minutes longer, sipping my tea until I finished it, thinking about what I ought to do next. I could go by the sheriff's department to see if Kanesha was in and would see me. Or I could simply text and say I needed to talk to her. Probably texting would be better. When she was on a case it was hard to catch her in her office.

I pulled out my phone and sent her a brief text that I really needed to talk to her. I made it short and slightly ambiguous on purpose. Let her think I'd found out something potentially important and maybe she'd respond more quickly.

I left the restaurant and made my way to my car in the lot behind the hotel. Thankfully for my head, what I had consumed of that Long Island iced tea had worn off. I heard my phone buzz, heralding a text message. Expecting to hear from Kanesha, I was slightly surprised to see the message was from Helen Louise. Her message was simple: *When you're done with lunch, come to my house. Barb is here.*

The name didn't register for a moment, but then I realized whom Helen Louise meant. Barbara Lamont was with her at home. That must mean Barbara wanted to talk, or already had been talking, about Carey and Irene Warriner. I quickly responded to Helen Louise's message to let her know I was on the way.

During the brief drive to Helen Louise's house, in the same neighborhood where I lived, I speculated on what had prompted Barbara Lamont to seek out Helen Louise. I couldn't imagine that this summons related to something else entirely. It had to have something to do with the murders. I debated a moment on stopping by my house to pick up Diesel, since he was often such a calming influence, in case Barbara was upset.

I had to go by my house anyway, and stopping to pick up the cat wouldn't take more than a minute. I pulled into the garage and hurried into the kitchen. I found Azalea there with both cats while the housekeeper worked on that evening's dinner. I said a quick hello, explained that I was on the way to Helen Louise's, and I wanted to take Diesel with me. Both he and Ramses had swarmed around me. Azalea stared at me briefly as if she hadn't understood me, then she nodded.

"One thing, real quick. Mr. Dan asked if he could bring his friend, the lady whose husband was killed, to dinner tonight. I told him you wouldn't mind."

"Not at all," I said, amazed at this news. Perhaps now I'd have my chance to observe the two of them more closely together and to find out more about Irene's relationship with her husband. "What time did you tell them?"

"Six o'clock, same as usual," Azalea said.

I nodded. "Come on, Diesel. No, Ramses, you stay here with Azalea. Diesel and I are going to see Helen Louise for a little while." When he heard Helen Louise's name, Diesel went straight to the door. Ramses tried to follow, but I scooped him up. "Not today," I told him, and put him down by Azalea.

Diesel and I made it out the door without Ramses escaping. Diesel hopped into the backseat, and I drove us the few blocks to Helen Louise's house. The cat preceded me up the walk to the front door. Helen Louise must have heard my car, because she opened the door before I had a chance to knock. She glanced down at Diesel in surprise.

"Did you take Diesel to lunch with you?" she asked, leading the cat inside and motioning for me to follow.

"No, but I stopped on the way to pick him up." I gave her a quick kiss after she closed the door. In an undertone, I said, "What's going on?"

"Barb wants to talk to you about the murders," Helen Louise said. "She hasn't told me much yet, just came by the house about half an hour ago." Diesel rubbed against her legs, and she patted his head absentmindedly. "We're in the kitchen."

Helen Louise led the way, Diesel right by her side. I followed them, impatient to find out what Barbara Lamont wanted to talk about. Would she have information that could shed more light on the murders?

"Here they are," Helen Louise called out as we entered the kitchen. "This is the famous Diesel."

Barbara Lamont came into view, sitting at Helen Louise's rustic farm table. She wore an oversized wool sweater, handwoven by the look of it, and her face was pale. When I drew closer, I thought she might have been crying. She clutched a wineglass in one hand, but she set it down as Diesel came closer to her.

"Hello, Charlie. Diesel is gorgeous. I've never seen a cat this big." She held out her fingers for Diesel to sniff. He did so, then started rubbing his head against her hand, a sure sign that he felt comfortable with her. "How sweet," she said as she began to stroke his head.

"He's gentle and affectionate," I said. "He obviously likes you, or he wouldn't have allowed you to rub his head. He can be picky about that."

"Charlie, how about some wine?" Helen Louise asked.

I almost shuddered. The thought of alcohol did not appeal. "I'd rather have tea or coffee, if that's okay." I would have to tell her later about my drink in the hotel bar with Miss Dickce.

"Of course." Helen Louise smiled. "I'll put the coffee on now. I think we'll all be ready for it before long." She gestured toward the table. "Make yourself comfortable."

I pulled out the chair across from Barbara Lamont, who had taken a chair on the short side of a table that could comfortably accommodate eight people. I didn't want to make her uneasy by sitting too close to her.

"How've you been?" I asked her. "I know you've been shaken badly by Carey Warriner's death."

Barbara gave a jerky nod and reached for her wine. After a couple of sips, she looked down into the wine. "I'm terrified, too," she said.

Diesel meowed loudly, and she glanced down at him, puzzled.

"He can tell that you're upset," I said gently. "It's his way of trying to reassure you. He's quite empathetic."

"That's amazing," she said, reaching out to stroke the cat's head again.

"What has you terrified?" I asked as Helen Louise rejoined us at the table. I exchanged a quick glance with her, and she gave a slight shrug. Evidently Barbara hadn't yet confided in her.

Barbara raised her head to look at both of us. She inhaled deeply before she spoke. "I'm terrified because I'm worried that Irene murdered that woman and then murdered Carey, and I don't know what I should do about it."

TWENTY-EIGHT

||||||||||||||||||||||||||||||||||||||||||||||||||||||||||||||||||||||||||||||||||||||

"What makes you think she might have killed them?" I asked, a bit stunned by Barbara Lamont's statement.

Without asking, Helen Louise refilled Barbara's wine-glass and received a teary smile in thanks. Barbara had more wine before she responded to my query.

"It was something she said to me one day about a week ago," Barbara said. "We were in my office at work. She had come to talk to me about a committee issue, and then, all of a sudden, she started talking about Carey."

"Was she upset?" Helen Louise asked.

Barbara nodded. "One minute we were calmly discussing the committee, the next she started ranting about Carey. I knew he'd been acting a bit strange recently, but there was more to it than I knew, she said."

"When you say 'acting strange,' can you explain what you mean?" I asked.

"Carey loved Irene, and he'd always been a little bit jealous when another man admired her," Barbara said.

"But he'd simply make a joke out of it, comparing Irene to Helen of Troy or Nefertiti, and talk about her power over men. I think Irene found it amusing. At least until a few weeks ago." She paused to have more wine.

"Coffee's ready," Helen Louise murmured. She got up to see to it, and Barbara didn't appear to notice.

"What changed?" I said.

"Carey seemed to grow more suspicious. She said he'd started to ask her questions about what she did during the day, whom she'd seen or talked to, where she'd been. Questions like that."

"All at once?" Helen Louise said as she placed a mug of coffee in front of me, and I smiled my thanks.

"No, it didn't happen overnight, but it did get worse pretty quickly, Irene said. He frightened her, she told me." Barbara shuddered. "He hadn't become physically abusive, but he would shout at her when they were at home. He would keep on and on with the questions until she was ready to pack up and leave him. She threatened to do it a couple of times, and that stopped him, at least briefly."

"How horrible for her," Helen Louise said. "I'm surprised she didn't walk out. That was a dangerous situation, if his behavior was escalating. He might have hurt her at some point."

"That's what I told her." Barbara shook her head as she rubbed the back of her neck with one hand. "But she loved him. She was sure she could persuade him that he had no reason to be jealous, but it didn't work. I saw it for myself."

"During bridge?" Helen Louise asked.

I remembered then that Barbara had told us on a previous occasion that she often played bridge with the Warriners, with either Dan Bellamy or Armand d'Arcy as a fourth.

"Yes, one night last week, when Armand was our fourth," Barbara said. "Irene suggested that she and Armand be partners, and I would play with Carey. He had a fit over that and insisted that Irene and I play as partners instead. To placate him, that's what we did. Irene hardly spoke to Armand that night, and he was careful not to talk to her that much, either. It was such a strain. I hated every second of it." She gave us a grim smile. "I finally pleaded a migraine coming on to put an end to the evening."

"I can imagine the duress you were under. D'Arcy and Irene as well," Helen Louise said. "It sounds to me like Carey Warriner was mentally ill. Something might have triggered it. I wonder if there was any type of mental instability in his family."

"I asked Irene that same question, and she said not any that she knew about," Barbara said. "She couldn't explain why he had changed, didn't understand it at all."

"We know he was violent toward d'Arcy," I said. "What about Dan Bellamy? I know that he and Irene were spending time together preparing for their presentation at the bookstore. Didn't that upset Carey?"

Barbara stroked the back of her neck again. "No, and that's weird, come to think of it. He didn't see Dan as a threat, I guess, only Armand."

"Dan is an attractive guy, and he shares interests with Irene," I said. "Why wouldn't Carey Warriner be jealous of him?"

"I don't know," Barbara said. "Dan's a pleasant man and a great bridge player, one of the best I've ever played with, honestly. But"—she paused briefly—"I don't know, he always seems so aloof. He liked Irene and Carey, I guess, or he wouldn't have spent so much time with either of them, but he was never flirty with Irene the way Armand is. I just put it down to his being French."

Helen Louise picked up on one comment. "Was Carey spending time with Dan on his own? The way Irene was?"

Barbara nodded. "I believe so. Irene said they had become close recently. I'm not sure why, since Dan is, well, Dan, but I guess he and Carey got along well together."

"What's that silly word they use nowadays to label men who are good friends?" I asked.

"You mean *bromance*." Helen Louise rolled her eyes. "Ridiculous term, as if friendship needed romantic connotations. Perhaps Dan Bellamy is gay and fell in love with Carey."

"No, I don't think he is," Barbara said. "I could be wrong, of course, but I know Dan mentioned an ex-wife once. And I never saw him look at Carey that way, or at Armand, either, and they're both really good-looking."

"It's far too easy to misperceive a person's sexuality," Helen Louise said. "I have to remind myself of that from time to time. Sounds like Dan and Carey Warriner were simply good friends, like Charlie and Stewart."

I still hadn't heard from Kanesha, and that was unusual. She was always busy working on something, however, and I knew there was no point in texting her again.

Helen Louise was explaining to Barbara who Stewart was. She nodded. "I know him. He's hilarious. We were on a committee together. I didn't realize he boarded with you, Charlie."

I nodded. "He's become one of the family now."

"That's nice," Barbara said. "I really miss my family, especially now. They're all in Colorado." She looked at Helen Louise with a faint smile. "Could I have some of that coffee? I'm about to get maudlin, drinking all this wine. I don't want to embarrass myself."

"Of course," Helen Louise said. "How do you take it?"

"Black is fine," Barbara replied.

I waited until she had her coffee and had taken a couple of sips before I steered the conversation back to Irene and Carey Warriner.

"You told us at the beginning," I said, "that you were afraid that Irene had killed Dixie Compton and Carey. Why do you think she would have killed her husband?"

Barbara frowned. "Irene told me last year about a man she'd been in a relationship with who had been extremely possessive. I had never seen her really angry, but she was in a towering rage when she talked to me about him. It took me a while to calm her down. She told me she'd do whatever it took to get out of that situation if it ever happened again—even if it meant killing the guy. She sounded pretty grim when she told me that. And then Carey started acting up."

"And then she found out he was having an affair with Dixie Compton?" I said.

"She told me she thought he was involved with another student," Barbara replied. "Irene wasn't sure who it was until she was murdered. Then she realized the woman had signed up for her class as well as Carey's."

"Had she seen them together?" Helen Louise asked.

"I don't think so," Barbara replied. "At least, Irene never said so. The other day in my office, she said Carey had taunted her by saying that if she could have an affair with Armand, then he could have an affair, too. When Irene asked him with whom, all he said was *Wouldn't you like to know?*"

I'd have to share with Helen Louise later what I'd learned from Viccy Kemp during my lunchtime eavesdropping session with Miss Dickce. I wondered whether Carey's alleged affair had begun before or after his behavior turned violent. That could be an important point.

"Do you really think Irene Warriner killed Ms. Compton?" Helen Louise asked. "She'd have to have known who she was in order to do that."

"True," Barbara said. "She told me she didn't know who the woman was until after the murder, but she might have lied to me about that. I hate this. Irene has been my best friend, and now I feel like I don't know her anymore. She frightened me when she got so angry."

"That's the terrible thing about murder for those who survive," I said. "It affects how we see those around us who were somehow connected, and sometimes the effects are long lasting."

Barbara sipped her coffee, her expression troubled. "If Irene told me the truth about not knowing who Dixie Compton was beforehand, then she didn't kill her. If that's the case, then she wouldn't have killed Carey." She brightened for a moment, then her expression clouded again. "Unless it was in self-defense. The way he'd been acting, maybe he finally attacked her, and she had to defend herself."

"That's possible," Helen Louise said. "But if she did do it in self-defense, why didn't she call the police right away? There were enough witnesses to her husband's erratic behavior to back up her claims."

"I hadn't thought of that. Surely Irene would have," Barbara said hopefully. "Maybe that means she didn't do it after all."

Helen Louise and I exchanged glances. Barbara had grasped at an answer that made her feel better. Both Helen Louise and I knew that Irene Warriner might well be the killer, but I didn't want to upset Barbara any further.

"Maybe so," I said. "I think you need to tell Deputy Berry everything you've told us, though."

Barbara started to protest, but Helen Louise patted her hand and said, "Listen, Barb, I've known Kanesha for years. She's smart, and she's fair. She's not one of those cops who settles for an easy answer. She wants the truth, and if Irene didn't kill anyone, then Kanesha will establish that by finding out who the murderer is. You can trust her. Both Charlie and I do, I promise you."

Barbara let go of a pent-up breath. "I guess you're right. If you trust her, then I guess I should, too. I just want this nightmare to be over."

Helen Louise patted her hand again. "We all do. Any information you can give may help do that."

"All right," Barbara said. "So should I call her and ask to see her? I'm not sure what the right way is to do this."

"I'll text her for you." I picked up my phone again. *If this doesn't get a quick response from her*, I thought, *then something big must be going on.* I prefaced the message with 911 to get her attention.

It worked, because she responded by calling me within thirty seconds. "Hello," I said.

"What's the emergency?" Kanesha said. I could tell from her tone that she wasn't happy with me.

I explained quickly that Helen Louise and I were with Barbara Lamont, and that Barbara had some potentially critical information for her.

"I'll be there in ten." Kanesha ended the call.

I relayed the message to Barbara and Helen Louise. Barbara suddenly looked apprehensive.

"Do I have to talk to her by myself?" she asked. "I know it sounds silly, I'm too old to be acting like a kid, but the thought of facing her by myself makes me nervous."

"If Kanesha says it's okay, then one of us can stay with you," Helen Louise said. "I tell you what, give me a dollar."

"What?" Barbara said, obviously startled. "Why do you want a dollar?"

Helen Louise's request puzzled me at first, but then I realized what she was doing.

"Is your law license up to date?" I asked.

"It is," Helen Louise said. "You never know when you might need it." She turned to Barbara. "If you give me a dollar as a retainer, then I can act as your attorney and insist on being present."

Barbara scrambled for her purse and discovered that Diesel was asleep on top of it. "Wake up, kitty, I need my purse."

Diesel had been unnaturally silent during all this, I now realized. I wondered if Ramses had run him ragged today, and he was sleeping it off. It wouldn't surprise me. Now he meowed loudly in protest, but he got off Barbara's purse. Barbara picked it up, rooted around, and found a five-dollar bill. "That's all the small change I have."

"That will do," Helen Louise said. "I'll give it back to you later." She set the bill on the table in front of her. Kanesha would understand the significance, I was sure.

True to her word, Kanesha arrived in ten minutes. Helen Louise went to open the door. When they came into the kitchen, I stood to greet Kanesha. She nodded in response. She looked over at Barbara Lamont.

"Dr. Lamont, I understand you have things to tell me," Kanesha said.

Barbara nodded, then looked in mute appeal to Helen Louise.

"I've agreed to act as Dr. Lamont's attorney for this interview," Helen Louise said, her hand resting on the five-dollar bill. "She's understandably worried and concerned that the information she is going to give you won't be misinterpreted."

Kanesha's rigid posture told me that she wasn't happy about this development, but there wasn't much she could do about it. "Very well." She turned to me. "In that case, I think we can excuse you, Mr. Harris." Her eyes shifted toward Diesel. "And your cat."

"Of course," I said. "I'll take my leave, ladies. But, Deputy, I really do need to talk to you later."

Kanesha frowned, then nodded. "I'll be in touch after I hear what Dr. Lamont has to tell me."

"Fine," I said. "I'll be at home. Come on, Diesel, time to go." We left the kitchen and exited the house. I drove the few blocks home, slowly, mulling over Barbara Lamont's information. I had the feeling that something she had told us was important, but now I couldn't say exactly what it was. I hoped I'd figure it out soon.

TWENTY-NINE

!!!

Thirty-five minutes after Diesel and I returned home, Kanesha rang my front doorbell. Azalea let her in, because I was in the den with both cats, halfway dozing on the sofa. Kanesha joined me in the den, pulling out my desk chair and taking a seat.

"How did it go with Barbara Lamont?" I asked after the preliminary greetings were out of the way.

Kanesha cocked an eyebrow at me. "Fine. Useful information."

"Are you anywhere near making an arrest?" I asked.

"Getting closer," she said. "Now, what is it you want to talk to me about?" From the impatient expression, I knew she was in no mood for me to dither around, trying to fish information out of her.

I suppressed a sigh and got to the point. First, though, I did ask whether she had heard from Viccy Kemp. She shook her head.

"Should I have?" she asked.

I nodded. "You need to talk to her. She can corroborate that Carey Warriner was having an affair with Dixie Compton. She can explain to you how she is sure of that fact."

Kanesha nodded. "All right. Anything else?"

I told her about the lunch earlier today and passed along the information I had gleaned from Melba's friends. I left out the remarks made about how intimidating Kanesha was, as well as the silliness about me being like Lord Peter Wimsey.

"Melba can attest to all this, of course," I concluded. "And Miss Dickce, too."

Kanesha had pulled out her notebook once I started and had jotted down a few notes. Now she looked at me, her expression inscrutable as always. The silence grew slightly uncomfortable, at least for me. Diesel stirred restlessly on the sofa beside me, and Ramses suddenly hopped off my lap and made a beeline for Kanesha. Before I could stop him, he hopped into her lap. She stared at him in astonishment.

"Ramses, get down," I said sternly, but the kitten ignored me. He rubbed against Kanesha's mid-region and began to purr. She began to stroke him, tentatively at first, then with more assurance. He curled up in her lap and settled down while she stroked.

I would have loved to pull out my phone and take a picture to have proof of this, because I wasn't sure anyone would believe me if I told them about it. I didn't want Kanesha to get annoyed with me, though, and I figured she would. She must have encountered Ramses at her mother's house. I wondered if she had given him any attention there. He obviously felt perfectly comfortable with her.

I had to smother a chuckle as I watched. I knew Kanesha wouldn't appreciate that, either. Instead I asked a question. "Did you learn anything new from what I told you?"

Kanesha raised her head to look at me. Her hand stilled, and she removed it from the kitten's head. "The mention of Ms. Compton's husband is new," she said. "We haven't been able to trace one yet, so I suspect that she could have been lying. Or she married in another state. We'll keep digging, because the husband, if there is one, is an obvious suspect."

"What about Barbara Lamont's evidence?" I asked.

"Suggestive," Kanesha replied.

She seemed determined to frustrate me, even more so than usual. Might as well go ahead and poke the bear another time or two, I reckoned. She hadn't made a move to go yet, so it was worth a try.

"What about the murder weapon used on Carey Warriner?" I asked. "Have you identified it yet?"

"No, we haven't," Kanesha said. "It could have come from anywhere. Mrs. Warriner claims that none of her kitchen knives are missing, and no one else has admitted to having lost one. No telling where the killer disposed of it."

"That's really frustrating," I said.

Kanesha shot me a look of irritation.

I hastened to ask another question. "Based on what you know right now, who do you think is the best candidate for the murders?"

"Irene Warriner," Kanesha said. "If we can really prove that her husband was having an affair with Ms. Compton, that gives her a prime motive in both killings."

"Do you believe she acted on her own in her husband's murder?"

"I don't think she could have," Kanesha said. "He was a big man, and I doubt she had the strength to dispose of his body by herself."

"Do you know yet where he was killed?"

"We haven't found any evidence that he was killed at his home," Kanesha said. "According to Mrs. Warriner, he walked out of the house a few minutes after they reached home. Dan Bellamy stayed with her for a few minutes, and then she asked Bellamy to go look for him."

"Dan told me that. He was the one who found the body," I said. "Do you think they're both telling the truth?"

"I think one or both of them has to be lying," Kanesha said. "If Mrs. Warriner killed him, she got Bellamy to help her move the body. We found evidence that Warriner was in Bellamy's car, but that could have been from the ride home Bellamy gave him when he was released from jail."

"Have you found any witness to the dumping of the body? Or information from the Warriners' neighbors about what happened at their house that night?"

Kanesha shook her head. "So far, all we've drawn are blanks. We'll keep digging, but I'm not hopeful that we'll turn up anyone who saw any part of what happened."

I understood her frustration even better now. The killer had been both shrewd and lucky not to have left any recognizable trace. But surely there had to be something.

"I've heard that Carey Warriner came from a wealthy family in Georgia," I said. "Have you been able to confirm whether that's true?"

Kanesha nodded. "Yes, he was a pretty rich guy. Mrs. Warriner doesn't have a copy of his will, or at least she claims not to. I've been trying to get in touch with the family's lawyer in Atlanta, but so far, no luck."

"It seems logical that he would leave everything he had to his wife," I said.

"Until we can confirm that," Kanesha said, "I can't do much." She removed Ramses gently from her lap and stood.

The kitten yawned and rubbed against her leg. "There's something I'm missing. Some connection that has to be there, but I can't figure out what it is." She shrugged. "There are still too many gaps in what we know about all these people's backgrounds."

"Who all are you including in that group?" I asked.

"Bellamy, d'Arcy, Dr. Lamont, and Mrs. Warriner," Kanesha replied. "And potentially Ms. Compton's husband, or even ex-husband."

"I'm sure you know about her dubious career here in Athena," I said.

Kanesha gave a short bark of laughter, surprising me and startling Diesel and Ramses. The kitten jumped away from her and ran out of the room. She didn't appear to have noticed.

"Yes, I'm aware of all that. I started investigating those connections right away. Anyone concerned in that had cast-iron alibis, so no help there," she said. "I've got things to do. If you think of anything, let me know."

I started to get to my feet, but she held up her hand. "I can find my own way out."

I subsided back onto the sofa and watched as she strode out of the room. I considered what she had told me. I wasn't surprised that she considered Irene Warriner the chief suspect. Things didn't look good for the new widow. She was the most obvious person in both cases. Her own best friend was worried that she could have killed both her husband and his alleged lover.

Perhaps for once, the obvious suspect was the murderer. The problem lay in collecting enough indisputable evidence to charge her with the murders and bring her to trial. And would Dan Bellamy be proven to be an accessory, by helping Irene Warriner dispose of her husband's body? I agreed with Kanesha that Irene couldn't have handled her husband's corpse on her own, but perhaps she had lied about his being gone. While Dan Bellamy was out looking for Warriner, Irene could have lured him out of the house on some pretext and killed him away from home, in that man's yard.

Like Kanesha, however, I had the uneasy feeling we were missing something. I couldn't figure out what it might be, but I kept hoping that an idea might surface in my crowded thoughts about the case. Surely there would be a break soon.

I checked my watch. Nearly three thirty, so I had over two hours before dinner. I hoped that Dan Bellamy did bring Irene Warriner, as he had said to Azalea he would. In the meantime, I decided to do some digging into these people's backgrounds. I doubted I could find things that Kanesha's team couldn't, but I might pick up on something they had overlooked.

I retrieved my laptop, and once the browser was open, I went to the Athena College website to look at departmental pages. First the English department, where I looked for information on Irene Warriner. According to what I found, she had earned her Ph.D. from Emory University. There was the Atlanta connection. I wondered if Carey Warriner had also earned his degree at Emory. A quick check of the history department page yielded the information that he had. They had probably met while at Emory, if not before. The dates on their terminal degrees were the same.

Searching for the Warriner name, coupled with Georgia or Atlanta, yielded numerous hits. I didn't try to read everything, but what I did read corroborated the fact that the Warriners were indeed a rich clan. I also found the announcement for Irene Elizabeth Murray's marriage to Carey Alan Warriner, son of Mrs. Judson Warriner and the late Mr. Warriner. They had been married in Atlanta seven years ago, and they had honeymooned in Paris and Venice.

I didn't find anything else that seemed pertinent to the case. I didn't turn up anything on Irene Murray until the wedding announcement. On to Armand d'Arcy, then. According to the music department's page, he was a graduate of McGill University in Montreal, with a doctoral performance degree. His instrument was the baroque bassoon.

I found a few articles in French, but they were beyond the comprehension of my rudimentary grasp of the language. I saved a few of the links to share with Helen Louise, who spoke and read French easily after her years studying in Paris. From what little I could gather from the articles, they were mostly about his music studies.

I checked Dan Bellamy's and Barbara Lamont's credentials as well. Both had Ph.D. degrees from respected graduate schools, Dan's in Texas and Barbara's in Colorado. Research on Barbara Lamont's name didn't yield anything of interest. On to Dan Bellamy. I found little on him, other than that his middle name was Carson.

Feeling frustrated, I went to the college library site to use some of the databases to which I had access there. I could search newspapers from around the country, for example. I didn't know whether the sheriff's department had their own access to this, but if not, they could use the databases available through the public library. It also had access to these newspapers.

Half an hour later, I had the beginnings of a headache along with mounting exasperation. I had found mentions of the professors in the local paper, short puff pieces on their work as part of an ongoing series on Athena College's younger teachers. Nothing much of interest, although in the piece on Dan, he did mention having grown up on the Gulf Coast, though whether in Mississippi or Louisiana wasn't clear. He referred to both in the article.

I also searched Dixie Belle Compton but turned up nothing, not even another person with a similar name. Only various companies called Dixie Belle or Bell, and a few street addresses. I decided to try my luck in a genealogical database.

A broad search yielded nearly a hundred hits on Dixie Compton, but no Dixie Belle among them. I ruled out most of the hits on the basis of dates. I figured the late Ms. Compton was no older than forty, maybe forty-five at the outside. That narrowed the list down to five hits. I began checking them each in turn.

No luck. On a whim I searched for the name Dixie Belle with the age limit.

I hit pay dirt.

THIRTY

||||||||||||||||||||||||||||||||||

I found a Dixie Belle Lee born about thirty-six years ago in Biloxi, Mississippi. She seemed a likely candidate. I searched her full name, with date parameters, in the newspaper index, and I got a couple of hits. One was a marriage announcement from eighteen years ago, when Miss Dixie Belle Lee married one Lewis Smathers in Baton Rouge. The dates fit, and the grainy picture of the bride-to-be could be Dixie Belle Compton, I thought, though I really couldn't be sure.

Four years later, according to the second hit, Mrs. Dixie Lee Smathers, a divorcée, married Ray David Bellamy in Biloxi, Mississippi. Mr. Bellamy was described as an employee of an oil company. I was pretty sure Dan had said his brother's name was Ray, but that they'd had different fathers. I tried to recall the conversation. Had Dan mentioned the name Compton? Or had he let us assume that was his brother's surname for some reason?

More details of the conversation came back to me. Dan

had never directly said that his brother's surname was Compton, though he had definitely said they had different fathers. He had allowed us to assume that Compton was his brother's name. But why?

Maybe he didn't want the name Bellamy associated with the murder, especially of a woman who'd had an ugly reputation as a gold digger in Athena, involved in scandals with married men.

Who was Compton, then? Was he the third husband, the one to whom she referred in the history department? Viccy Kemp said she'd heard Dixie refer to a husband, and from the context it sounded like she was married.

Yet searching the name Dixie Compton hadn't brought up a valid result. I couldn't figure it out. Was there a Compton? Or had she simply changed her name to distance herself from her second husband and his brother?

I searched for Ray Bellamy in the genealogical database and found a death record. He had died four years ago. That much at least was true.

Kanesha hadn't mentioned any of this, so it seemed obvious that her staff hadn't uncovered it. I wrote her an e-mail, detailing my findings. After I sent it, I texted her to request that she check her e-mail immediately.

Five minutes later, she called.

"How did you find this? We obviously missed it," she said, sounding annoyed.

That's why it pays to work with a librarian. I dismissed my snarky thought and hastened to explain.

"I see," she said. "Thanks for this. Dan Bellamy obviously has more questions to answer. I don't like it when people lie to me."

"I'm wondering now if there *is* a Mr. Compton involved in this," I said. "Could he be the missing connection you've been looking for?"

"I don't know," Kanesha said. "So far we haven't turned up anybody by that name here in Athena, even registered in one of the hotels or motels. I'm wondering if she changed her name for some reason."

"I think maybe she did, but I don't know why," I said. "There's got to be a reason, though. Have you turned up anything in Dan Bellamy's background that might shed light on this?"

"Not so far," Kanesha said, "other than a birth certificate and his driver's license. Education records. That's about it. I'll have my guys search the records again for Ray Bellamy, instead of Ray Compton, and see what they turn up."

I gave her the death date I'd found, and she thanked me.

"One more thing," I said. "Dan is supposed to be bringing Irene Warriner to dinner here tonight. I'm not sure why. Would you have time to drop by? At six."

"I think I'll make time," Kanesha said. "This could prove to be pretty interesting. See you later." She ended the call, and I laid my phone aside.

I heard the front doorbell ring. I wasn't expecting anyone, but sometimes Laura dropped in unexpectedly while she was out running errands. She didn't have classes on Tuesday or Thursday afternoons, I recalled. I hurried to the front door, and Diesel scurried ahead of me.

Laura, baby Charlie on her hip, diaper bag on the opposite shoulder, stood on the stoop.

"Sweetheart, this is a lovely surprise," I said, reaching out for my grandson. He came to me readily, and Laura laughed as she stepped inside.

"He's always happy to see his grandfather," she said. "So am I." She let the diaper bag slip off her shoulder to the floor and gave me a quick kiss on the cheek.

Charlie gurgled and flapped his hands at me, and I held

238

him slightly away from my body, my hands grasping either side of his torso.

"What have you been up to this afternoon, young man?" I asked. He gurgled again. "You haven't started walking yet, have you?" He smiled.

"Not yet," Laura said, "but he's a champion crawler. We just came from the pediatrician's office. He had a checkup."

"Come on into the kitchen; I know Azalea wants to see you both." Diesel stood on his hind legs, his front paws braced against my side, as he nuzzled at the baby's bottom. "Yes, I know you want to see him, too, Diesel." I headed for the kitchen, asking Laura over my shoulder, "What did the pediatrician have to say?"

"That your grandson is in the top percentile in every category," Laura said with obvious pride. "He's healthy as a baby horse, to boot."

"Of course he is," I said to Charlie. "You're amazing, young man." Charlie laughed and made more noises. I took that as his agreement. "Look who's dropped by for a visit," I said to Azalea when I entered the kitchen.

She turned away from the stove and started beaming the moment she spotted Laura and baby Charlie. "Let me see that precious angel." Azalea held out her arms, and Charlie seemed ready to jump. I hastily handed him over before he could wriggle loose. Azalea crooned to him.

I gestured for Laura to take a seat. "Would you like something to drink?"

"I'd kill for a cup of coffee," Laura said. "Just one, mind you. I had one earlier today, and I try to limit myself to no more than two a day."

She had explained to me early on, after Charlie was born, that both her doctor and Charlie's pediatrician had told her it was safe, as long as she didn't consume a lot of caffeine every day, or any while she was actually nursing.

"Coffee coming right up." I prepared the coffeemaker and then joined her at the table.

Azalea still had Charlie, bouncing him on her hip and singing to him in a low voice. He seemed enthralled by whatever song she had chosen. I couldn't quite make it out.

Laura gazed fondly at Azalea and her son. "She's wonderful with him, isn't she?" she said softly.

I nodded. Azalea had a gift. If she was around when either Charlie or Rosie was fussy, she could calm them quickly. I wasn't sure how she did it, but the babies obviously found her safe and soothing.

"What all is new with you?" I asked, one eye on the coffeemaker. "You look excited, even more so than from a good report from the baby's doctor."

"I am," she said. Diesel settled down beside the chair with his head on her feet. He rubbed against her shoes, marking them.

"We had a department meeting this morning, and I wanted you to be the first to know," Laura went on. "Frank was there, of course."

Laura had returned to her job in the college theater department this semester, now that she felt she could leave baby Charlie in the capable hands of the nanny she and her husband, Frank, shared with her brother, Sean, and his wife, Alex.

"I hadn't told you about this before," Laura said, "because I had no idea whether it would work out. You know how we always do a play in the spring semester with a guest actor."

When I nodded, she continued, "I can't tell you who that is going to be yet, but I think it's going to be somebody I worked with in Hollywood."

"After the time you spent there, you certainly ought to have some good contacts," I said.

"I did," she said. "But I've been gone for a couple of years now, and memories are short in Hollywood. If we can get the person I want, it's going to be great. And, the best part is, I'm playing the lead female role."

"Congratulations, sweetheart," I said. "I know you've missed acting. Is it a good part? Do I know the play?"

Laura shook her head. "It's a fairly new play by a writer with connections to Athena. It's called *Careless Whispers.*"

"Sounds like a mystery," I said.

"It is, and a fun one."

"When do you start rehearsals?" I asked.

"Not until early March," she said. "The run is set for late April. But, speaking of mysteries, how is it going with those campus murder cases? I'm sure you're in it up to your eyeballs."

She didn't sound censorious, as her brother probably would have. He had always been more critical of my sleuthing activities than Laura, though I know she had the same concerns about my welfare that Sean did.

"I am involved," I said, "in an advisory capacity." I wasn't sure I wanted to tell her that one of the suspects was currently living in my house. Actually, I hadn't thought about Dan as a serious candidate for the role of murderer until this afternoon. I couldn't understand why he would lie, at least by omission in this instance, about his late brother.

Laura giggled. "I know what that means. Kanesha is doing her best to keep you from getting too involved, but you're still going around, snooping." She sobered. "Promise me you'll be careful, Dad. You know we all worry."

"I know, sweetheart," I said. "I promise, I'm not going

to do anything foolish." I checked the coffeemaker again, and it had finished brewing. I got up to prepare coffee for Laura and me. Azalea never drank it, or else I would have made some for her. She continued to keep the baby occupied. Ramses danced around her feet, having suddenly appeared from wherever he'd been all this time.

Laura took her coffee like I did mine, with cream and sugar. She accepted the mug gratefully and took a long sip. "Ahh, much better."

"How much do you know about what's happened?" I asked, curious to discover what kind of gossip was going around campus. The theater department, like every other department at the college, stewed over every bit of scandal attached to faculty, staff, or students.

"Two murders," Laura said. "One professor and one student, who may or may not have been having an affair."

That was worse than I expected. "Any bets on who the murderer is?"

Laura looked uncomfortable. "I hate to say it, but most people think it has to be Irene Warriner. I've met her a couple of times, and she seems like a perfectly nice woman. I have a hard time seeing her killing anyone, but if her husband really was cheating on her, well, who knows?"

"It's possible that he was," I said. "Has there been any talk about Mrs. Warriner having an affair?"

"Yes." Laura grimaced. "She's been seen in the company of two men, one big blond guy who I think is from the history department. The other one is that gorgeous Frenchman with the lovely accent. Music department, I think."

I nodded. "Yes, Armand d'Arcy. He's actually Canadian, from Quebec, and he does have a noticeable accent. Teaches early music and plays the baroque bassoon."

"I'll have to pay more attention the next time the early-music group on campus gives a concert," Laura said. "I've never seen a baroque bassoon, or heard one, either, that I know of." She took another sip of coffee. "Some people are saying that she's had affairs with both men. Who's the blond guy?"

"Dan Bellamy," I replied. "He's a history professor. His specialty is Regency-era England. That's the period she writes about in her historical fiction. Remember, I told you about her. Lucy Dunne."

"Right," Laura said. "One of these days, when I actually have some time to read for pleasure, I want to try one of her books." She glanced at her son, still happily swaying on my housekeeper's hip. "That imp of a grandson doesn't give either his father or me much time to relax, between work and looking after him. Cherelle is a godsend, I have to tell you." She directed her last remark to Azalea.

Azalea nodded. "She's a fine girl. Loves looking after babies."

"She has your gift with them," Laura said, and Azalea smiled.

Laura glanced at the kitchen clock and groaned. "I hate to go, but I've got to get home. Frank and I have to get ready for dinner with some of our colleagues tonight. It'll take me two hours to get him ready." She giggled. "Frank, I mean. Cherelle will be taking care of Charlie this evening." She rose.

"I'm sorry you have to go so soon," I said, "but I understand. We're happy to see you and Charlie even for a few minutes."

Azalea handed Charlie to his mother, anxiously watched by Diesel. Ramses meowed loudly, wanting to be noticed, and Laura said hello to him and called him a good boy. That seemed to appease him. He had learned his name quickly and generally responded to it. Except when he was too intent on mischief, that is.

I grabbed the diaper bag, and Diesel and I escorted Laura and Charlie out to the car. I strapped Charlie into his car seat under Diesel's supervision, and Laura slid into the driver's seat.

"Thanks for the coffee, Dad," she said. "You be careful, all right? Don't do anything rash."

"I won't, I promise," I said. *Besides having a potential murderer or two in the house for dinner tonight*, I added silently as she backed out of the driveway and drove off.

THIRTY-ONE

I had little doubt as to what my children—and their respective spouses—would have to say if they knew that the prime suspect in the two murders, Irene Warriner, was coming to dine at my house tonight. With Dan Bellamy, who remained a large question mark in my mind. What was his role in all this? Accessory to murder, perhaps, helping Irene dispose of Carey Warriner's body.

As Diesel and I made our way back to the kitchen, I took comfort in the fact that Kanesha would be present. With her, and possibly Haskell as well, in the house, we should all be safe enough. I began to relax.

Azalea stood once again at the stove with Ramses watching her intently.

"Do you know if Stewart and Haskell will be joining us for dinner tonight?" I asked.

"Yes, they'll be here," Azalea said. "I've already laid the dining room table for five, unless somebody else is coming."

"Better make it six," I said. "Kanesha is going to join us."

Azalea turned quickly to face me. "What on earth for?" She didn't sound pleased.

"Business," I said. "I don't want to say anything more, but I need her here tonight."

Azalea turned back to the stove. "If you say so."

"I'll go set the other place. Helen Louise is working at the bistro tonight." I was glad of that. I didn't want her to be involved in any unpleasantness that might take place in my dining room tonight.

"All right," Azalea said. "Everything will be ready by five thirty, and you can set it all in the dining room or serve from here."

"Thanks. What's on the menu?" The aromas were tantalizing, but they mingled and were hard to separate.

"Tomato soup. Stewart asked for that, now that it's turning cold outside," Azalea replied. "Salad, pork chops, asparagus, and mashed potatoes."

"Sounds, and smells, wonderful." I headed for the dining room. Diesel remained in the kitchen.

Once I finished setting the extra place at the table, I went back to the kitchen. I checked the time. Nearly five thirty. Azalea would be leaving soon.

"Would you mind taking Ramses home with you for tonight?" I had thought about it while I was in the dining room. Unless I put him in his crate, he would be a pest at the table, egging Diesel on with his naughty behavior. He would howl if I put him in the crate when he could smell the food.

Azalea frowned at me. "Why do you want me to take him?"

I explained my reasons, and she shrugged. "All right, I guess it can't hurt." She checked her various pots and pans one last time and then made preparations to leave.

She scooped up Ramses and put him in her bag. His head peeped out, and he meowed as if saying, *Look at me.*

"You be good for Azalea," I told him, and he meowed again.

Once he and Azalea were safely out the door, I checked the stove to make sure everything would be okay while I dashed upstairs to freshen up. Diesel trotted up the stairs after me.

I changed my shirt. I had discovered a small stain, no doubt from lunch earlier today, and didn't want to look grubby in front of my guests. When I reached the head of the stairs, Diesel ran down ahead of me. I heard sounds issuing from the kitchen. I hurried down and found Stewart standing over the stove.

He turned when I greeted him. "Hi, Charlie. Azalea told me that Dan is bringing a guest tonight. Irene Warriner, I think she said. Is that true?"

"Yes, it is. Are you okay with that?" I asked.

"Why not? It's been a long time since I dined with the chief murder suspect," he said cheekily. "I'm sure this will prove to be an interesting evening."

"You haven't heard the best part," I said. "Kanesha is going to be here, too."

He eyed me shrewdly. "Something's up, then. Are you narrowing in on the killer? Is it really Irene Warriner?"

"I don't know. She's the prime suspect, for various reasons, but I found out that Dan has been less than truthful about something."

"And what would that be?" Stewart asked.

"He led us to think that Compton was his brother's name," I said. "Not a huge lie, I suppose, but still, he lied by omission, if nothing else."

"That's a stupid thing to do," Stewart said. "He had to know that the cops would find that out."

I shrugged. "I'd have thought so, but who knows? Listen, before anyone else gets here, can you think of anything Dan might have told you about his background? Where he grew up, that kind of thing? You said you chatted with him at the gym."

Stewart frowned. "I'll have to think about it. At one point he mentioned the Gulf Coast. Biloxi, I think. He never said anything about his brother or his brother's wife." He paused, and after a moment, he resumed. "I seem to recall he said something about growing up kind of poor. He worked his way through school. Got a couple of scholarships, but they weren't enough to cover everything. I got the impression his parents couldn't do much for him in the way of financial support."

"That's interesting," I said. "Anything else?"

Stewart shook his head. "No, he really didn't talk about himself that much, other than the occasional remark about his students." He grinned suddenly. "You know we professors always gripe about our students when we get together."

I laughed. "Yes, I've heard that. Haskell will be here, too, won't he?"

"Any minute," Stewart said after a glance at the clock. He gestured to the stove. "Do you want to dish this all up and put it in the dining room, or should we let people fill their plates here?"

"Whatever you think," I said. "I'm fine either way."

"I say if we're going to entertain a murderess at dinner, then we should do it properly," Stewart said with an arch look. "I'll get everything ready to put in the dining room on the sideboard."

"Tell me what to do, and I'll help," I said.

Diesel, as usual, watched us carefully as we worked to get all the food safely transferred into the proper containers and then into the dining room. The time had just gone six when we finished and I heard someone at the front door.

I walked into the hallway to see Haskell heading upstairs in his uniform. He liked to change out of it when he didn't have to go back out later. He'd be back down quickly, efficient in anything he did. While I stood there, I heard a key in the lock. The door opened to admit Dan Bellamy, accompanied by Irene Warriner. I moved forward to greet them.

Irene looked wan and tired, which didn't surprise me. She had to be under tremendous strain. Dan, beside her, looked calm and unruffled, though he did glance at Irene with a concerned expression.

"Good evening, Mrs. Warriner," I said. "Welcome. I hope you'll enjoy dinner tonight."

"Thank you, and please call me Irene," she said, taking my extended hand. "May I call you Charlie?"

"Of course," I said. "And this is Diesel, if you remember."

Irene looked down at my cat, who had come up to her. She reached out and stroked him tentatively. "I thought about bringing Jonesy, my dog," she said. "He's so lonesome by himself, but I didn't know how you felt about dogs."

"Stewart has a poodle, and he and Diesel play well together. Of course, Diesel is a good bit larger," I said. "He hasn't been around many other dogs, though, so I'm not sure how he would react to a strange one."

She continued to stroke Diesel's head, with more assurance, and Diesel seemed happy for her to do so. Dan removed his coat and hung it on the rack, then he assisted Irene with hers.

"We'll be eating in the dining room tonight," I said. "If you'd like to wash your hands, there's a powder room under the stairs there." I indicated the door.

Irene smiled. "Thank you, that would be lovely. If you'll excuse me." She moved past us, and I turned to Dan. "How are you doing? I haven't seen you lately."

Dan shrugged. "I'm fine. I've been busy with my classes as usual. Not much time for anything else."

"You've been looking after Irene, though," I said.

"A bit," Dan said. "Thank you for allowing me to bring her here for dinner. I thought it would be better for her than sitting at home by herself with the dog. If she goes out anywhere, people stare at her and whisper behind her back. It's been a considerable strain on her."

"I can certainly understand that." The doorbell rang, and I excused myself to answer it. Diesel reached the door before I did. I opened the door to admit Kanesha.

I don't know why I'd expected her to show up in uniform. Probably because I rarely saw her wear anything else. She had changed, however, into a smart black pantsuit with a white blouse and a string of pearls around her neck.

She noted my surprise but did not say anything. "Good evening, Kanesha. I'm glad you could join us."

"Thank you for inviting me," Kanesha said. "I always enjoy my mother's cooking."

I let that little jab pass by. I shut the door behind her. Diesel regarded her for a moment, meowed, then trotted into the kitchen.

Dan stood looking at the deputy, his expression unreadable. I had wondered how he and Irene would react to Kanesha's presence tonight. They were free to leave, of course, but since Kanesha appeared out of uniform, maybe they would relax a bit and stay. I wondered at Kanesha's strategy. I didn't think her being out of uniform was going to stop her from being on duty. She was rarely ever *not* on duty.

"Good evening, Dr. Bellamy," Kanesha said. "I hear that you're a fan of my mother's cooking, too."

At this cordial remark, Dan seemed to loosen up somewhat. He nodded. "Yes, she's a wonderful cook. Reminds me of my grandmother and the meals she used to make."

Irene Warriner emerged from the powder room and at first didn't seem to realize who Kanesha was. Then her expression changed, and for a moment, I thought I read panic in her eyes.

"Good evening, Mrs. Warriner," Kanesha said.

"Good evening, Deputy Berry," Irene replied. "I must admit I didn't expect to see you here tonight."

"I'm a friend of the Harris family," Kanesha said blandly.

I looked up to see Haskell coming down the stairs. He always did it fast, and I envied him his ability to do it without stumbling and breaking his neck. These days I was a lot more cautious. He wore dark slacks and a white shirt, collar open at the neck, his sleeves rolled back to expose tanned wrists.

"Good evening, everyone," he said.

I was watching Irene to gauge her reaction to the presence of another deputy. She closed her eyes briefly and inhaled, as if to steady herself. Surely Dan had told her about Haskell and his connection to Stewart and that he would possibly be present at dinner tonight. I doubted either Dan or Irene had expected to see both him and Kanesha at dinner, though. Irene now looked even more pale than before.

"Let's go into the dining room, shall we?" I said in a bright tone. "Azalea prepared an excellent meal for us. Stewart has been busy making sure everything is ready." I led the way, and Dan and Irene followed me. Kanesha and Haskell, with Diesel, brought up the rear.

I discovered that Stewart had filled the water glasses, and there was a pitcher of iced tea on the sideboard. He greeted everyone and directed them to their places. He had Irene sit to my left at the head of the table, with Dan across from her. Kanesha sat next to Dan, and Haskell next to Irene. That left Stewart at the other end of the table facing me. Azalea had earlier removed the leaf to accommodate the small number of this dinner party, so there were no gaps between anyone.

"Now, who would like iced tea with dinner?" Stewart picked up the pitcher and glanced around. "If you'd like something stronger, I believe there's wine in the fridge. It won't take a moment to get it and a wineglass."

Everyone opted for tea, and Stewart filled the glasses, making a circuit around the table, starting with Irene. I watched her covertly, and I saw her hand shake a little when she reached for her water glass. She sipped at the water like she was dying of thirst.

Stewart took his seat and looked at me. I hadn't planned to say grace, as I always did at family meals. I gave a slight shrug. Stewart made the decision. "I'll say grace," he said.

Dan looked startled, as did Kanesha, but they both bowed their heads. I fancied I could feel the tension emanating from Irene while Stewart intoned a simple prayer. After we had all said *Amen*, Stewart picked up the platter of chops and began passing them. He directed me to begin serving myself with the asparagus near my place.

For a minute or so we were all occupied with sending the various dishes around the table. I was surprised that Stewart had changed his mind about putting everything on the sideboard. I wondered what had occasioned the change. I thought about various mysteries I'd read over the years, and I realized that he might have decided it was safer this way. It would be harder for someone to put poison on anything.

I pushed away that macabre thought. I didn't think Irene or Dan would dare try to poison someone tonight. Surely that hadn't been Stewart's reason, but I wouldn't put it past him.

Once everyone had been served, I glanced around the table. Irene stared at her plate, Dan kept darting glances at Kanesha, but Haskell seemed undisturbed by the atmosphere of unease. I was about to introduce a mild topic of conversation, the weather, when Irene shocked everyone by suddenly rising from her chair.

"I can't do this," she cried. "It's too much. I know you're here to try to trap me." She pointed a finger at Kanesha. "You think I'm a murderer." She sobbed out the last word. "Then go ahead and arrest me and get it over with." She sank back into her chair, suddenly gasping for breath, and then she fainted and slid out of her chair onto the floor.

THIRTY-TWO

||||||||||||||||||||||||||||||||||||||||||||||||||||||||||||||||||

I sat immobile, shocked by Irene Warriner's collapse. Haskell, however, responded immediately. He thrust her chair out of the way and knelt beside her while I watched, praying that my fanciful notions of poison were no more than that. The only person in the room who might have tried to murder her was Dan Bellamy, and I couldn't figure out when he would have had an opportunity to do so.

I glanced at Dan beside me and was startled by his expression of anguish. He appeared to be frozen into place. Suddenly he burst into movement, knocking his chair back as he stood. "Oh my Lord, Irene. What's wrong with her?" he demanded. "Save her, don't let her die."

Kanesha grabbed him before he could charge around the table to get in Haskell's way. He tried to shrug off her arm, but she exerted her strength and forced him back into his chair. "Bates knows what he's doing," she said. "Stay out of his way."

Dan glared at her, struggling to break free of her grip, but something in her expression must have convinced him she meant to keep him where he was. He subsided, but Kanesha didn't let go of his arm.

"Call 911," Haskell said tersely. "Labored breathing. I'll do mouth-to-mouth if necessary."

I was still too shaken to respond, but I saw Stewart, phone in hand, fulfilling Haskell's order. Kanesha released her hold, and Dan went around to assist Haskell.

"Don't let her die," Dan said, his tone verging on frantic. "She can't die on me." He no longer conveyed the manner of the detached friend. Now he had apparently let his true feelings for Irene surge to the surface, and I thought, *He's in love with her after all.* His naked fear for Irene's life had stripped away his façade.

I heard the doorbell, and I jumped up. Diesel, who had been cowering under my chair, darted out of the room. The emergency services personnel had responded in record time, I thought, as I hurried to let them in.

I flung open the door, after pushing Diesel out of the way and telling him to stay where he was. I expected several EMTs to rush in, but to my astonishment I found Armand d'Arcy on my front doorstep.

"I must find Irène," he said as he stepped inside. "Take me to her immediately. I must speak with her." When I did not respond right away, he said in tones of rising impatience and panic, "Where is she?" He reached out as if to shake me, but the sound of approaching sirens, growing ever louder, stopped him.

"She has collapsed," I said. "The EMTs are coming here. You must get out of the way."

He darted around me and started looking into each room along the hall until he found the dining room. He disappeared inside. I wanted to go after him but knew that Kanesha would deal with him. I needed to stay where I was to guide the EMTs.

The time until the EMTs appeared on the walk, rushing toward the front door, seemed interminable but probably was no more than a minute and a half. Diesel had disappeared up the stairs, and I knew I'd find him on my bed, his head burrowed under a pillow.

I directed the emergency crew to the dining room and trailed after them. There was nothing I could do, but I wanted to know if Irene Warriner was alive. The thought of a guest dying in my dining room was intolerable, but my concern was for Irene herself.

When I reached the doorway and looked inside, I saw that Haskell had yielded his place to the crew. He now had a grip on Armand d'Arcy, who was screaming in French and struggling to get to Irene. Kanesha had her hands full with Dan Bellamy, who seemed to want to attack d'Arcy. Stewart had placed himself between the two duos, ready to run interference, I supposed, if necessary.

One of the EMTs, a tall, muscular-looking woman, stood to address Kanesha. "She's stable for the moment, but we need to get her to the ER. Can you clear the room?"

"Yes," Kanesha said. "To the kitchen." She forcibly turned Dan toward the door and pushed him forward. I moved hastily out of the way to let them pass. A few seconds ticked by, during which I heard d'Arcy still yelling in French. Then Stewart and Haskell forced him, struggling the whole time, out of the dining room. He seemed frantic to get to Irene. Had he completely lost his mind? What did he think he could do for her at this moment?

Stewart and Haskell didn't give him a chance to do anything. They frog-marched him to the kitchen with me in their wake. I was prepared to coldcock him if he somehow got loose. I abhorred violence, but d'Arcy had irritated me to the point of being willing to hit him, if that was what it took to ensure his cooperation.

I was concerned about Diesel, but I knew that he would be perfectly safe upstairs in my bedroom. I kept pace with the trio ahead of me, and when we reached the kitchen, I shut the door to the hall and stood with my back to it.

Dan Bellamy occupied a chair, and Kanesha stood at the sink, filling a pitcher with water. D'Arcy had not ceased his ranting, and Kanesha calmly came toward him with the water. D'Arcy was too worked up to realize what she intended, and the cold water shocked him into silence. He evidently swallowed some of it and started coughing. Haskell thumped him on the back, and after a tense few moments, he subsided.

D'Arcy stumbled toward the table, one foot sliding in the water on the floor, but the sight of Dan Bellamy appeared to enrage him all over again. He launched himself at Dan and hit him with such force that Dan went over backward in his chair.

By the time Dan hit the floor with d'Arcy on top of him, however, Kanesha and Haskell reached them and dragged d'Arcy away. Stewart knelt by Dan. I was relieved to see that he appeared to have suffered no significant injury, but it took him a moment to right himself. With Stewart's help, he managed to get up off the floor.

I scrambled to find a couple of dishcloths to wipe up the water. In the meantime Kanesha was telling d'Arcy that unless he ceased his belligerent actions immediately, she would handcuff him to a chair. D'Arcy appeared finally to recognize the voice of authority. He sat when she pointed to a chair but regarded her with a sullen expression.

I glanced at Dan as I placed the sopping cloths in the

sink. His own expression, directed to d'Arcy, was murderous. I couldn't blame him for his anger. I wondered whether he would press charges against d'Arcy for assault. I wouldn't blame him if he did. What was behind this outrageous behavior of d'Arcy's?

Haskell left the kitchen, and I wondered whether he was headed upstairs to retrieve his handcuffs. Probably not a bad idea, I figured. In the uneasy silence that prevailed in the kitchen, I could hear him running up the stairs. Stewart remained near Dan.

"I want to press charges for this completely unprovoked assault," Dan said, his voice cold and controlled.

"All right." Kanesha pulled out her phone and tapped in a number. After a moment, she identified herself to the person who responded. She gave my address and requested a squad car to pick up d'Arcy.

As she put away her phone, she glanced between the two men. D'Arcy had not reacted to Dan's statement or to Kanesha's phone call. Haskell reappeared, now in uniform, complete with handcuffs and gun. Kanesha informed him that backup was on the way, and he nodded.

Still d'Arcy did not react. He and Dan glared at each other, and the tension in the room made me want to hurry upstairs and join Diesel. I stayed where I was, however. I knew I might have to talk to the police, although with Kanesha and Haskell as witnesses, they wouldn't need much corroboration from Stewart or me.

D'Arcy spoke, startling me. "You should not arrest me. He is the one who should go to jail." He pointed at Dan, who started to rise from his chair. One look from Kanesha, however, stopped him.

"Why should I arrest him?" Kanesha asked in a mild tone. "You are the one who attacked him."

Haskell walked over to stand beside Dan and indicated

that Stewart should join me on the sidelines. He promptly did so.

D'Arcy snorted. "Because if you do not, he will harm *ma belle* Irène. His attentions to her are unwelcome, and he knows this. He knows that she prefers me, and this makes him angry."

Dan laughed, a harsh, grating sound. He rattled off a few words of French, and d'Arcy's face suffused with red. He half rose from his chair, but Kanesha's hand on his shoulder stopped him.

"What did he say to you?" Kanesha asked.

"What you would expect from one of his sort," d'Arcy said. The contempt in his tone obviously riled Dan, but with Haskell next to him, Dan didn't dare move. "What is it you say in English? A guttersnipe, *oui*, that is the word. He is a guttersnipe."

I hadn't heard anyone use that epithet in real life, though I had encountered it in historical fiction often enough.

Stewart murmured in my ear. "Dan called him *un salaud*."

A bastard.

I recognized the word as one Helen Louise had informed me was insulting to a French speaker. The two men obviously loathed each other, both jealous of the other's interest in Irene. Did she actually favor one over the other? Or were they both imagining that she, so recently bereaved, had romantic feelings toward either of them?

If Irene had been committing adultery like her husband, however, this proprietary attitude of d'Arcy's would be more understandable. Particularly if he were the man with whom she'd been having the affair. Until tonight Dan had never demonstrated any strong feelings toward Irene. How they behaved with each other in private, however, could have been completely different.

Considering that both of these men were in love, perhaps deeply so, with Irene Warriner, I had little trouble considering that one of them had murdered Carey Warriner. But why would either of them have killed Dixie Belle Compton? If I could answer that question, I thought, I would know who killed Warriner.

Unless Irene Warriner had killed her in a fit of jealousy over her husband's affair.

Which brought me back to square one. Her collapse at the dinner table notwithstanding, Irene Warriner was as capable of having killed two people as either of the men in my kitchen. I hoped Kanesha had more information at her disposal than I did and would soon bring this case to a close. My nerves couldn't take much more of this.

I marveled that Dan had said nothing to counter Armand d'Arcy's accusations. I eyed him uneasily. Now he appeared cold, remote, completely detached from the situation. What was going through his mind? Why didn't he speak up in his defense, or at least denounce his rival? I couldn't understand it.

When the doorbell rang, Stewart announced that he would admit the police. I was thankful they had arrived. The sooner both men were out of my house, the happier I would be. I decided that I would ask Dan to find other accommodations until his renovations were complete. I would be happy to refund the money he had paid me. I remembered then that I hadn't yet made it to the bank to deposit the check. I would simply tear it up and give it back to him. Relieved by my decision, I felt slightly better.

Two Athena police officers appeared in the kitchen, led by Stewart. Kanesha explained the situation, identifying the two men. One of the officers asked Dan if he wished to press charges. Dan replied in the affirmative, and the other officer cuffed Armand d'Arcy and issued a

brusque command to accompany them to police head-
quarters. The first officer escorted Dan out, following his
colleague and d'Arcy.

"You go with them," Kanesha said to Haskell, and he
left the room. "I'm going to the hospital to check on Mrs.
Warriner," she informed Stewart and me. "Sorry about
the ruined dinner," she added.

I had completely forgotten about dinner in all the drama.
I wasn't sure I still had any appetite, but I would certainly
put the food away. No reason for it to spoil.

"Will you let us know how Mrs. Warriner is doing?" I
asked. "How serious is her condition, do you think?"

"To answer your second question, I think she might
have had a panic attack brought on by stress," Kanesha
said. "Not anything I expected, or I wouldn't have accepted the invitation to dinner tonight. I will let you know
how she's doing once I find out more." She nodded and
headed out of the kitchen.

I turned to Stewart. "Do you feel like eating?"

Stewart grimaced. "Would you think me terrible if I
said I do?"

"Not at all," I said. "Go ahead. I'm going to check on
Diesel, then I'll start putting the food away."

"Don't worry, I'll do it," Stewart said. "Are you sure
you don't want anything?"

I hesitated, and my stomach betrayed me by rumbling.
Lunch had been over six hours ago, after all. "Maybe a
little something," I said. "After I check on Diesel."

Stewart nodded and I left the room.

I didn't have to go far to check on my cat. I found him
coming down the stairs. He had somehow figured out that
things had calmed down and thus felt it safe to return. I
was relieved to see him. He greeted me with a couple of
loud, complaining meows, and I smiled.

"Come on, boy, let's go to the dining room, and I'll find you a treat or two." He followed me happily then.

We found Stewart calmly eating, even though his food had cooled. I looked at the table. So much food untouched on the plates. I sighed. I hated to throw it out. I picked up my plate and told Stewart I was going to the kitchen to warm it in the microwave. He nodded.

"Come on, Diesel," I told the cat, and he followed me.

I set the plate in the microwave and selected the time and power. While the plate rotated in the microwave, I watched it, my thoughts drifting back to tonight's melee.

Jealousy. That seemed to lie at the root of the murders. I remembered that Miss Dickce had mentioned Shakespeare's *Othello*, a powerful example of malignant jealousy. For the first time in my life, I thought, I had encountered something similar.

The microwave pinged, and I gingerly withdrew my plate and set it on the table. I retrieved a fork and sat down to eat.

Jealousy.

Othello.

I laid my fork aside as a thought struck me. Could my wild notion possibly be right?

THIRTY-THREE

||||||||||||||||||||||||||||||||||||||||||||||||||||||||||||||||||||||||||||||||||||||

I picked up my fork again and stuck it into something on my plate. I was too distracted by my thoughts to pay much attention to what I was eating. I almost burned the roof of my mouth and my tongue on the first bite, however, and that brought me back to earth. I let the food cool for about thirty seconds before I attempted another bite, but I blew on it before I put it in my mouth.

Diesel placed a large paw on my thigh to remind me that I had promised treats, and I pulled off a bite of pork chop and gave it to him.

My wild idea about how jealousy played its role in the two murders was formed by something I'd heard tonight and that needed corroboration. Kanesha might already have the information. I wished she would hurry and call to let me know about Irene Warriner's status. If I were correct in my thinking, Irene wasn't the murderer, but she was the reason that two people had died. I could be completely off base, though, and might have fingered the wrong person. Only getting more information would tell me whether I was correct.

Stewart walked into the kitchen and took his plate to the sink. He turned to me. "What do you want to do with the plated food? I'm planning to save Haskell's for later. Do you think I should do the same for Dan?"

"No," I said. "I intend to ask Dan to leave the house first thing in the morning. I'd rather he go tonight, but that is probably too much to expect. I don't have any idea how long it will be before he finishes at the police station."

"He might want to go to the hospital afterward," Stewart said. "I didn't think he was in love with Irene Warriner until this evening."

"I'm not completely convinced that he's in love with *her*," I said.

Stewart appeared not to have noticed my slight emphasis on the pronoun. "Frankly, I thought he might be one of those people who simply isn't interested in a relationship with either sex. We see a lot of attractive men and women at the gym when we work out, and I don't recall ever hearing Dan make a comment about any one of them." He laughed. "Trust me, that's unusual."

"I agree."

Diesel evidently was still convinced that he hadn't had enough to eat, because I felt the paw of demand on my thigh again. "I'm going to have to put both of us on a diet," I told him, even as I gave him another bite of pork chop.

"What about the food?" Stewart reminded me. "I won't save Dan's, but I hate to throw out everyone else's when nobody had time to even taste it."

"I don't want to save what was plated," I said. "But whatever wasn't plated we can keep, along with Haskell's dinner, if you think he'll want it."

"He probably will," Stewart said. "Okay, I'll put away

what we can save, then I'll clear away the rest. I don't want to be the one to tell Azalea, though, what happened to her delicious dinner."

"I won't, unless I have to," I said. "I'm sure she'd understand."

Stewart grinned. "She might find some way to blame Kanesha for it. You know how they are."

"They're too much alike," I said. "That's the problem."

Stewart left the kitchen, and I got up to put my plate in the sink. "That's all, Diesel." He meowed sadly in response before trotting off to the utility room. I leaned against the sink cabinet and considered what to do.

I debated texting Kanesha with my questions, but I thought that might aggravate her unnecessarily. Considering how easily I irritated her in general, I didn't need to go to extra lengths. I stood a better chance of getting information from her if I waited to hear from her first.

Instead I focused on what I would say to Dan when he returned to the house. I'd prefer to talk to him with Haskell here, because I wasn't sure how he might react. I feared there might be pent-up rage waiting to boil over, since he had restrained himself, for the most part, during the scene with Armand d'Arcy. D'Arcy was so obviously the volatile type, one who boiled over easily, whereas I thought Dan was the opposite, the type to stew for a long time. When he did erupt, it might be epic, compared to d'Arcy.

How could I frame what I wanted to say to Dan in a polite, inoffensive way?

I heard Melba's voice in my head. *I want you to get the hell out of my house. That's what you say to him.*

I shook my head. No, I couldn't do that. *Dan, I think it best if you find somewhere else to stay while your renovations are completed. I don't feel comfortable with this arrangement any longer.*

That sounded polite enough, I reckoned. Would he be offended? I wasn't sure. A reasonable person ought to understand why I thought it best he remove himself from my house. But how reasonable was he?

Why hadn't Kanesha called?

Surely she ought to be able to get information out of the ER staff more quickly than a mere human like I could. If nothing else, I thought, she could get hold of that cardiologist she dated for a while and get him to run interference for her, if her badge wasn't enough.

Diesel came back from the utility room and dropped three pieces of his dry food on the floor by my feet. He looked up at me before he picked one up again and crunched it in his mouth. He went through the same routine with the other two pieces.

"See, I told you that you weren't going to starve," I said.

In response he began to clean his right front paw and ignored me. I grinned and rubbed his head, and that earned me a couple of chirps.

Come on, Kanesha, call me.

I halfway expected the phone to ring, but it didn't. I stirred restlessly from my position against the sink and went back to my usual place at the table. Diesel followed me and stretched out on the floor near my chair. Perhaps I should follow his example and go to the den, stretch out on the sofa there, or up to the bedroom. I half rose, then sat down again. I couldn't settle.

I pulled out my phone and laid it on the table, almost willing it to ring. It lay there, inert, silent, frustrating me. Stewart, carrying three plates from the dining room table, bustled back into the kitchen. One plate he set aside on the counter, the other two he took into the utility room to dump into the garbage there. He came back in a moment and set those two in the sink. Then he found the plastic wrap to put over Haskell's plate and set the covered plate in the fridge.

"Now for the leftovers," he said.

"I should help," I said.

Stewart waved me away. "No, I'll do it." He glanced at me, his gaze shrewd. "I know the mood you're in. You think you've got this thing figured out, and you're brooding over it. Am I right?"

I responded with a rueful grin. "Waiting to talk to Kanesha. I need information."

"Then stay right where you are," Stewart said. "I'll be Donny Domestic and you be Sherlock, sans pipe or cocaine."

I rolled my eyes at his retreating back. He was irrepressible.

I glared at my phone, and it startled me by ringing. My heart racing, I looked at the number of the incoming call. Finally.

"Hello," I said to Kanesha. "How is she?"

"Panic attack, like I thought," Kanesha replied. "They've given her meds, and they're checking her heart and so on, but they're pretty sure the stress got to her and brought this on. Evidently it's not the first time."

"I'm glad she's okay," I said. "Do you think this was guilt-induced? Do you believe she committed the murders?"

"I don't think she did," Kanesha said. "I have someone else in mind for the part."

"So do I," I said. "But I need information from you to clinch it in my mind."

"Like what?" Kanesha asked sharply.

"Background," I said. "Childhood stuff, really."

"Like who had a deprived childhood and who didn't, you mean?"

"Pretty much," I said. "My idea rests on the fact that the killer grew up pretty poor and is looking for money."

Kanesha caught on immediately. "In that case, I can tell you, both d'Arcy and Bellamy come from poor backgrounds. Not much money in either case. Same thing with Barbara Lamont."

Barbara Lamont. Hearing her name startled me, because I had basically eliminated her from my calculations. She might have grown up poor, like the other two, but I couldn't see how she otherwise might fit the profile I'd built up in my mind.

Unless . . .

No, I thought she was in love with Carey Warriner, not Irene. Both Helen Louise and I had thought so. D'Arcy and Bellamy were in love with Irene, not Barbara Lamont.

I expressed these thoughts to Kanesha.

"Interesting," she said. "Dr. Lamont never admitted to me that she was in love with Carey Warriner, or Irene Warriner, for that matter. Not something I considered, really. Is there anything else?"

I'd been so caught up in my thoughts I'd nearly forgotten she was still on the line.

"There are a couple of things. Have you found any trace of Dixie Compton's alleged current husband? And when do you think Haskell might be home again?"

"Still no trace of a current husband," Kanesha said. "We're working another lead, however, that may explain that situation with regard to her source of income.

"Now, for your second question," Kanesha said. "Bates won't be home until the business at the police department is done. He'll be keeping an eye on Bellamy and will escort him back to your place."

"Good," I said. "I wasn't looking forward to facing him on my own."

"What do you mean?" Kanesha asked.

"I'm going to ask Dan to leave my house and go back to his place," I said. "I don't feel comfortable with his staying here after what happened tonight."

"I see. Can't say I blame you," Kanesha said. "Frankly, I can't understand why he wanted to rent a room at your place. Can't be just to eat my mama's food."

Had Kanesha made a joke? I wasn't sure, given how she felt about her mother working as my housekeeper.

"He told me he needed a quiet place to work while he's having renovations done to his house," I said. "He's working on a book, and he doesn't want to be distracted by the commotion that comes with renovations."

"That's interesting," Kanesha said.

"How so?" I asked.

"That isn't what he told me," she said. "He told me, twice, that he was in the process of selling his house. The new owners would be moving in soon, but he hadn't had time to look for a new place."

"Maybe he's having renovations done that the new owners insisted had to be finished before they took possession," I said, though I thought that a bit far-fetched.

"If that was true," Kanesha said, "why didn't he tell us both the same thing?"

THIRTY-FOUR

||||||||||||||||||||||||||||||||||||||||||||||||||||||||||||||||||||||||||||

I felt a sudden chill.

Why, indeed, had Dan told Kanesha and me different stories about his reasons for renting a room in my house?

"I think maybe I should come back to your house," Kanesha said, "and wait for Haskell to bring Bellamy back there."

"I think you should, too," I said. "When you get here, I'll tell you the slightly crazy idea I came up with to explain what's behind these murders."

"I'll be on my way soon," Kanesha said. "I'll probably be there before Haskell gets back with Bellamy. Is Stewart still there?"

"Yes," I said. "He just walked into the kitchen."

"Stay together, just in case." Kanesha ended the call.

Stewart set down the containers he had brought from the dining room.

"Was that Haskell on the phone?" Stewart asked.

"Kanesha," I said.

"What did she have to say about Mrs. Warriner?" he asked as he looked for lids to the pots. When he didn't find them, he used plastic film to seal the pots.

I relayed to him what Kanesha had told me about Irene. Then I told him about the discrepancies in what Dan had told Kanesha and me about his reasons for renting a room here.

"That's strange," Stewart said. "Why would he lie about it? Or fail to tell the whole truth about it? That doesn't make any sense."

"I'm not sure," I said. "I can't imagine why he would want to be in my house, particularly. I suppose you and Haskell had talked about where you lived, and he thought it was a good option. Maybe it's no more than that."

"We did tell him about you," Stewart said, "and what a great landlord you are." He grinned, but the grin faded quickly. "Still, something doesn't feel quite right about it." He looked at me oddly, I thought.

"What?" I asked.

"Surely it can't have anything to do with your penchant for getting involved in murders," Stewart said.

"Unless he was planning to murder two people that he thought I was somehow connected to," I said, "I don't see how that would play into it."

Stewart frowned. "Hang on a minute. Didn't the first murder take place before he moved in here?"

"I believe it did," I said after thinking about it briefly, "but he asked you about the possibility of living here before the first murder, didn't he?"

Stewart nodded. "Yes, you're right. I'd forgotten. Still, it might have been premeditated. His intention to live here, that is."

"Like the murders were premeditated?" I asked.

"I guess so," Stewart replied.

271

Diesel could sense my unease. He stirred restlessly on the floor and meowed. I tried to reassure him with a few pats on the head, but I wasn't sure it worked.

"I'm going to take Dante a few bites of pork chop if you don't mind," Stewart said.

"Of course not," I said. "He's welcome to them. Don't be upstairs too long, though. Kanesha said we should stick together, just in case."

"In case of what?" Stewart asked.

"I'm not sure," I replied. "She ended the call before I could ask her."

"Surely she doesn't think Dan is going to attack you." Stewart shook his head in disbelief. "He'd have to get away from the police department and Haskell first. I don't think that's going to happen."

I felt reassured by Stewart's certainty. "No, you're right. But don't take too long, anyway."

"All right," Stewart said. "Back in two minutes, promise." He moved quickly out of the kitchen, and moments later I heard him run up the stairs.

I relaxed slightly, feeling better. Then I heard the front door open, and I tensed up again. I turned to see who came into the kitchen, hoping it would be Kanesha.

I was shocked to see Dan Bellamy. For a moment I couldn't catch my breath. Haskell appeared behind him, though, and I relaxed again.

"Have you heard anything?" Dan demanded. "How is Irene? I haven't been able to find out."

I caught Haskell's eye. He made a slight movement of his head. Hoping that I followed his cue correctly, I said, "No, I'm still waiting to hear from Kanesha."

"That's not good," Haskell said. "Kanesha would have called by now if Mrs. Warriner was going to be okay. EMT told me she looked like a heart case."

Dan looked almost panic-stricken at our words. He stumbled to a chair and dropped into it. "Oh God, don't let her die. She can't die." Elbows on the table, he cradled his head in his hands, palms against the eye sockets. He trembled, obviously in great distress.

"I hope it isn't her heart," I said. "She's so young, but of course anyone can have heart problems." Diesel moved closer to me, obviously unsettled by the tensions in the room.

Dan lifted his head and stared at me. "No, she can't, she just can't."

Was he playing the role of a distraught lover? I wondered. Trying to convince us that he was terrified of losing her?

Terrified of losing her money.

The thought came unbidden to my mind. I was convinced that the motive was nothing more than greed, pure and simple. Dan had been willing to murder two people to get to Irene Warriner, not only for what she would inherit from her husband but also for the money she would earn through her new contract for more books.

With Haskell there to protect me, I decided to gamble. The more I had thought about what lay behind the murders, and the contemptible way in which Carey Warriner must have been manipulated, the angrier I had become.

"It's a shame, isn't it?" I said with faux sympathy. "With Irene goes all that money." I shook my head. "The Warriners will get to keep it after all."

Dan looked at me, uncertainty in his expression.

I nodded. "All your planning, all that work, going down the drain when Irene kicks the bucket. You didn't count on her having a bad heart, did you?"

"What do you mean?" Dan glared at me.

"Exactly what I said." I tried to inject as much contempt

as I could into my tone. "You weren't thorough enough, though, were you? Didn't do all the research you should have, covered all the bases. You didn't think to look into Irene's medical history, and it's blown up in your face."

Dan laughed. "You're crazy, you know that? You think you're that old bat on TV, the one who's always finding dead bodies wherever she goes. You need help."

"Jessica Fletcher?" I laughed. "Well, maybe, but in this case, I'm not the crazy one. How on earth did you think you were going to get away with it? You're smart, I'll give you that. You couldn't have earned a Ph.D. without some intelligence. But you're not smart enough to get away with murder."

"So explain to me—if I really am a murderer—how I went about it," Dan said, seemingly oblivious now to Haskell's presence, he seemed so intent on me.

"Charlie, don't," Haskell said in a low voice, his tone harsh. I paid him no mind.

"I haven't completely figured out your relationship to Dixie Belle Compton," I admitted. "I suspect there was more to it than her having been married to your brother. Your brother, by the way, not your half brother. It wasn't too hard to find that out." I shook my head. "Really, you should have foreseen that one."

"Go on," Dan said.

"The way I see it, you promised her a cut of the proceeds, once you had Carey out of the way and managed to talk Irene into marrying you," I said. "But maybe she decided not to play along, or maybe she wanted a bigger cut. Anyway, you got angry and struck her. You probably didn't intend to kill her, but that's the problem with you guys who take a while to boil over. When you do boil over, you don't know how to control yourselves." I shook my head again. That gesture appeared to annoy him. I knew I was taking a risk, but I was relying on Haskell if Dan tried anything.

Dan laughed. "Interesting story. Obviously there's more."

"At some point, you must have read *Othello*." I paused to see if that struck home. His jaw tensed ever so slightly, just enough for me to think I was on the right track. "When you first began to think about how to screw up the Warriners' marriage, you thought about Iago. You had already seen that Carey could be a little possessive of Irene. Then along comes Armand d'Arcy, who is way too obvious in his adoration of her. But that fit your plan all too well, didn't it?

"All you had to do was feed Carey's possessiveness by convincing him that Irene returned d'Arcy's feelings. You assured him that all you and Irene talked about was her research in your period, but she had let on to you that she was interested in Armand." I paused for a moment. "Let me know if I'm going too fast for you."

Dan's jaw tightened again. "Please, continue."

"All was going well," I said. "You got Dixie Belle to enroll in both their classes. I'm sure before they finish with you, they'll find out you paid for her classes. She referred to you as her husband, did you know?"

Dan breathed a little harder. I had to wonder if they had indeed been married. Well, Kanesha would have to find that out.

"But there was a hitch with Dixie Belle. She was willing enough to seduce Carey Warriner. After all, he was an incredibly handsome guy, with lots of charm. He probably had to fight off students all the time, and not just the women." I shrugged. "By then, you'd poisoned him enough against Irene that he must have thought he might as well screw around with Dixie and get back at his faithless wife."

"Charlie," Haskell said in a warning tone. Again, I ignored him.

"You ought to write fiction," Dan said, trying to sound contemptuous but failing.

"You're disappointing me, you know," I said, "with these lame, predictable comments. But I shouldn't be surprised. Anyway, back to the story. For whatever reason, Dixie Belle started giving you problems, you got angry, lashed out, and suddenly had a dead body on your hands. You panicked, not so much about killing her, but losing your bait with Carey. Probably you'd never intended to kill anyone, but at some point, you must have realized that Carey's widow would get a lot more money than if he'd simply divorced her. Am I right?"

He ignored that. He continued to glare at me. I could feel the hatred emanating from him. That disturbed me, but it also convinced me I was right.

"So then you had to murder Carey, too, if you were going to end up with the big prize. He really played into your hands by attacking d'Arcy after your presentation with Irene that night. I wonder if you put that into his head." I shrugged. "No matter, he would have erupted sooner or later. He ended up being hauled to jail, and you, playing the loyal friend, stayed until you could take him home. Now, here's where I get a little fuzzy on the details. You didn't kill him before you took him home, because otherwise Irene would have figured that out. So you took him home but counted on him to be too angry to talk to his wife. Carey left the house; you said you'd go look for him. You found him and killed him. End of story." I was vaguely aware that Stewart had returned to the dining room, and I felt, rather than saw, Haskell move closer to me.

Dan continued to look at me, cold rage in his eyes.

I decided to push a little further. "What I don't understand was why you wanted to rent a room here. You obviously knew about my past experiences. You should have realized I'd be smart enough to catch on to you. So what made you do it? It really was the stupidest thing you could have done, you know."

He caught me completely off guard. Haskell, too. Dan had his hands around my throat before I even realized he had launched himself at me. Haskell reacted quickly, but it was really Diesel who saved me, I'm convinced. I heard the cat scream with rage, and the next thing I knew, Dan stumbled back, yelling that Diesel had clawed his eye out. Haskell felled him with one blow before he could retaliate, and Diesel climbed into my lap, anxiously meowing and chirping.

EPILOGUE

IIIIIIIIIIIIIIIIIIIIIIIIIIIIIIIIIIIIIIIIIIIIIIIIIIII

I caught grief from everyone over my stunt. I shouldn't have done it, I knew, but my temper got the better of me. Once I'd had my wild idea about Dan's playing Iago, I got angry. I thought of poor Irene Warriner. I was convinced that, at some point, she would go the way of the hapless, loyal Desdemona if Dan managed to get her to marry him. Somehow, I felt sure he would have, though he'd have had to get Armand d'Arcy out of the way to do it. From what I'd seen, though, Irene hadn't been enamored enough of d'Arcy to make him much of a threat.

I also thought about Carey Warriner, a promising career cut short, the students who would be deprived of his eloquence, his passion. Such an obscene waste.

There was also poor Dixie Compton, used by her brother-in-law in tawdry schemes to bilk married men out of money, jewels, cars, and whatever else she could get. Evidently his salary as a college professor wasn't enough, so he basically prostituted Dixie in order to earn money for them both. Kanesha had dug deep enough into both Dixie Belle's and Dan's past to discover that Dan had used his sister-in-law coldly, and she had, sadly, been willing to let him. I felt angry on her behalf. She had deserved better. I still felt a bit guilty over turning down her offer to study together. She was looking for a friend, I thought, and I hadn't been willing to be one.

I had driven myself nearly around the bend trying to figure out why Dan had come to board at my house. I figured Dixie must have told him she had met me and probably even that she had asked me to be her study partner. Perhaps he had feared she had told me something and decided he wanted to be able to keep a closer eye on me. Then, too, after her murder he had definitely put himself in the right place to keep tabs on the investigation. He had already known about my connection with law enforcement through his connection with Haskell and Stewart at the gym.

I had come to the realization, almost too late, that Dan was a sociopath. He had charm, otherwise Stewart and Haskell wouldn't have befriended him, nor would Stewart have recommended him as a boarder. He had carried off the nice-guy routine pretty well, though when he had tried to implicate Irene Warriner in the murders, he had made me uneasy. Like most sociopaths he had also overestimated his intelligence, his ability to con me and those around him. I figured he had thought that, despite my involvement in previous investigations, he was far too canny to allow me to catch on to the truth about him.

He had been busy with various plans to spread confusion. Not only had he tried to implicate Irene Warriner—a shrewd move to throw me off the scent that he really was interested in her—but he also had told Armand d'Arcy about the dinner with Irene at my house. He had admitted as much to Kanesha. Ultimately, of course, his attempts to throw me off base had failed. I had goaded him beyond bearing by taunting him.

Once my family found out about what had happened, Sean actually yelled at me, and for once in her life, so did Laura. That shook me pretty badly. Helen Louise didn't yell, but she wouldn't talk to me for three days after she found out what I'd done. Stewart and Haskell wouldn't look me in the eye. Kanesha had lost her temper, and I felt like I'd been skinned alive by the time she finished.

Azalea didn't fuss at me, but she did manage to work my grandchildren into several conversations, telling me how important it was that I stick around to see them grow up. What a shame it would be if I did something foolish to keep that from happening.

For a few days there, I felt friendless. Even Melba was mad at me. Diesel and Ramses were my only companions. I was thankful for my cats, and I was rethinking my idea about giving Ramses to Azalea. I might change my mind again at some point, but for now, he was going to stay with Diesel and me.

I indulged Diesel a bit too much, probably, for several days, giving him extra treats and spoiling him even more than usual. I felt like I owed him my life. If he hadn't attacked Dan the way he did, I think Dan might have broken my neck before Haskell could have stopped him. Diesel hadn't clawed either of Dan's eyes out, but he had left him with a badly scratched face.

Eventually, by the end of the week following my crazy stunt, as it would no doubt go down in the family annals, my loved ones began to thaw toward me. Laura brought baby Charlie over to see me, and Alex brought Rosie. I sat down in the living room, both children in my lap. Diesel sat on the sofa beside me, anxiously watching the babies. Laura and Alex faced me.

"Dad," Laura said, "you have to be more careful in the future."

Alex smiled. "We love you, and we know you too well to think that you'll ever give up being nosy."

Laura spoke again. "But you have these little ones who need their grandfather, okay? You have to be around for them, and for any others that come along in the future."

"Deal?" Alex asked, one eyebrow raised.

Diesel meowed as I regarded my grandchildren. Around the lump in my throat, I responded to Laura and Alex.

"Deal."

Turn the page for a sneak peek at the all-new Cat
in the Stacks mystery by Miranda James

CAT ME IF YOU CAN

Coming soon from Berkley Prime Crime!

"Do you regret saying *yes* so quickly when I asked you to do this?" I glanced over at Helen Louise Brady, taking my eyes briefly from the highway ahead. I had to be careful because I wasn't used to driving in the mountains.

Helen Louise laughed, and in the backseat, Diesel, my Maine Coon cat, chirped loudly.

"I do admit to having second thoughts, maybe even third," Helen Louise replied, a note of mischief in her tone. "You caught me by surprise that night. I certainly wasn't expecting *that* question."

"No way you could have," I replied, my attention once again focused on driving. "I hadn't really planned it. You know how I am. Occasionally a thought hits me, and out of my mouth it leaps." I shot her a wry grin.

Helen Louise laughed again. "I do know how you are, and your ability to surprise me is one of the qualities I love about you. Asking me to go along with you on this, especially after popping that *other* question, came out of the blue."

I had asked Helen Louise to marry me a couple of months ago, and to my delight she had said *yes*. I had given thought to *that* question before I posed it to her. There was nothing spontaneous about it. We hadn't yet set the date, though the family knew a wedding was in the offing. Everyone seemed happy about the pending nuptials.

"I hope this isn't pushing you too far outside your comfort zone."

"It's been years since I've done any such thing," Helen Louise said. "Other than make occasional speeches at one of the local clubs or in a church committee, that is, but I used to do it frequently when I was practicing law."

"You feel comfortable with the subject, don't you?" I still felt anxious, worried that I had pressured her, though I had tried hard not to.

"Talking about books I love to other readers?" Helen Louise grinned. "I'm not a librarian doing readers' advisory, my love, but I think I can manage."

"I know you can," I said. "As long as you're sure you're okay with doing this, and I didn't push you into it, I'm happy."

"Then be happy, Charlie. You've never pushed me into doing anything before, and I doubt you will in the future. I'm not all that pushable." Helen Louise tapped my shoulder lightly. "I'm happy to talk about Elizabeth Cadell to the group. Frankly, I'm curious to find out whether anyone in the group is familiar with her work."

"I vaguely remember Cadell from my early public library days. I never read her, though, until you insisted."

"And you liked her."

I ignored the smugness and said simply, "Yes." Cadell's gentle blend of mystery and romance had charmed me, especially when I was in the mood for a cozy read.

Diesel again chirped from behind us, evidently in need of being noticed. Helen Louise twisted herself around to reach back and rub his head. He rewarded her with his deep purr, the source of his name.

"This is my first visit to North Carolina," I said when Helen Louise settled back into her seat and faced forward again. "I've always heard that the Asheville area is beautiful."

"I went there once, probably thirty years ago," Helen

Louise replied. "Before I gave up law and headed to Paris to study French cuisine, of course. Had to depose someone who lived there. It is a beautiful area. I love mountains."

"After all those years in Houston, where the only thing close to a hill or a mountain is a freeway overpass," I said, "I am certainly enjoying the different terrain." I grimaced. "Though having to learn to drive in the mountains as we go is a bit nerve-racking."

"You're doing fine," Helen Louise said. "You had no problem during the pass down from the Gatlinburg area into Cherokee." Cherokee, North Carolina, was a town on the reservation of the Eastern Band of the Cherokee Nation, in the western part of the state just over the Tennessee border. We had stopped there briefly to look around before continuing our journey. We both wanted to return to Cherokee after our sojourn in Asheville to explore a bit more.

"Thanks," I said. "Honestly, though, I was so tense coming down, especially with that one guy in the truck going about three miles an hour. I felt like ramming him out of the way."

"I could tell," Helen Louise said, the barest tremor of amusement in her voice. "I'm glad you didn't succumb to temptation." She glanced at her phone and its GPS. "We're not that far from Asheville now. Only about another half hour, maybe forty minutes."

"That's good," I said. "This scenery is spectacular, I must say, but I'm not able to enjoy it as much as I'd like."

"I told you I'd be happy to drive," Helen Louise replied.

"I know, and I appreciate it," I said. "But I do better with heights if I'm at the wheel. Otherwise I can get a little too freaked out."

"Charlie Harris, you are a mess, a psychological mess," Helen Louise said in a mock-tragic tone.

"But you still love me anyway," I replied airily.

"Lord help me, I do." Helen Louise giggled.

A sound suspiciously like a snort came from the backseat. If cats could snort in derision, Diesel would certainly do it.

"That's enough from the peanut gallery," I said.

Diesel warbled in response. He always seemed to know when I was speaking directly to him.

"Ramses wanted to come, too, and he wasn't happy at being left behind." Ramses was a Christmas present from a young friend. He was still too kittenish to trust out of his home environment. Diesel was several years older and well seasoned.

"I'm sure he wasn't," Helen Louise said, "but Azalea will spoil him even more rotten than she already does."

"I've no doubt of that." Azalea Berry, my housekeeper, had become devoted to Ramses after claiming for years that she didn't like cats in the house. She even displayed affection for Diesel, calling him "Mr. Cat" for some reason known only to herself. Diesel didn't appear to mind.

"This should be a lot of fun," Helen Louise said. "It's nice to get away from the everyday routine for a few days."

"I'm happy to be having this time with you, and neither one of us distracted by work," I said.

"Henry promised to call me only in the case of an extreme emergency," Helen Louise replied. Henry managed Helen Louise's French bistro in Athena, and he was more than capable of running the business and baking up to Helen Louise's Paris-trained standards.

"That's good," I said. "I promise not to look for mysteries anywhere."

Helen Louise laughed. "We'll be talking a lot about

mysteries every day, thankfully all fictional. That's enough for a vacation."

"No argument here." In recent years I had found myself involved in several murder investigations, and though I fancied I had a knack for solving them, I wouldn't mind if I didn't encounter another one for quite some time.

We chatted in desultory fashion, with the occasional feline comment thrown in, the rest of the way to Asheville. As soon as the highway exit came into sight, Helen Louise switched into navigator mode. She fed me the directions step-by-step to the boutique hotel where we would be spending the week.

"That's where we would turn to go to Biltmore." Helen Louise pointed to the left not long after we exited the highway. Biltmore, the Vanderbilt estate, was the major tourist attraction in Asheville. We would view it sometime this week, depending on the schedule set up by Miss An'gel and Miss Dickce Ducote, the sponsors for the mystery week. The sisters, the leading lights of Athena society, were dear friends of ours, and it was thanks to their connections we would have a special tour of the Vanderbilt estate.

"Take the next left," Helen Louise said, "and then the first right after that. The hotel should be on the right about a block later."

"Easy enough." A few minutes later I pulled the car into a circular drive before a lovely red brick building. According to the information we had found online, the Hindman Hotel was originally built as a home for a local family of prosperous merchants in the late nineteenth century. At some point the family fortunes shifted and the house became the property of an ambitious hotelier. Alas, this building was all that was left of his once-hopeful empire.

The Ducote sisters had reserved the entire hotel, with its twenty bedrooms—several of which were luxurious suites—for the week of our gathering. The pictures we saw online promised a beautiful setting for our stay here, and I had selected one of the small suites for Helen Louise, Diesel, and me. Miss An'gel had assured me that Diesel would be welcome at the hotel. I would have left him home otherwise, albeit reluctantly.

I opened my door, got out, then stuck my head in to ask Helen Louise if she wanted to go in with me. Diesel took that as his signal to jump into my vacated seat and then out onto the driveway. "You stay right there, boy," I told him in a stern tone. He warbled.

"You two go on in," Helen Louise said. "I'll stay here."

"Okay." I shut the door and glanced down at my cat. "You stay right by my side, you hear?"

Diesel warbled again, and he stuck by me all the way to the reception desk inside. He looked around the whole time, his nose occasionally quivering as it caught some intriguing scent. When I stopped at the desk, however, he sat by my feet and stayed there.

A young man stepped up to the desk from a door in the back. "Good morning, sir." He gave me a toothsome smile. "How may I assist you?" His name tag read *Arthur*. Tall, muscular, and handsome, he looked to be in his early twenties.

"Good morning, Arthur." I introduced myself. "I have a reservation for this week."

Arthur nodded. "Yes, Mr. Harris." His fingers tapped at the keyboard, and after a moment he said, "A reservation for yourself and Ms. Brady, as well as a cat." He frowned. "There must be some mistake. We don't allow animals unless they are service animals. Is your cat a service animal?"

"No, he is not," I said.

"Then I'm afraid we can't allow him." Arthur frowned.

"I was assured that I would be allowed to bring the cat. Miss An'gel Ducote, who arranged to reserve the whole hotel for the week, told me so."

Arthur swallowed as his eyes grew wide. "Oh, yes, Miss Ducote," he said, his voice almost a whisper. "Then there is no problem, Mr. Harris. My apologies." Arthur now became obsequious almost to the point of irritation. He babbled about numerous amenities, then tapped a bell for a bellman, and kept assuring me that I would love the hotel and so on.

I suppressed a grin. I had seen this effect before. Miss An'gel had a forceful personality, and not many, certainly not this youth, could withstand it.

The bellman, a man about forty, appeared, and Arthur directed him to the car. "Suite four," he said. "Thomas will bring your bags up to your suite, and if you'll leave him your keys, he will also park your car for you. Valet service is included."

"Thank you, Thomas," I said. "The keys are in the car along with the other member of our party, my fiancé, Helen Louise Brady."

Thomas nodded, his eyes fixed on Diesel, who had approached him to sniff at his shoes. "Does he bite or scratch?" Thomas asked, his voice steady.

"No," I said. "He's friendly."

Thomas rubbed Diesel's head after the cat sniffed his fingers. "He's the biggest cat I've ever seen outside of a zoo."

I explained about the Maine Coon breed, and Thomas nodded. I noticed that Arthur appeared rooted behind the desk, though he was peering over it at my cat.

Thomas left to take care of the bags and the car, and

Helen Louise appeared moments later. Arthur escorted us to our suite on the second floor. He opened the door with a flourish and stepped aside, waving us into the room. "I'm sure you'll be very happy with your accommodations."

Diesel preceded us into the suite, and at first glance, I decided Arthur was correct. The suite had beautiful furnishings, reminiscent of a bygone area of luxury. Everything looked perfect.

Except for the body sprawled on the sofa.

Miranda James is the *New York Times* bestselling author of the Cat in the Stacks Mysteries, including *Six Cats a Slayin'*, *Claws for Concern*, and *Twelve Angry Librarians*, as well as the Southern Ladies Mysteries, including *Fixing to Die*, *Digging Up the Dirt*, and *Dead with the Wind*. James lives in Mississippi.

CONNECT ONLINE

CatInTheStacks.com

☐ MirandaJamesAuthor

Ready to find
your next great read?

Let us help.

Visit prh.com/nextread

Penguin
Random
House